T0265720

MURDER AND THE
MISSING DOG

Also by Susan C. Shea

French Village mysteries

LOVE & DEATH IN BURGUNDY
DRESSED FOR DEATH IN BURGUNDY

The Château in Burgundy mysteries

MURDER VISITS A FRENCH VILLAGE *

Dani O'Rourke mysteries

MURDER IN THE ABSTRACT
THE KING'S JAR
MIXED UP WITH MURDER

* *available from Severn House*

MURDER AND THE MISSING DOG

Susan C. Shea

**SEVERN
HOUSE**

First world edition published in Great Britain and the USA in 2024
by Severn House, an imprint of Canongate Books Ltd,
14 High Street, Edinburgh EH1 1TE.

severnhouse.com

British Library Cataloguing-in-Publication Data
A CIP catalogue record for this title is available from the British Library.

ISBN-13: 978-1-4483-1092-0 (cased)
ISBN-13: 978-1-4483-1336-5 (e-book)

All Severn House titles are printed on acid-free paper.

Typeset by Palimpsest Book Production Ltd.,
Falkirk, Stirlingshire, Scotland.
Printed and bound in Great Britain by
TJ Books, Padstow, Cornwall.

Praise for Susan C. Shea

"The quirky village residents make this an appealing
series debut"
Library Journal on *Murder Visits a French Village*

"Ariel is a sympathetic amateur sleuth . . . and the mystery is
nicely framed by a view of expat life in France and the details
of restoring a chateau"
Booklist on *Murder Visits a French Village*

"A comedy of errors full of amusing characters, a fine feeling
for life in small-town France, and a suitably twisty mystery"
Kirkus Reviews on *Dressed for Death in Burgundy*

"Francophiles will look forward to Katherine's next adventure
in Burgundy"
Publishers Weekly on *Dressed for Death in Burgundy*

"A Miss Marple-like investigation . . . immerses the reader in
the life of an American woman trying to fit into an insular
French village"
Booklist on *Love and Death in Burgundy*

"A pleasant getaway from hard-core killers"
New York Times on *Love and Death in Burgundy*

"The outlandish antics of the eccentric locals add to the
humor. Suggest to fans of Rhys Bowen's early 'Evan Evans'
series for the humor, the characters, and the charming setting"
Library Journal on *Love and Death in Burgundy*

About the author

Susan Shea spent more than two decades as a non-profit executive before beginning her first critically praised mystery series in 2010, featuring a professional fundraiser for an art museum. Since then she has created two different mystery series set in France, the most recent being the Château in Burgundy mysteries with Severn House. She's a regular on *7 Criminal Minds* blog, is past secretary of the national *Sisters in Crime* board, a past board member of the Northern California chapters of *Sisters in Crime* and *Mystery Writers of America*.

She lives in Marin County, California, where two cats pretty much rule the house!

https://susancshea.com/

For Tim, always, in loving gratitude

Acknowledgements

Research for this book involved calling on pre-pandemic memories of the Musée de la Resistance and the Burgundian châteaux I've visited. A pause to thank the people long ago who created these memorable forts and castles, and the people today who care for them and allow visitors to peer into corners and ask silly questions. Thanks again to the friend who introduced me to the area and at whose house I stay during my visits. A special chew toy for her ebullient dog, who shall go nameless. Thanks to Christina, my wonderful agent whose advice is sterling, and a special thanks to Vic and Laura and everyone at Severn House who made this a much better book.

ONE

As she drove to Katherine Goff's village home on a blustery March morning, blond hair caught up in an unruly ponytail, Ariel Shepard was celebrating, or at least mentally basking in her success. Over Burgundy's coldest, wettest winter months, she'd concentrated on making parts of her inherited château livable. There was heat everywhere but in the tower, hot and cold running water in all the faucets, snug window framing on the ground floor and the next one up – which was in France the first floor – and a scrubbed if not fully furnished kitchen in which a few pots, a French *cafétière presse* for morning coffee and a tea kettle had to suffice until she felt more settled.

Pointed to a master craftsman who still did caning by hand meant that eight lovely old chairs she had found in an upper-floor room of her mansion were safe to sit on, even if the table they surrounded still needed refinishing. Another furniture restorer in Auxerre had brought a handful of the upholstered chairs whose skeletons Katherine deemed worth the cost back to life in fabric tones of rose and cream. The man was as slow as molasses on a cold day, but it wasn't as though she had needed the lounge chairs to entertain company yet.

The workman that her friend and café owner Tony had recommended for replastering the walls had whistled while he repaired the jagged spaces the British electricians and Andre the plumber had knocked open in their search for old wires and pipes. Ariel could see the patches, but the plasterer assured her three or four coats of paint would make that disappear. The painter recommended by the plasterer was due to come by soon to talk about the bulk of the interior painting. Ariel's nervous 'four coats of paint?' was dismissed by Katherine, who explained new plaster was damp and the painter wouldn't even put on the primer until it got warmer inside.

'Darling, when I paint your frescos, I won't touch the walls until the walls have been painted and let to dry. Which reminds me, let's decide which rooms get the fresco treatment so I can case them out.'

Ariel said aloud more than once as she surveyed the progress, 'Dan, my darling, what do you think? Would you be proud of me?' It had been more than a year since he had collapsed in their New York apartment, but she could still close her eyes and see him poking around in the run-down, vacant château, eyes alight with pleasure at discovering the place while they were on their honeymoon. He had meant the gift of the modest château to be a surprise for her, thinking he had all the time in the world to restore it before bringing her back. Now, the challenge was hers alone, but it had helped her focus on something other than her loss since she had arrived.

Her new friends, chief among them Katherine, an American ex-pat artist with eccentric enthusiasms and seemingly endless creative energy, had lent her their opinions, expertise and connections. It was taking a village, several in fact, but Château de Champs-sur-Serein was coming back to life. It was also taking money, piles of it, and Ariel was watching her bank account nervously. That's why she'd told Katherine that the purely decorative parts of the restoration for its upcoming life as a bed and breakfast destination would have to be inexpensive finds from flea markets.

'My little shop,' Katherine had said, cackling. 'You shall be my best customer.'

Ariel slowed to ease around the sharp turn and into the Goffs' driveway in Reigny-sur-Canne. The old pear tree was still barren of leaves, and Katherine's beloved hollyhocks were nothing more than dead stalks leaning against the wall.

At the sound of her car, the kitchen door opened and two shaggy dogs, one large and black, the other small and dirty white, ambled out to greet her. The aroma of roasting chicken escaped from the open door.

'Watch out. If they rub up against you, you'll be covered in mud,' Katherine said, drying her hands on a faded vintage apron as she followed them out. She was a petite woman whose style of dress was firmly dated to the 1930s, and she hunted the flea markets relentlessly for finds that defined her aesthetic.

Ariel tried unsuccessfully to maneuver around the dogs, glad she had worn an old raincoat and boots. The friends exchanged the French *bis* in the air next to their cheeks and retreated into the house, leaving the dogs outside to wander over the patio and desiccated garden.

'I hope I'm not too early, but you said best to get in and have time to check out what you've collected before any other customers come in to snap up your treasures.'

'As if.' Katherine cackled.

Her laugh was a high-pitched sort of giggle but not girlish somehow. More knowing, Ariel thought, like a good witch perhaps.

'These days, my earliest customer is likely to be my only customer. Michael says not to worry, that business will take off when the summer visitors arrive to see Sophie Bellegarde's family home.'

Another château, this one restored to emphasize its historic purpose, but one that wasn't open to paying guests, which was a relief to Ariel, who needed hers to bring in euros if she was ever going to break even on the repairs.

'Is Michael around?'

'Off to Paris first thing for the day via the TGV fast train to check out a recording studio. He wants to put down some vocals here before going back to the States to finish the new album. It's all a blur to me, but I never cease to be in heaven that his luck has changed and he's a hot property according to his new agent. My dear husband deserves every bit of good fortune.'

She whipped off her apron and tossed it on top of the combined washer-dryer whose dryer function she almost never used. 'Here, I've got my coat. I'll call the dogs in so they can muddy the furniture some more and then we can walk to the shop.'

The two women headed down the hill into what might be called the center of Reigny-sur-Canne if a shabby crossroad embellished by one minimally functional café could be called anything as aspirational as a center.

'Did I tell you the mysterious woman you see around Noyers came back last week with another treasure? I can't figure her out. She looks poor, is completely unsocial, but has brought in lovely things. I figure she's selling off her own personal treasures, piece by piece, just to survive, and it breaks my heart.'

Ariel knew who she meant. Madame Toussaint prowled around Noyers-sur-Serein like a dark wraith. Gossip had it she had been abandoned by her only relatives and left to fend for herself and her handsome dog. 'I'm surprised Pippa hasn't come up with a fantasy for what the poor old woman is doing, given her search for suspicious happenings she can turn into novels.'

Katherine snorted. 'Don't get me started on that girl. Oh dear, we'll have to stop and say hello to Madame Pomfort.'

Reigny's self-appointed social lioness and town crier was working in the abandoned church garden she had claimed as her own several decades previously and which she guarded against all comers. Her face was completely hidden under an ancient straw hat that tied beneath her chin. She might be elderly, Ariel thought, but a passerby wouldn't think so, watching her bring her hoe down savagely on a weed that had foolishly tried to tuck itself among the pruned branches of a rose bush. When she heard them coming, she whirled around.

'*Bonjour, Madame. Viens ici vite!*' the widow called, beckoning with her free arm and hurrying over to the garden gate.

Ariel thought, not for the first time, that Madame must have cut discreet eyeholes in the hat brim because, otherwise, how could she see everyone and everything that passed her?

'*Bonjour, ma chérie,*' Katherine called back. 'Shoot,' she said in a low voice to Ariel, 'I'm not supposed to use endearments when speaking to the women in the neighborhood. My American habit of assuming friendships that haven't been cemented by decades of connections leads me into danger all the time.'

Madame Pomfort's downturned mouth said she had heard and disapproved of Katherine's familiarity as much as ever, but Ariel wondered why she was distressed.

The woman unlatched the gate and stepped through. 'This was bound to happen once those Bellegardes took over our village for their benefit. I warned everyone, did I not, that vagrants and rude people and *voleurs* would descend on us?'

'What's happened?' Ariel looked around but saw no streams of threatening, swaggering strangers, much less curious strangers begging to spend money in Reigny.

'Well, it is you who should be the most concerned, Katherine, since it is happening at your' – here Madame paused to sniff, her long nose adding emphasis – 'shop. I saw it with my own eyes not ten minutes ago.'

'Saw what? I'm on my way there now. Surely no one has broken into it?' Katherine's face registered fear. 'A small negative cash flow is one thing, but the loss of so many exciting finds would be a catastrophe.' Katherine's hand went to her mouth. 'I blame myself for not asking Michael to fix the back window that doesn't close properly.'

Madame Pomfort would not be distracted from her most severe warning. 'A vagrant, a homeless person just sleeping in your doorway. What does he think – that we shall all feed him, give him our own money, let him sleep in our houses? We will be run out of our homes, next thing.' Her mouth turned down into a dramatic frown to register all kinds of nasty possibilities. 'We will not be safe in our beds at this rate.' She clutched one gloved hand to her heart, waved her hoe around and her voice trembled.

Ariel frowned. A vagrant wasn't a good thing overall, but Madame Pomfort had a habit, fed by an overactive imagination and old biases, of seeing the fall of civilization in anything that disturbed the routine of the village over which she reigned by dint of willpower. The gardener had taken off her apron, settled her long-handled hoe at her side and was clearly not going to miss any action from this invasion.

As the defenders of Reigny's safety rounded the bend and the whitewashed old house that now housed the little shop on the ground floor came into view, Ariel saw there was, indeed, someone curled up in the recessed doorway. But the beret, slightly askew on a head of gray hair, and the long shapeless coat were familiar.

'Could it be Madame Toussaint from Noyers?' Ariel asked. The poor woman had probably arrived before dawn and was exhausted by what must have been a long walk.

Katherine made a clucking noise and hurried forward. For Madame Pomfort's benefit, she said, 'She brings me little things to buy. She's harmless, but she's quite old.'

Ariel stepped closer. 'I'll wake her gently. No need to hold that over her.' Madame Pomfort had advanced slowly to about six feet away and the hoe was poised as if to strike the small bundle of a woman.

'Madame,' Ariel said, bending over the huddled form. 'Madame, wake up, please.'

The woman was sleeping so soundly that she felt guilty disturbing her, but, really, this was no place to take a nap. Ariel would insist on driving her home, perhaps after a coffee here.

When she still didn't respond, Ariel shook her shoulder lightly, and the woman rolled over from her hunched position, her beret falling off. Her eyes were open, dried blood covered her face in rivulets and her gray hair was matted with blood.

Ariel stopped breathing. The old woman wasn't sleeping; she was dead.

Madame Pomfort was screaming in a voice that would be an excellent replacement for an air raid siren. Over the sound, Ariel heard her own ragged breathing and guessed Katherine would have screamed too except that she seemed to be having trouble finding enough air to keep from fainting. The dead woman's gaze gave Ariel the impression she was looking at her for help. Katherine sat abruptly in the deserted street.

Maurice, the owner of the little café up and around the corner from Katherine's shop, materialized, jogging and carrying a broom and a cell phone. 'I heard the noise,' he said, wheezing as he stumped over to the little group. Ariel's ears were buzzing, and the activity around her was not entirely in focus.

'Bloody hell,' a voice rang out in a strong British accent.

Pippa, Ariel thought through the haze, *Pippa is here. Pippa will call the gendarmes and I can go home and get into bed and maybe this will not have happened a second time, finding someone who ought to be alive but was not.*

A tractor bouncing slowly through the intersection from one rapeseed field to another stopped, and the farmer jumped down from the seat to join the rapidly expanding number of onlookers. He too had a cell phone, and Ariel said in a shaky voice, 'Someone call the sheriff please.' Ariel remembered meeting the commune's only law officer, a decent if lethargic man who was likely to be sitting down right now to his breakfast roll and espresso at the café.

Pippa pulled Katherine to her feet. 'Let's get you away from the traffic, love. Can't have farm equipment running you over. Come on, Ariel, you too. You don't look much better.'

Ariel tore her eyes away from Madame Toussaint's face and backed away. Madame Pomfort had already retreated halfway up the street but looked like she was not going any farther.

Pippa pointed behind them. 'How about here, across the street, not too close to . . . well, you know? This house is unoccupied, and the steps are deep enough to sit back safely. Is she really dead?'

The next few minutes were a blur, but soon Henri, the sheriff, came barreling down the street, napkin in hand, and, out of breath from the unaccustomed exercise, was on the phone the next minute to the mayor, shouting so loudly everyone could hear him. '*Vite! Elle est morte! Morte! Oui, oui.*'

'Not a dream then,' Ariel said as though speaking to herself in a whisper. 'She isn't asleep or passed out from hunger.'

Katherine's eyes had filled with tears that were dribbling down her cheeks. 'She had come to the shop to sell whatever small treasure she was going to sacrifice from her past life, and someone killed her while she waited.'

Pippa said, 'Hang on. Killed? She might have fallen and hit her head. I didn't get close, but is she someone you knew then?'

Ariel nodded. 'You must have noticed her in Noyers – the old woman who walks everywhere with her dog? I hope you're right, and that it was a fall, because if someone wanted to rob her of what few euros she had, they could just grab her bag and run. She'd never catch them.'

'Where's her bag?' Katherine asked. 'What had been in it that she wanted to sell today?' She stood up. 'I need to see her, see if she has her purse.'

Ariel tugged at her sleeve. 'I'm not sure that's a great idea. Won't the gendarmes expect us to leave things as they are?'

'Philippe's on duty today, so I expect he'll be sent with his partner and one of the bosses.' A small piece of Ariel's brain registered something in Pippa's voice that wasn't her usual pride. Or was a fledgling author's appetite for a plot beginning to surface?

Several more residents of Reigny had arrived and stood around, shifting from one foot to the other as they waited. The sheriff announced in a loud voice that the mayor had called the gendarmerie in Avallon and no one was to get too close to the victim.

Nevertheless, perhaps because she didn't understand French, Pippa crept near and started to take a photo, but Henri yelped at her.

'*Non, non,*' he said, putting up his palm and glaring at her. 'It would be unseemly.'

Pippa retreated, her face red.

Delphine, the mayor and a farmer's wife, wearing run-down slippers, and a scarf tied under her chin, showed up with a plastic grocery bag full of bottles of water for everyone. 'You must hydrate when you're upset – I read in the newspaper.'

She explained she had not yet opened the *mairie* when the sheriff called her on her cell phone, and she and Henri agreed that no one should leave until the police had the chance to question them.

Madame Pomfort needed a chair, Delphine said with a quick glance at the woman leaning heavily on her hoe handle, and Maurice asked if he could bring one from the café. Henri waved his approval, and Maurice huffed his way back up the street and around the bend, doubtless on a second mission as well, to fill his wife in on the situation. She could then get on the phone and tell half the village.

'Henri,' Katherine said, pulling herself to a standing position but keeping one hand on the crumbling stucco of the empty house. 'My friends and I know this woman. She came into my shop several times. She always had a large black carryall with her, and I wonder if you can see it from where you are?'

The sheriff walked around to the far side of the doorway then shook his head. 'Not that I can see, but it could be underneath her, Madame Goff. We shall have to wait for the gendarmes to learn more.'

As if on cue, the two-note siren of France's police vehicles sounded from outside the village, and everyone stepped back. Maurice's café chair arrived, and Madame Pomfort tugged it bit by bit closer to the doorway where the victim lay.

A little car with its flashing blue light came around the corner and skidded to a stop. The driver's and passenger's doors opened simultaneously, and two gendarmes stepped out in their blue uniforms, putting their caps on as they surveyed the crowd. Philippe did a double take when he saw Pippa, who raised her hand halfway to her shoulder in an aborted greeting before dropping it. He frowned and walked toward the body with his partner, a young woman with wide shoulders and a barrel body.

Ariel edged over to Pippa and whispered, 'Who is she? I think I've seen her before.'

'Transferred from the Medoc last year. Philippe says she's good enough but awfully tough.'

'Tough as in what?'

Pippa shrugged. 'I'm not quite sure. She's new and I guess there's some teasing going on at the station.' Her tone changed. 'I get the feeling she's not easy to intimidate.'

'That's good, isn't it?'

Pippa made a noncommittal noise, and Ariel looked back at the new cop. She noticed that the woman was quite pretty, even frowning as she was now, leaning toward Philippe and saying something under her breath. She stepped up close to the old woman's body and squatted down next to it, then pulled out her cell phone and began taking pictures.

Philippe turned around and spoke to the small crowd, pointedly not looking directly at his girlfriend. 'Good – everyone's here who arrived when the body was first discovered, yes? No one has left?' He looked over at Delphine and Henri, the two people in charge of village matters. They in turn looked around and then nodded. 'Very well. While Officer Lannes calls for the inspector, I need to talk to each of you. Separately. Is there a place?'

Delphine said they could come to the *mairie*, but the winter rains had created a leak in the only large room, and there was, *désolé*, no heat at the moment. 'The furnace repair is next week and I'm working in my thickest coat.' She grimaced.

'The café then,' Henri said. 'If there are customers, they can sit outside. You can close it, can't you, Maurice?'

Maurice looked unhappy, bobbing his head this way and that as if to say, 'Yes, but . . .'

Ariel looked over at him. *Really? A woman's dead in front of him and he's afraid to lose a one-euro espresso sale? Tony would never hesitate*, she thought. Tony owned and ran Noyers-sur-Serein's busiest café and had proven himself a good friend when she first arrived in France to take on the challenge of restoring her château. He would have jumped at the chance to be at the heart of anything interesting.

Reigny's café owner may have felt a wave of disapproval from his neighbors or seen the look on Philippe's face because he said after a pause, '*Mais oui, immédiatement.*'

A new car arrived before the group could begin its trek up the street, and a tall man in a winter-weight suit and a wooly scarf unfolded from the back seat, his uniformed driver looking unconcerned, as if dead bodies were always lying around.

Ariel groaned. 'It's the gendarmerie's Brigadier Allard,' she said to Katherine in a low voice. 'Did Philippe tell them he thought it was murder?'

Not low enough. He turned toward her, dipped his head slightly and said in English, 'How can this be, Madame Shepard? Another body and you here? I would have thought you would choose to stay close to your house after, well, after the last tragedy.'

Her French would have been adequate for the words, and the sarcasm didn't need translation.

'*Bonjour, Brigadier,*' she chose to reply in French. She was determined to speak his language unless she ran into words beyond her vocabulary. 'I just got here, wasn't even right here actually, when someone said a person was sleeping in front of Katherine's shop.' Ariel waved her arm, first in Madame Pomfort's direction then toward Katherine.

'Me neither, *moi non plus,*' Katherine said, jumping in quickly. 'We know nothing – well almost nothing, but Ariel recognized her from Noyers, and then so did I.'

Allard ran his hands through his thick, short hair. 'Very well. I will speak with you – with everyone,' he added, turning to glare at the assembled watchers, 'but first I must speak to my officers. Wait here.'

Katherine sat back down at the curb. 'What will Michael say? He will think I somehow butted into this, and he's likely to get mad again.'

Pippa edged back over to them. She had been standing slightly apart, and Ariel thought she might be trying to avoid being recognized by Philippe's boss, since Philippe had been dressed down once or twice for letting information leak to his girlfriend.

'That would be so unfair. Don't worry – I'll explain everything to him.'

'Please don't,' Katherine said with a small groan. 'It's not that he doesn't like you, Pippa, but he does think you lead me into trouble, like with the reporter last year.'

Pippa made a face. 'Not quite my fault then, was it? I mean, she wormed things out of everyone. Anyway, he's not daft – he'll understand this is different. This involves you directly, right? I mean, it's your shop she died at. If it wasn't an accident, you might even be in danger.'

Ariel said, 'That's enough, Pippa. Katherine's upset. We're all upset, and meanwhile there's a fragile old woman still lying there, and if I can't cover her decently, I intend to go around the bend in the street, so I don't have to sit here feeling useless.'

'Got it,' Pippa said and took Katherine by the arm. 'Steady on. We can sit on the church steps on the way to the café. It will give us time to think. What we need to do now is try to figure out why she was here and what might have happened.'

'No,' Ariel said, realizing as she spoke that the particular kind of headache Pippa could ignite was coming on fast. 'We don't have to figure out anything. For one thing, there's nothing that clearly points to a homicide. The gendarmes may decide that it was an unfortunate accident.'

Pippa's mouth registered her skepticism, and she raised her eyebrows.

'Right now, there are two police cars and four gendarmes within a hundred feet of us, and I promise you they have begun working on that already,' Ariel said. 'One of them, I might point out, is your fiancé, and I don't think he'd be happy hearing you say you plan to conduct your own investigation.'

Pippa shifted from one foot to the other. 'Boyfriend, maybe, but no longer fiancé. He's so bossy and sides with his superiors against me. Anyway, his mother hates me, the old hag.'

Ariel wasn't up to a discussion of Philippe's professional obligations or name-calling, although she had a hunch Pippa would change her views of the monster mother if Philippe proposed they get married tomorrow.

Philippe and Officer Lannes had gone into a huddle with Allard. In murmurs the watchers couldn't hear, the officers must have been filling him in on the little they knew. Ariel pointed to the church steps and gave Allard a questioning look as the three women walked slowly past them the hundred meters to the building. Allard nodded. As they conferred, the gendarmes' heads dipped in turn to the corpse and then to Katherine and Ariel, whose stomach lurched again. When they had finished, the brigadier walked over to them.

'*Bonjour, Madame Goff,*' he said. 'You speak French, I understand? Good. You own this shop, *oui*?'

'*Oui.* I'm Katherine Goff, and that is my new shop. I was on the way to open it. I know this woman, poor thing.'

'Perhaps you will tell us who she is.'

'My friend Ariel knows more, but I can tell you she came into my shop every Thursday for the last month or more to sell small things.'

He frowned. 'So you don't actually know who she is.'

Ariel broke in. 'She is Madame Toussaint, a widow who lives alone in Noyers. I've only spoken to her a few times, but the people who've lived there longer can tell you much more about her, I'm sure. She goes everywhere with her dog. Oh, wait. Where is her dog?' She looked around. From where they now stood, she could see in all directions around the little intersection. No dog hovering anxiously, no dog sitting and waiting. There had been no dog in sight when she and Katherine came around the corner. 'The dog is missing.'

'Dogs turn up. She might not have brought it with her, and the dog is not my problem at the moment.' Turning to Katherine, he began quizzing her on the dead woman's appearances at the shop.

'She came in to ask me to buy some lovely old trinkets. She didn't give me her name and wanted to be paid in cash.'

'And did you?'

'Did I what?'

'Buy them, Madame Goff.'

'Yes.'

He nodded. 'Very well. I will speak to you separately when we have determined if it was a crime.'

Ariel stared. 'I turned her over and saw blood—'

'You moved the body? Interfered with the scene? It is the role of the gendarmes to deal with these things.' He had been speaking in heavily accented English at first, but as he became agitated, he switched to French.

'That's not fair,' Ariel said, her voice rising and attracting the attention of the small crowd. 'I thought she was asleep. We all thought she was asleep – the neighbor thought she was a vagrant. I only shook her shoulder to wake her up. She might have been alive and sick. We might have needed to get help. And, by the way, you know I speak French, so you don't have to keep translating.'

'*D'accord.*' The brigadier gave her a skeptical look along with his okay and walked away to rejoin the two officers.

Pippa took her arm. 'What was he saying? He doesn't think you killed the old woman, does he?'

Ariel closed her eyes and began counting to ten – slowly. 'For heaven's sake, Pippa. How could you think that?'

Katherine exhaled a noisy breath and pulled the hair that had escaped in the slight breeze back into her gray ponytail. 'He thinks we shouldn't have touched the woman, even to help her.'

More police sirens approached, and Philippe herded the bystanders back toward the café. A police van appeared, heralded by sirens, the driver going way too fast for the road, and another police car followed close behind.

Ariel looked back. Two people exited the van and began pulling on white coveralls. Maybe the police did think that someone had decided to kill a harmless old woman who clearly wasn't able to defend herself. Reigny had no roaming bands of muggers in spite of Madame Pomfort's dire warnings, and Jean, the swaggering local thief, was not violent and more of a nuisance. He had a habit of lifting tools and anything else in people's yards that was easily portable, storing them in his messy compound then offering them for sale – often to the very people he had stolen them from, with the patently untrue explanation that he had bought them at a flea market. So had someone snuck into town, seen her and seized an opportunity to grab a handbag? Was that likely? Was someone after her specifically? And did her death have anything to do with what she'd sold to Katherine?

Ariel stopped suddenly in the road. Could that possibly mean her friend was in danger too, perhaps for having those items in her store? She hated to sound like Pippa, but Ariel had been to Katherine's shop a few times already. She visualized enticingly cluttered sawhorse tables covered with vintage lace tablecloths and piled high with miscellaneous tableware, diminutive glasses, candle holders, and chipped jugs and jardinières. There were several baskets in the corners of the shop that held rolls of wall-papers salvaged from who knew where, delicate and flower-covered designs. Ariel had her eye on them, seeing them on the walls of her château, even though none of the remnants was itself large enough to paper an entire room.

A deep shelf in the front window of the shop held several painted wooden statues of religious figures, the paint now faded and chipped but the reverence in the work still obvious. The back wall held a much-degraded tapestry, its backing showing through in several places. Katherine swore it was from the fifteenth century and said she was researching the subject, which might require a trip to the Cluny Museum in Paris.

Every space not crammed with treasures her eagle eye had discovered at Burgundy's numerous *vide-greniers* held large or small paintings of hers, almost always charming medieval fanta-sies. Invariably, they featured the same young woman – her neighbor Jeannette, the teenage daughter of widower Jean and big sister to two rambunctious younger brothers. Ariel loved the paintings, which was why she had asked Katherine to paint at least two large murals somewhere inside Château de Champs-sur-Serein when the place was ready.

But was any of that likely to attract a robber? It wasn't as though the shop, which had no name yet ('I'm waiting for inspi-ration, and in the meantime, it's the only shop in Reigny, so how can it be a problem?'), looked successful enough to tempt anyone looking to steal money. There were no valuable antiques, although Ariel recollected a locked glass cabinet near Katherine's desk that held a small collection of baroque-style silver and vermeil pieces, much more valuable than the bits and pieces scattered everywhere. Perhaps someone had scouted the shop and seen those pieces. Had Madame Toussaint interrupted a robbery?

Soon enough, it was her turn to be questioned. Brigadier Allard beckoned her in from the small terrace. When she sat down, expecting to be grilled, he frowned at her for a moment before breaking out in a wide smile. 'Well, well, Madame Shepard, here we are again. But of course I have not the smallest suspicion you cracked that old lady on the head and left her there to die.'

'So you think someone did? Kill her, I mean?'

'Not yet. I will gather the preliminary evidence and pass it along to a *juge d'instruction*. If he thinks it is suspicious, we will explore that fully.'

'I don't want it to be murder. Madame wasn't sweet-tempered or friendly, but she was a part of Noyers, obviously intelligent but very old, maybe in her nineties. And then, who quotes Sartre these days? I liked her for that.'

'I shall hope for the same outcome. Until then, there is such a thing as coincidence, and I cannot conjure up the slightest idea why it is anything other than that in your discovering her. So what I want is your eyes and ears.'

After that, it was easy to talk with him. She was able to describe the walk down the hill from Katherine's house, Madame Pomfort's shrill alarm and the sight of the old woman, first from a distance looking like a bundle of rags and then her horror as the victim's body rolled slightly and she saw the blood-streaked face. No one was on the street when the shop first came into view, and none of the people who gathered in the next few minutes had acted suspiciously.

'My friend said the woman had been in her shop a few times and that she carried a black bag with whatever item she hoped Katherine would buy from her that day. Did you find it?' Ariel asked.

'No bag, no small thing one might sell, nothing in her pockets. We would not have known who she was had you not identified her. Now, we have to wonder what might have been in a bag if, indeed, she had it with her. Later, we will take a look at the items in the shop and see if anything is missing. For now, the officers will visit every house in Reigny to see if anyone noticed or heard anything at all.'

He got up, the signal that their interview was over.

Ariel turned back at the café door. 'The dog. I know it's not your priority, but that dog was always with her. I worry that it's frightened and lost. Your officers might ask the local farmers or people who live a little away if they saw it. It was always on a leather leash, so it may be dragging that. I hope it didn't get stuck somewhere.'

'A name for the dog?'

'No, I never heard her call it by name. It's a reddish-tan color and very much like one you'd see in an eighteenth-century painting of a hunt. Definitely not a mutt.'

'Very well then. We're looking for a black bag and a red dog. I can see my officers will have their hands full.' He smiled again and bowed slightly.

Maybe a touch sarcastic, but not such an intimidating man after all, Ariel thought as she walked the rest of the way back to Katherine's house. She'd forgotten that he was so good-looking in spite of that military haircut.

TWO

'The shop, the empty quarters upstairs, and the entire intersection is off limits,' Katherine said, rolling her eyes.

The three women had retreated to Katherine's crowded little living room. Katherine had scooped bunched-up velvet drapes off the small settee and a stack of oversized drawing papers from an ottoman as she waved them in.

'Too early for wine, even for me, although I'm still in shock. I'll start some coffee. Shoo,' she added in a stern voice to the scraggly yellow cat that she had once told Ariel had come with the house she and Michael had bought years ago. It was sitting on top of the desktop computer crammed into a corner and paid no attention to Katherine until she waved her hand directly in front of its face, at which point it looked blankly at her before jumping down soundlessly and heading to the kitchen.

Ariel knew the coffee would be strong, so she asked for a *café crème*, and Katherine nodded.

'*Bien sûr*. You too, Pippa?'

'I'll pass,' Pippa said and winked at Ariel. 'My mum and dad raised me to stick with tea, and I had an ocean already today. Somehow it takes the edge off even the worst moments.'

While Katherine was busy in the cramped kitchen, Ariel looked around and marveled. The room was crowded with old wooden furniture and what Ariel could only call 'stuff' – cracked, leather-bound books piled everywhere, two hulking armoires so full that the doors wouldn't quite close and a costume of some kind tacked up on the wall. An impressive stone fireplace mantel was draped in what might once have been decorative branches, or perhaps just kindling. It was no wonder that, rain or shine, Michael preferred to play his guitar and compose music on the patio. What delighted Ariel, however, wasn't the cacophony of it all but the fact that the room was intriguing, beguiling, popping with rich color and pattern. Katherine had something in her DNA, a sense of design and style, that Ariel was convinced she'd never achieve. Katherine's living room wasn't something that would work for Ariel's formal home, but the sophisticated use of color and pattern might translate into elegance if she could just figure out how.

Coming in from the kitchen with two ceramic bowls of coffee, the old-fashioned way of drinking the brew when the French added milk, Katherine said, 'It's too cold to paint in my little shed, and I think it's going to rain. I'm irritated at my drawings without my darling Jeannette to model for me, and I was counting on sorting through wallpapers today.'

'Where is Jeannette?' Pippa asked.

'There's no school this week, so she's taken the boys to Avallon to buy new shoes. They will not stop growing.'

'Not to steal them, I hope?' Pippa said with a snort.

'Pippa, don't be unfair. Their father may be a bit of a thief, but Jeannette has reformed, and she is determined her brothers won't pick up the habit.'

'I might prefer they did. These days, it seems chasing my cats is their main after-school activity.'

'Your cats have a feline ability to melt into the background, and I don't imagine two loud, clumsy boys really frighten them. Anyway, Michael and I agreed we'd slip a little money to Jeannette. Even in the wilds of Burgundy, kids notice things like sneakers.'

'That's true enough, I guess. The cats all reappear at the door when it's dinner time. I count them each night. Okay, I have to leave, words to put on paper. Not sure I can be productive, given the poor woman who died right near my house, but my editor awaits.' Pippa jumped off the ottoman and left them with their coffee.

Katherine shook her head in mock disapproval. 'Have you noticed she manages to slip "my editor" into the conversation at least once a day?'

'Well, why not? She's made a success so far out of her mystery-novel writing dream.'

'Agreed. It does worry me that she expects our little community to supply all the deadly plots though. I will tell her point-blank not to use Madame Toussaint as a way to make money. It's indecent.' Katherine drained her cup. 'Let me put the chicken in the refrigerator and I'll go back to your place with you. We can think about which walls should be papered and which painted.'

'Perfect. There are days like today, chilly and overcast, when rambling around by myself in that big house is depressing.'

'No ghosts?'

'No, Christiane's memory has become a good one.' The visiting scholar had been killed on the château grounds as part of an attempt to cover up another crime. 'Now, it's just the call of so much left to do. The small amount of furniture that I had sent from New York in the shipping container vanishes in those high-ceilinged rooms, and, anyway, it's out of place. Mid-century modern means mid-twentieth century not nineteenth, much less fifteenth.'

As she pulled into the château's forecourt, at the center of which was the rim of a fountain or the base of a statue, Ariel tried to put the tragedy of the morning aside and concentrate on her mental list of what had to be done this week. She couldn't afford to let the momentum on her project slip if she had any hope of opening it to guests next year.

Unlocking the big wood doors with their iron fittings, she waved Katherine into the mansion. 'I need a distraction from this morning's shock, and there's nothing I can do for Madame Toussaint anyway. Let me show you what's on the to-do list.'

They climbed the two-story staircase with its handsome iron balustrade.

'Solid now,' Katherine said. 'I remember wondering if it would hold me when we first looked around, and I'm quite light.'

'For that, we needed the metal worker Jean-Paul remembered from an earlier commission. I was lucky he had a week between jobs to tackle this, and he said it was nowhere near as difficult as most of the repairs he's done.'

'Speaking of your charming Jean-Paul, I don't hear French pop music coming from his boom box. Is he finished here?'

'Jean-Paul will never be finished, and after the fright from last year, I think I owe him employment for a lifetime. He is a perfectionist in woodworking, for one thing. I decided now that the ground-floor and first- and second-floor windows are done, I should look to the top floor.'

Katherine squinted up the staircase. 'How many floors are there? I get confused.'

'A kind of sub-basement where all the pipes and boilers are, the big basement kitchen above that, then this ground floor, which must have been part of the original fortress because there's a set of steps at the end of the room near the massive stone fireplace that connects it to the old tower. Eventually, it became the public floor where parties took place. The space opposite it must have been a baronial dining room, the kind with a twenty-foot table. Empty now of course.'

'And upstairs?'

'The second floor has those big bedrooms, four of them with a wide hallway large enough to have its own furniture running from front to back. And, above that, the top floor with a few small rooms, which must have been the servants' quarters. There's a long, low-ceilinged room there too – remember, where those stacks of old furniture we scavenged from last year were stored? So five levels, although two are below the main entrance level.'

'Plenty of room for ghosts from long ago, I imagine,' Katherine said as she reached the landing.

Ariel shrugged. 'A woman in Noyers said her mother always told her the servants' rooms were haunted, but since the château hasn't been lived in since the 1970s, that's ancient gossip, more for the fun of telling it than based on any testimony. It's a large space and I need to put it to good use, maybe even as my winter bedroom if we can't solve the problem of heating the tower.'

'Ah, the tower. That's what made you fall in love with the property, isn't it?'

'Yes, the source of my romantic, rose-covered fantasy. That's before I knew it was a remnant of a medieval fort and was still imbued with medieval forms of comfort, which is to say none. I keep asking myself how Dan would have transformed it. Probably by throwing more money at it than I can afford, but it can still be my warm-weather retreat until more money comes in than goes out. The roses still climb up the stones, and Raoul has already pruned and fertilized them.'

'When will Jean-Paul begin on the servants' quarters?'

'Soon hopefully – I need to talk to him about it and see when he might be free.'

They walked to the end of the first-floor hallway.

Katherine looked out the window at the land behind the mansion. 'Then there's this, and the front entrance.' Her eyes were bright. 'Don't tell me you're going to get the landscaping done in the next couple of months?'

Ariel grimaced. 'Hardly. The drive and forecourt need to be done first, to create a suitably important first impression. On this back side, there's the remains of a handsome allée, but the box shrubbery and the woods behind need considerable tending. I might tackle a rose garden over there though.' She pointed to a churned-up space where Andre had installed underground lines to a septic field farther away. 'In the meantime, Raoul's turned out to be a passionate gardener, a job much more to his liking than all that replacement stonework he did last year. He and his wife keep a small potager, he told me, and he's been here every day getting the ground ready for the herbs and lettuces, and the rest. Funny, I don't see him now, which is unusual.'

During her first year, while she struggled to deal with the most urgent needs of the neglected mansion, Raoul's job had been to repair obvious faults in the stonework around the foundations, the wide and tall front steps up to the entrance, and a crumbling low stone wall that had been built close to the building. Katherine had recommended him, adding that she suspected he was a communist 'of the old school', whatever that meant. He had been silent most of the time, marking the minutes until he could quit for the day. But he had done good work, and Ariel had come to count on his stolid presence.

Later, drifting down the worn stone steps from the entrance level to the basement kitchen with her friend, Ariel registered how comfortable the room felt now that it was scrubbed and bright with electric wall sconces and metal-sheaved overhead lights. There was a bowl of oranges on the long wood table, and a rack for wines on one wall.

'Still pretty primitive for cooking,' Ariel said, 'but I can whip up an omelet or pasta. Here's my dream though. Cooking classes, real Burgundy classics, part of vacation packages at the château. What do you think?'

'The kitchen's so big, and you could almost walk into that

fireplace. Great atmosphere for visitors who want to be in a grand old kitchen that served the gentry.' She cackled. 'I hope it doesn't mean hiring some la-de-da fancy chef though. He'd probably demand celebrity fees.'

Ariel held up her hands, wriggled them and said, 'I had a brainstorm, and I can't wait to spring it on her. Regine, who turns out mouth-watering, purely Burgundian meals every day at Tony's café. She's such a generous soul, and nothing fazes her. A woman chef. What do you think?'

'You haven't asked her yet?'

'She and Tony are in Corsica on vacation, chasing the sun. They get back tomorrow.' Ariel stopped short. 'Oh no. They'll hear about the old woman's death as soon as Tony opens the café, and Regine will be affected the most. You know, she was in the habit of delivering a meal to Madame Toussaint now and then? I shouldn't be talking to her about my hopes for making money now.'

Katherine was silent for a long moment. 'It's funny how life goes on, rolling right over tragedy most of the time. Usually, we're only stopped in our tracks when someone close and meaningful to us dies. Still,' she said, touching Ariel's hand for an instant, 'you're right. Wait a week or two to propose your excellent idea. Tony may wonder how he could manage without her even for a day, but her job with you would only be for a weekend or two every month during tourist season, right?'

'Yes, and I bet she'd make up enough coq au vin and vegetable terrine to keep his regulars happy when she's not on the premises.'

'Speaking of food,' Katherine said in a brisk voice, 'it's getting late. Come back to Reigny for dinner. The chicken is done, and Michael would love to see you. No omelet by yourself tonight. It's been a bad day, and we need wine and rich food to settle our stomachs and our thoughts.'

THREE

The next morning was a March surprise – blue skies and a hint of warmth in the sun. Ariel took an apple out on to the steps facing the back of her property, turning her face up to the sun and letting herself daydream about a manicured vista all the way to the tree line. Somewhere, a small flock of birds was chirping, but otherwise it was silent.

The other surprise was that Raoul still hadn't turned up – unlike him where working on the garden was concerned. From the moment last year when he had stopped a villain in his tracks, Raoul had become a member of the restoration team rather than a silent old man focused solely on his tasks. He had helped Jean-Paul replace the rotten beam over the front entrance with its Latin motto, and then became enthusiastic about creating a kitchen garden for her.

Her to-do list for the day included more of the slow business of scraping faded wallpaper off the walls of one bedroom, standing as high on the ladder as she dared to reach the crease between the ceiling and the wall, from which the paper dangled in ribbons. The crick in her neck had become an ache, and she realized she would go to great lengths to put off climbing the ladder today.

Driving over to Raoul's house in Reigny to see if he was okay was obviously more important. After all, his wife worked a few hours a day at the *supermarché* at the outskirts of Avallon and maybe he could use a little company. She'd bring the seed catalog that had arrived in her Noyers post box. That would cheer him up. She'd stop by Pippa's as well. The wallpaper could wait for a few hours. A stern interior voice – her mother's perhaps? – pointed out that the sagging wallpaper would not spontaneously re-adhere itself to the wall, but Ariel had learned to tune out her mother's voice many years ago.

Reigny was sunny too, and a few residents had taken advantage of the weather to go for strolls with their dogs, who romped or sniffed coded messages on tree trunks along the way. The deciduous trees were still barren, but new grass was sprouting along the verge and in some pockets along the riverbank. Maurice had put several tables and chairs on his café's narrow patio. Ariel drove past slowly, thinking she might see Raoul there.

Two boys in ill-fitting pants and sweaters were dancing around, banging into unoccupied tables, one holding a baguette like a sword. Jean's two sons – Jeannette's brothers.

'Must be a handful,' Ariel said under her breath and remembered that Katherine had rather grandly offered to give them art lessons.

She passed Katherine's shop. There were no lights on, and police tape still marked off everything from the curb to the closed door. One blue-and-white police car was parked outside, but there were no officers visible. An involuntary shiver rushed through her body.

She drove a bit farther, to a small street on the left with run-down houses that crowded the pavement on both sides. Raoul's house, mustard-painted stucco over stone, with parts of the stucco missing, was one of only a few before the street petered out and became a dirt lane. Smoke from the chimney signaled someone was home.

As she stepped out of the car, she heard insistent barking from inside, a dog that took its sentinel duties more seriously than Katherine and Michael's two beasts. When she knocked on the heavy door, no one came, but the barking didn't stop. She knocked again, promising herself she wouldn't do it a third time and upset the animal further, since its barking had become almost frenetic.

Just as she was turning away, the door opened slowly. Raoul leaned out, his expression wary. 'Ah, it's you, Madame Ariel,' he said. 'Excuse me – I was busy with something.'

'Good morning, Raoul. I thought I'd stop in to see if you're feeling well. I thought you might have the flu since you haven't been in my garden for a couple of days.'

Raoul's grizzled face and permanent stubble didn't look any different. His iron-gray hair stood at all angles, as it always did when he was at the château, as if he had just run his dust-covered hands through it, which he probably had. He frowned at her, but she reminded herself that was his default expression.

'Your poor dog thinks I'm here to steal your wheelbarrow,' Ariel said. 'Maybe if I come in, he'll stop barking?'

Raoul turned back to the interior of the house without opening the door further and yelled, '*Ferme-la*!' Telling the animal to shut up in no uncertain terms seemed to work. Then he turned again to Ariel. 'Sorry, Madame. That dog is a nuisance.'

'Is he yours?'

Raoul shook his head. 'My sister-in-law's.'

'Does she live in Reigny – your sister-in-law, I mean?'

'No, a bit away, closer to Montbard, but my brother is in hospital and she wanted to spend an overnight with him.'

'I'm sorry. Do you need to visit too? We can put off the garden work.'

'I already went to see him. He is stubborn – he will be fine.'

The dog had been quiet for a moment, but now it started up again. 'Pardon, but I can't invite you in. He is not so friendly. Did you need to talk to me about the garden?'

'No, just a sense of when you might return for work, although, again, it isn't as important as being there for your family.'

He chewed his lip for a moment then nodded. 'Tomorrow. It does not matter for the plants anyway. They will do better if we wait another week or two to put in the little seedlings.'

Ariel realized he wasn't going to ask her in. He wasn't even as carefully dressed as he was when he came to work, so perhaps he'd just thrown something on to answer the door. If he wasn't feeling good, he obviously didn't want to share that with his employer.

'In the meantime, here's a catalog you might like,' she said. 'If you see something that you think will fit into my garden, let me know and perhaps I can order it.'

'Thank you,' he said, although he didn't come farther out of the doorway to reach for it.

Ariel stepped forward and put it in his hand. She tried to be discreet, looking past him to the dark interior of the house, but there was nothing to see except an old armchair and what was probably a tool bag propped against it.

'I will be there tomorrow,' he said again, with a brusque nod, and closed the door abruptly.

Ariel blinked. *I shouldn't be surprised*, she thought. *That's pure Raoul.*

Pippa's car wasn't in her yard, although Ariel spied four or five cats perched on rough stone walls or sunning themselves on the front steps. Reluctant to drive back past the scene of Madame's death, Ariel took the longer way back to Noyers-sur-Serein and wound up entering under the old gateway arch and into the center of the little town, where she found a parking place next to the *épicerie*, the little grocery store.

When she brought several bottles of Badoit water and some yogurts to the counter, the owner leaned over and said in a stage whisper that would not have kept anyone else in the store from hearing, if there had actually been any other customers, 'I don't suppose you've heard? Old Madame Toussaint was murdered – stabbed, I heard.' She nodded and cast a stern look at Ariel as if to suggest this should be a warning to Ariel. 'By someone in the next commune, a poor farming village. And just when her relatives were beginning to take notice of her. Such a tragedy.'

Ariel's mouth opened and closed again. This was either the rumor mill gone wild, or the store owner had a direct line to the brigadier. 'What?' she said. 'When did you hear this? I knew she had died. I was th— I mean, I knew she was found in Reigny but nothing about a stabbing, or a killer captured.'

'I heard it from Marine at the Post Office, and she heard it from her sister, whose husband delivers supplies to Reigny's café.'

Ariel didn't say anything else. It sounded more like a rumor, but even so, if the keeper of the shop everyone in Noyers came into for their staples and newspapers was eagerly dispensing her version of the facts, there was no way to avoid the gossip.

Sure enough, the red-cheeked baker at the boulangerie next door had heard the news too. While the woman bagged her *gougères* and lemon tart, Ariel had a thought and said, 'I know it happened very early in the day. She must have taken the bus to Reigny.'

'No, Madame, not possible. The only bus comes at ten and circles to Nitry in the same commune before it goes to Reigny. I know because the man who used to help me with the early bake was from Nitry and so he had to drive, which upset him. The petrol, you know.'

'But that doesn't make sense. Madame would have had to walk all the way, unless she stayed somewhere overnight, which I can't imagine. It must be six miles – ten kilometers. She was too old, surely?'

The baker settled her net cap more securely over her hair and shrugged. 'Well, you know, she walked, walked, walked around here for hours at a time, sometimes all the way to the ruins at the top of the hill. She and that dog.'

'Did you hear the dog seems to be missing?'

'Ah, no, what a shame. Poor thing probably panicked. And such a handsome fellow. Maybe he'll make his way home. I used to give him a piece of something when Madame stopped in for her bread.' She paused and raised a finger. '*Un moment.* You've made me think. I do the early bake myself now, more's the pity, and it's possible I saw her yesterday long before dawn. It's the picture of the dog in my head, you know. I was putting the first basket of baguettes here in the front window, and I'm sure I saw him straining on his leash to come to the door for his treat. There are no street-lights nearby, and I only saw his shape, and her holding the leash.'

Ariel's pulse quickened. 'You're sure it was her?'

'But of course. No one around here looks like her, you understand?'

'You must tell the gendarmes, Madame. It could be important. Have they come to you yet?'

'No, why would they? I know they talked to the people who live next door and on the same street as Madame Toussaint yesterday. The nosy couple who live across the street apparently told them she had visitors last week, if you can imagine Madame having anyone in her house. At least that's what my friend said.'

'I expect they'll broaden their inquiries today, but if they don't, you must call and tell them what you saw, all right?'

The baker straightened a basket of miniature tarts on the counter. 'I don't like to get involved, but I will see, if they come to my shop.'

Ariel put her packages in the back seat of her car and drove slowly down the block and into the parking square in front of Tony's, not wanting to take up a precious space in front of the food shops. The apartment over his café had not been rented after Ariel moved out and into the château. Tony joked that she'd be back the first time she heard a rat running down the hall, a comment that had made Ariel shudder and Regine lightly slap him on the head.

The café was open for early lunch, a few customers sitting outside at the rickety tables smoking cigarettes. Inside, Tony was stacking glasses behind the long zinc bar and turned to see her. 'Ariel, here already? I knew you hadn't forgotten us.' His lean face split into the grin that always made Ariel think of him as a pirate, a missing tooth behind his incisor making him look rakish.

'For heaven's sake, you've only been gone two weeks,' she said in mock reproach, 'but, yes, I missed you and Regine and my morning espresso – a double today, please. How was your time in the sun?'

'Wait 'til you see my Regine – brown as a nut. The water is so blue it's like paradise, although their red wine is not to my taste at all, far inferior to our burgundies. But you've heard,' he said, the smile disappearing. 'Madame Toussaint, that poor old woman, always minded her own business, never harmed a soul. Of course, Regine and I have only heard what people are saying, and every person's story becomes more extreme, so I expect most of it isn't the truth.'

Ariel looked around. There was no one else inside the café, and she said, 'Please don't tell anyone but Regine, but Katherine Goff and I discovered the body yesterday morning when we went to Katherine's shop to look at things for my house.'

Tony put his elbows on the bar and stared at her. 'But this is terrible, and after everything else. At least your impetuous writer friend wasn't there.' In the silence that followed, Tony's eyebrows rose precipitously. 'She was?'

'Afraid so, although the gendarmes came so quickly, including her boyfriend, that it tamped down her impulse to get involved.' Ariel managed a chuckle then grimaced. 'It's a mess. She was quite old and always looked kind of totter-y. I think it's possible she fell hard and hit the concrete step, but our friend Brigadier Allard isn't sure yet.'

'Ah, the brigadier, he was not so swift discovering the crime last year.'

Ariel nodded. 'He apologized, you know, and yesterday, he made a point of saying I was not a suspect.'

Tony leaned over to her and hissed. 'Not a suspect? Why would you be? *Mon dieu*, the man seems positively dim.' He shoved the last two glasses on the shelf and turned back. 'My advice? Don't speak to him or anyone else about the poor old woman's death. Let the police do all the investigations.'

'You're right,' Ariel said, sipping her drink and putting aside a desire to defend the head of the gendarmerie, 'and I hope to convince Pippa of that. But, Tony, there is a bit of a mystery, and maybe everyone in Noyers can help with it.'

He picked up his ever-present damp cloth and made to wipe the counter, which, when he glanced down, was clean. Throwing it on the bar, he said, 'I have decided I disapprove of mysteries, period.'

'Wait, this is simple. Madame's dog is missing. It wasn't at the scene of her death, and I worry it may be lost or frightened.'

'That dog never went anywhere on its own. Are you sure she didn't leave it in her house or in that fenced garden behind the house? I sometimes saw it there when I walked past the church.'

Ariel paused. 'Good point. I'm not sure. I mentioned it to Allard yesterday, when he interviewed everyone who had been at the scene, but you're right. Do you think it might have returned home after the gendarmes checked her house? I hope it isn't stuck inside.' She remembered the boulangerie owner's observation. 'Someone thinks they saw her and the dog before dawn yesterday, together as usual, but it's possible Madame circled back from the boulangerie and put the dog in the house.'

'Then they would have found it no matter how lazy they are. Most likely he ran away,' Tony said, 'and he'll find his way home. Dogs are smart that way.'

Ariel finished her coffee and put two euros on the bar. Tony shook his head and pushed one back at her.

'I think I'll walk up that way just to satisfy my curiosity,' she said. 'It's such a lovely day, and I don't want to spend it all in the car. I'll come back for dinner – that is if Regine is going to cook today.'

'Of course she is; even made a simple lunch for the regulars. She said she's happy to have her own kitchen again. She's off to Avallon to the butcher so she can stock the freezer with duck, veal and chicken. We admire our butcher here, but his beautiful meats are rather expensive for what I can charge my customers.'

The walk along the street to Madame's house was one of Noyers' charms. Three half-timbered houses in a row lent a medieval flavor to the main street and had actually been constructed in that time. The ground floor of one of them was a shop selling delicate hand-painted ceramics, and its next-door neighbor was in the process of being fitted out to be a wine bar.

After them there were small, stuccoed buildings on each side of the street, all of which had started as private houses. The ones closest to the center of town were now small businesses – her hairdresser's first, a jeweler, then a bookstore that sold books in French and German but not English, and a small restaurant that served vegetarian dishes. Whether they were still homes or not, every window had a box with the promise of flowers imminent. Some had tidy plants in the ground under the windows where space permitted. The street was cobbled, and the whole thing could have been a movie set, at least until you reached the end of the street and Madame Toussaint's corner house. No window boxes. In fact, the outside of the building showed signs of disrepair – shutters with peeling paint hanging off window frames, little piles of stucco debris underneath crumbly exteriors and a crooked iron railing that went around the exterior.

There were no signs of police presence, and the door appeared to be locked. She knocked, but there was no response, not even the barking she would expect if an abandoned dog was inside, frantic to get out.

She walked around to the side where the next street intersected it and peered over the iron railing that fenced in a small garden. The remains of a few cabbage plants and limp greens that might signal turnips kept company in a raised box. A double row of roses sat toward the back of the garden, and Ariel was surprised to notice they had been expertly pruned and were beginning to leaf out. Perhaps Madame was more enthusiastic about beauty than edibles?

Someone cleared a throat behind her, and Ariel spun around, feeling guilty for spying.

'You won't find her here,' a man with only a few wisps of

hair said. He had splotchy skin and eyes that watered, and he pulled his scarf closer around his neck. 'Are you a relative?'

'*Bonjour, monsieur.* No, I was a friend. I know she has died. I just wondered if her property was secure and if her dog might have found its way home.'

'Friend?' he said and coughed. 'I would not have said she had a friend, but then, there's much I did not know about my neighbor, it seems.'

'Perhaps I'm overstating our relationship. I saw her around, and we did speak now and then. She wasn't very social, was she?'

He barked a laugh, which caused him to start coughing again. 'Not social? If my wife or I so much as asked her how her garden was coming, she would glare as though we were asking for some privileged information.'

'Well, obviously she cared about her roses,' Ariel said, smiling to lighten the conversation.

'She had a gardener tend to them. Her roses were her vanity. She liked having people on the street, especially during the tourist months, stop and take pictures of them.'

Ariel was surprised. Vanity had not seemed to be one of Madame's faults. She certainly hadn't dressed for approval or spoken in dulcet tones. But the roses? As poor as she was, how had she paid a gardener? 'You live nearby?'

'Across the street and up one house.' He turned and pointed to a house that must have been very like Madame's a long time ago but which was as unalike as possible now – a tidy gravel walk, bordered by freshly painted iron railings, the house's walls painted beige over smooth stucco, pale-green shutters tightly attached to every window and window boxes under the ground-floor windows. The boxes were already showing geranium leaves and buds.

'You are the American at the château, yes? We see you at the café now and then. Regine is a much better cook than my wife, but don't tell her – my wife, I mean.' He managed a small smile through closed lips.

'Ariel Shepard,' she said and held out her hand.

'Monsieur Legrand. The police came to ask questions. My wife didn't want to speak with them, but I told them what little

I could. Lived alone. Talked to herself when she was out walking. I noticed she bargained hard when the food sellers set up the farmers market on the town square, so I guess she didn't have much money. Unless' – and here his tone changed to signify a possible secret – 'she was a miser and had lots of money she did not want people to know about.' He raised his eyebrows and gave Ariel a knowing look.

Ariel hadn't thought of that. Was Madame not entirely who she seemed to be? After all, she had sold some fine silver pieces to Katherine. If the police searched her home, would they discover a Madame Toussaint no one knew?

Monsieur Legrand coughed again. 'Her relatives will come as soon as they hear, I am certain.'

'Relatives? I didn't know she had any.'

'Not around until this past year, but they came a few times recently and must have been helping her around the house, getting rid of things in their big German car.' He paused to sniff disapprovingly. 'Perhaps bringing supplies also, you know? They were here again the other day, so perhaps they live not far away. I think they are well off. Fancy car, nice clothes and manners. The woman was a professional of some kind, I think. She had one of those silly little dogs with the long hair and flat faces. My wife loves them. I think they might as well be cats.' He laughed.

'Would you know how to reach them? Some of the townspeople want to help with the funeral.'

'*Désolé*. One minds one's own business of course, and the man and his wife didn't introduce themselves, only said they were here to visit his grandmother. But do not concern yourself – they will return. Where property is concerned, you may be sure relatives will present themselves.' He winked.

Ariel nodded.

'I must get back inside, where it is warm. My wife fusses over me.' With that, he backed away, ducked his head in a bow and walked briskly to the little path and his front door.

Ariel stood for a moment, looking at the expertly pruned rose bushes, each one with a name tag stuck into the ground in front of it that she couldn't read from outside the fence. The neighbor's suggestion might seem far out at first, but was it so unlikely? And if it was possibly true, then could it be motive enough for someone who knew to attack her in a robbery attempt that went wrong? In that case, the house would surely be a target too. Had the gendarmes searched it properly? She decided to call the brigadier. Not investigating, she reminded herself, just being an alert bystander.

Not an excuse to make contact with him? her inner critic asked. *Definitely not,* she huffed at herself, *just doing my civic duty.*

FOUR

As the day lengthened, clouds moved in along with a chilly breeze, and the sunlight disappeared. She checked her cell phone and realized she needed to get back to the château to meet an architect Andre had recommended, who would look at the bathroom construction project.

Her place was only about a kilometer from the town. She drove slowly up the drive from the pillars that marked the entrance to her property, looking at the neglected and dying plane trees that had once formed a grand allée and wondering again when and how she could improve such an unimpressive view.

She remembered an earlier visit by Christiane, the elegant Sorbonne scholar, in which the historian had looked out at the acreage beyond the dry moat as a possible site for a small orchard. Katherine had agreed and said, 'There's a man from somewhere around here who sells apples later in the year, but I don't know what kind. Have you researched the varieties for your orchard? It would look so perfect on that gentle hill.'

When she had arrived in Burgundy with the not-inconsequential proceeds of the Manhattan apartment, she had been optimistic about having adequate funds to bring Château de Champs-sur-Serein back to life. Now she was racing against a diminishing bank account to bring it to a status where she could advertise its bed and breakfast appeal. In her darkest moments, usually in the middle of the night, in the temporary space she had turned into a bed-sitting room, she wondered if she had gotten in over her head.

She needed a break. If Corsica was out for the same reasons drapery was a tug on her budget, then maybe Paris for a couple of days? A stop at l'Orangerie to breathe in the peace of the Monet water lilies murals, a long walk in the Jardin des Tuileries or lunch on a bench near the fountain at Jardin du Luxembourg, where children and their parents or nannies helped them sail little boats. Much as she loved Regine's cooking, perhaps she could treat herself to an haute cuisine dinner somewhere. Research was needed.

The idea improved her mood, and she made a promise to herself that she would set a date in the near future. She and Dan had visited all those places. Her stomach flipped and her mood sank. Go without him? It would make her loss more pronounced. She'd hear his voice at every corner she turned, at every magnificent view she sought out.

The clouds darkened as she stood at the window. They matched her mood. 'Enough,' she said out loud. 'I need food, I need a glass of wine, I need to be with the people I care about here. Paris can wait a little longer.'

She did a quick tour to make sure all the windows were closed and locked, that the hot-water heater was still on and most of the lights off, then locked up and ran to the car as the first raindrops fell.

'I guess a lot of people had the same idea,' Ariel said, smiling as Regine brought her a glass of red wine, 'although I expect most of us are just happy you're back and in the kitchen again.'

'Not as happy as I am,' Regine said.

She was, Ariel thought, tanned, and her suspiciously jet-black hair showed a whisper of a lighter hue above her forehead.

She frowned. 'The cafés there seem to serve sausages in every dish unless it's from the sea. But thoughts of poor Madame dying alone and not even in her own house make me sad.'

'Have you ever been in her house?'

'Only once.'

Someone from a nearby table called to her, and Regine excused herself.

Ariel looked around. If she wanted to ask Regine more about Madame's house and what might be in it, she'd have to prolong her meal. That would mean having dessert. Oh well, a slice of warm tart wasn't such a terrible thing to contemplate.

Ariel dug into the plate Regine had brought her and wondered how such a simple dish of stewed chicken, red wine and tomatoes could be so comforting. Maybe this was France's version of chicken soup. Perfect with a basket of baguette slices and herbed butter.

The café had almost cleared out, and Regine had served the

last apple tart. Tony was wiping down the imposing copper espresso machine that sat at one end of the bar, and Regine's new helper, a teenage boy whose single mother cleaned houses in Noyers during the tourist season, was washing dishes in the small kitchen tucked away discreetly behind a curtain.

Regine came over to sit with Ariel, plunking her wine glass on the table and lowering her hefty but shapely body into the chair opposite Ariel. 'I bet you know more than we do,' she said, grinning. 'You and your all-woman detective team.'

She was teasing. Last year, an overly eager local reporter who had rubbed everyone the wrong way had done a negative article about Ariel, Katherine, and Pippa. They had made a vow to stay out of the spotlight. Now, Ariel hesitated. Was she investigating, or just being nosy?

'The gendarmes were on the scene right away, and their chief is asking an investigative judge to determine if it was anything other than a tragic fall. Rumors are flying, and I guess if I had to explain my interest it would be because as crusty as she was, she was a real presence in Noyers. And Noyers is now my home.'

Regine reached across the table and squeezed Ariel's hand. 'You are one of us, and I happen to agree. Noyers will be a little less colorful without her, a little less – how should I put it – welcoming to people who are different. She is one less person to embrace.'

'You were kind to her. Tony says you brought her dishes from here?'

'Now and then. I wasn't sure she ate properly. She liked tonight's dish, for example, but refused my ratatouille outright. "Too much garlic," she told me. But she never turned down my veal-and-mushroom dish, or a container of leek-and-potato soup.' She smiled at the memory.

'Did she invite you in when you came over?'

'Never. But wait, once, not long ago, she told me she had sprained her wrist and asked me to put the covered dish on her kitchen table. Her wrist was badly bruised, and I asked her if she'd like me to drive her to the doctor in Avallon, but she insisted it didn't hurt; it was just too weak to hold a heavy dish. Her face looked bruised too. I asked her if she had fallen and she said she had, that her dog had pulled too hard on his leash when she was walking him late one afternoon.'

'I'm going to sound nosy, but did her house seem, well, like her, I guess?'

Regine took a long sip of her wine. 'I didn't see anything unusual. We all know she hasn't got any money. The room I was in was crowded with a few old pieces. A rough-looking kitchen table, an ugly armoire, some shelves stacked crookedly with plates and cooking pots, an old stove and even older refrigerator, some stacked cardboard boxes, probably things she needed to move up to the first floor for storage.' She paused. 'I should have offered to take the boxes upstairs, but I had the sense she didn't want me to stay – typical of her solitary behavior.'

Ariel tapped her fingers on the table. 'Regine, did you see any silver tableware, perhaps a tea service or a decorated bowl or plate? I ask because Katherine told me she was bringing some lovely old pieces to the shop and asking Katherine to buy them. It doesn't sound like what Madame would use in the kitchen you're describing.'

Regine's mouth turned up a fraction, but it was a sorrowful smile. 'No, it doesn't, and, no, I didn't see anything that fancy. Truth is, the room was not tidy. I remember feeling the itch to get in there and clean it. Madame would have been furious if I had even hinted at hiring someone to help with housework, even if she could afford it.'

'She must have had her personal treasure tucked away upstairs then. The gendarmes had had the shop surrounded with their crime scene tape, but maybe I can take a closer look at the pieces when they're finished there. It's curious that she had beautiful things and yet lived so sparsely.'

Regine stood up. 'Maybe it was her philosophy. I heard she was a communist in the old days. She might have inherited from a relative and felt uncomfortable about owning fancy things? You let Tony and me know how we can help. We will talk with our neighbors and the mayor and will make sure she gets a respectful send-off at the church.'

Something nagged at Ariel, but she lost the thought. 'That's a lovely idea, but someone – her neighbor – said her family has recently been in touch with her. Ah, a neighbor I ran into. He saw them. They may want to make the arrangements.'

'Too little, too late, if you ask me,' Regine said with a snort. 'But, yes, I will check with the priest in Avallon, the closest parish.'

Communist, that was it, what had tugged at her memory. Raoul was – at least she thought he was – a communist. Ariel tried to see Madame as a communist. They were both brusque, both old, not quite old enough to have been active in the occupation of Burgundy in the war surely? Ariel had no idea of her age, but the woman had quoted Jean-Paul Sartre and he had been a politically active leftist in the fifties, which would more likely date Madame's interest.

Yay, finally a small moment in France when my PhD is useful, her sarcastic inner voice cheered. Not so useful, really, since it had no bearing on Madame's death.

FIVE

The next morning, as Ariel was drinking the brew her little cafetière made, which had to stand in for real espresso until she stopped at the café, she heard Raoul's old car drive into the gravel forecourt and the car door slam. She finished the slice of yesterday's baguette, smeared with strawberry preserves, and headed out the back door to the site of what would, she hoped, be a tidy garden of lettuces and celery and tomatoes and who knew what else by late summer.

'Good morning, Raoul. Sorry the weather isn't as good as it was yesterday. The ground is a little muddy.'

He shrugged. 'I will continue setting the brick boundaries and work on the path from the garden to the door.' He looked at her running shoes, already slightly wet from the puddle in the ground outside the kitchen door. 'That bit has to be leveled, then sand and pulverized quarry stone rolled over it before much longer.'

'You're right. I don't know what I'd do without you, thanks. Did you have time to look at the Verisem catalog? I'm afraid I'd order one of everything, so best left to your greater judgement.'

Raoul ran a hand over his grizzled chin. 'Best to go easy, Madame Ariel. My wife's seedlings are where I'd start if you approve. Grown right here for our soil temperatures, you know?'

'Will you – or she – let me pay for them?'

He nodded. '*D'accord*, maybe a small amount. But I'm thinking you have much more space here in the back, and maybe you'll let us expand our own small garden some day? Your soil is stronger, and you have more sun.' He waved at the western sky behind him.

'Good idea – I love it. As soon as you've got my little kitchen garden going, please invite your wife over. We'll have coffee and look at what might work.'

Ariel excused herself and went upstairs to get dressed and call Brigadier Allard before she got too busy. Fortunately, cell-phone reception was good here on top of the gentle hill on which the château sat. Pippa had told her that was a good thing to mention when she advertised her bed and breakfast. When would that happen? Was it even possible she could welcome her first guests this year? No, she answered herself.

She was shrugging on a fleece jacket over jeans when there was another knock on the front door. When she opened it, a young man with startling violet-blue eyes stood there, smiling shyly at her.

'Lucas, how nice to see you. Come in.'

'Madame Ariel, I think you need a big bell or a knocker. I was not sure you could hear me,' he said as he edged in the open door.

She was reminded that Lucas Gaultier was like a wild colt, quick to turn and run.

'Are you offering to take on the task of finding me something that matches the house?' she said, not sure if he would want to work at the château again.

'Y-Yes,' he stammered, 'but I was not asking for work. You have others who can do this, I am sure.'

'I'd be delighted if you'd take that job off my to-do list, which is already far too ambitious. But why did you come by today? And can I offer you a *café presse*?'

He blushed. 'If it is not too much trouble.' He held out the sack he was carrying. 'I am still learning, hoping to become a chef, and I wondered if you would be so kind as to taste this and tell me, truthfully, what you think?'

'What is it?' she asked, opening the bag and peering at the covered glass jar.

'Duck confit with lentils and leeks. My own recipe. I have eaten so many versions, I can no longer be sure if it is any good.' He grinned. 'I think I am better at simple things like onion tarts and cassoulets. I bring my results to the community center where people who do not have enough food will eat anything and say they like it.'

Ariel laughed. 'I warn you, I'm not too different from those lucky people. My kitchen is still quite primitive, and I count on Regine and Tony to feed me well.'

'Ah, Regine, that one is a master cook,' Lucas said, nodding. 'When I can afford to eat there, I try to figure out on my own what she puts into her sauces. She won't tell me.'

They went down to the kitchen, and Ariel was pleased that Lucas had no reaction to the room other than interest in its potential. He had spent some frightening moments there one fraught day last year. While she heated the sample dish, he walked around, making suggestions that showed he was rapidly becoming a real cook.

'Delicious, and I'm guessing there's some unusual herb in it?'

The young man's face broke out into a wide smile, devoid of his usual diffidence. 'But if I tell you, then I am giving away my secret, am I not?'

'Like Regine? As long as it's not a poisonous mushroom,' Ariel said. It was so rewarding to see Lucas blooming after his tough times. She wondered if he had a girlfriend. He was easily the best-looking man she had met since she'd moved to Burgundy, like a male model only not surly, and way too young for her. Surely, though, a catch for someone his own age.

'You can add this to your repertoire with confidence,' she said as she handed him the washed jar, 'and please let me join your list of taste testers again.'

He took a couple of cell-phone photos of her door and promised he'd be back with ideas in a few days, and then he was gone, a colt who had suddenly got shy and galloped away. Ariel smiled as she walked back up the staircase. Sweet kid.

The police chief wasn't in, a brisk female voice told her, but perhaps she'd like to make an appointment if it wasn't an emergency? It had to be late afternoon. The brigadier was at a conference in Dijon and would be back in the office at five o'clock. Would that do?

'If it's not too late for him?' Ariel said. The voice assured her the chief worked late many nights.

So, perhaps not married? the little voice in Ariel's head said.

'Good. I will be there at five. *Merci, Madame.*'

What are you thinking? she asked herself. *I have friends, I have a life, my Dan has only been gone for a little over a year. I'm not ready, and even if I were, he hasn't shown the slightest interest in me as anything other than a suspect, an interfering American and a stranger in his country.*

Chiding herself, Ariel turned to her list of work to be done, most of which was in her head but memorialized in the little notebook she now carried in case she had an understandable brain freeze as the realization of how much everything cost threatened to overwhelm her:

1. Work on Bathrooms Plan B with Andre, with a budget of about half of what he'd probably propose.
2. Research some regional French cooking classes and decide how to make hers uniquely appealing.
3. Go to Katherine's shop and see what old wallpapers she could buy and enlist her friend's help in scouting for more if needed.
4. Invite Michael and Katherine to dinner at Tony's before he left on whatever new gig was on his schedule.
5. Decide if Madame's death was a homicide, and if so, make sure the crime doesn't go unsolved.

That last should have given her pause, but Ariel wasn't fazed. The old woman deserved a full accounting and justice. Not that she agreed with Tony about the brigadier or the gendarmes' skills, but sometimes it was the little things like what a woman carried in her bag that they passed right over. Madame's black bag and the engraved treasure she wanted to sell cheaply were likely not to be seen as important in their own right. Katherine and Pippa would understand.

Ariel added another item to her to-do list:

6. Invite Pippa and Katherine for an indoor picnic at the château right away.

She heard Andre's little truck scrunching over the gravel and met him at the door. An hour later, having listened to her plumber, she realized how naïve her decision to add a bathroom was. Andre had been optimistic, but then, he had no way of knowing what was, or more accurately, wasn't within her reach. Maybe bathrooms in each of the four rentable rooms wasn't going to happen. Maybe upgrade the one she had hoped to make an en suite feature and then one new one, so four bedrooms sharing two would work? They'd have to be pretty luxurious in that case. The simple bathroom on the servants' floor needed expansion too. The tub was rusty and there was no shower, only a bowl for washing.

The conversation with Andre was confusing partly because her conversational French, while better than her ability to read academic research on Jean-Paul Sartre and his friends, was short on plumbing vocabulary. Last year, she had had an involuntary crash course on building materials, furnaces and sewer systems, but there was always more to learn, and she added *conduites d'eau* to her little notebook as Andre explained the intricacies of adding new water lines within the walls.

'It can be done,' he assured her, and if only for one new bathroom not a major problem. Just more holes in more walls and more copper pipes.

Ariel asked him if he would take charge of the work, and he agreed but warned her it must be done by the end of July, before he and his wife left for their month-long vacation to the south of France.

'We go every year, and my wife would never agree to any postponement,' he said, following that declaration with a full-throated laugh and a slap on his pant leg that raised a small cloud of dust.

The French, she had learned, took the month of August off. Almost everyone. Almost everywhere, unless the business owner relied on summer tourists for most of his income. Restaurants, the dry cleaner, the shoe-repair shop, the plasterer and now her plumber.

She watched as his little truck swung on to the road toward the A6. The window, now handsomely framed in Jean-Paul's master craftsman's work, was waiting for drapes. Add that expense to the long list. For now, she wanted to talk to Katherine about something other than flooring, new walls and fixtures.

Michael Goff answered the phone, something he rarely did because his French was limited. 'She's over your way,' he said. 'Today's the day a fashion magazine she tells me she must have is delivered to the little grocery store in town. She's got my car and will fill it at the gas pump out front to save me a detour when I have to get up to Paris again in a few days. I want to drive this time.'

'She told me you were looking for a recording studio.'

'Yeah, but the one I went to was pretty primitive. I may go back to the one out here, although it's, how do they say it, "tray share"?'

Ariel winced. 'I called to see if she can get into her shop again. There are some things I want to look at. Also, I want to make sure I can play host to the two of you properly before you leave for the States again. I want a chance to hear more about what you're up to.'

'I won't be going for at least a couple of weeks, which is fine with me. Finish the album, which will probably sink like a stone, and do a couple of tour dates with my former bandmates. Between them, my wife and Pippa can conjure up trouble faster than a flea can bite. This death may be nothing more than an accident, but I see that glint in Kay's eyes, and see her and Pippa hunched over coffee, and I get to worrying.'

So they're suspicious too? Ariel thought. *OK, that item on the to-do list just moved up a notch.* 'I'll call her later, hoping it's not off bounds. Let her know, will you?'

They rang off, and Ariel tapped her phone against her teeth. When she and Katherine met later, she'd suggest the indoor picnic at the château to decide how they should proceed, and before that, she'd see what the brigadier had to say.

SIX

To prove to herself her motivations were professional and not personal, Ariel deliberately didn't redo her messy ponytail or put on lipstick before meeting Brigadier Allard at the gendarmerie in Avallon. Her blond hair was wisping around her face, and her bangs, which needed another trim, were getting in her eyes as the brisk March wind swirled around the street where she parked. The fluffy wool scarf she had chosen was long enough to wrap around her neck twice, and she held her camel-hair coat, a transplant from her New York life, closed with one hand as she pushed open the door to the police station.

Nothing had changed since her last visit. The dingy '*Pas de fumer*' sign was still there, as was the smell of cigarettes. The fluorescent overhead light was still casting a deathly hue. The man on duty at the window was still looking harassed and unhappy to see a member of the public who might require service.

'*Bonjour*,' Ariel said, putting on a smile intended to show she wasn't about to lodge a complaint.

'What assistance are you looking for, Madame?'

'The brigadier. I have an appointment.'

His glance sharpened. 'Ah, the American. Why didn't you say so?'

Ariel opened her mouth to protest that she hadn't had time and didn't know how her nationality came into it, but he had already pushed himself out of his chair on the other side of the door and opened it.

'Corporal,' he called over his shoulder, and a slender, dark-haired man who looked too young to shave trotted up behind him. 'To the brigadier, and don't waste time.'

That meant the boy sprinted up the stairs and was halfway down the hall before Ariel made it to the landing. He flung open the door to Allard's office and snapped his arm into a salute as Ariel caught up with him. 'Sir, your appointment.'

Allard's deep rumbling came from within. 'Good, good,

Corporal.' Then Allard himself appeared in the doorway, dressed in his uniform, rather than a suit and tie, and shooed the eager recruit away with a half salute.

'Come in, Madame. I haven't decided whether young Sahli will be a good policeman, but if eagerness counts, he's already scoring high.' He smiled.

'Is he French?'

'You do not know nearly enough Frenchmen, my dear lady.' Allard chuckled. 'But, yes, he is born and raised French, of Algerian grandparents who came here many decades ago and have fully absorbed themselves in French life. It is a sad fact today that there is more scrutiny of Arab and North African immigrants, but he is ours. A good lad.

'Now,' he said, sitting back behind his desk and placing his hands on it, fingers spread wide, 'how can I help you? My guess is it has something to do with the death of Madame Toussaint.'

'You must know rumors are racing all around Noyers. Everyone has a theory or is sure they have the most shocking information from impeccable sources. If you've determined this was an unlucky fall, you can tell me that, can't you?'

'I could if it were, but it now appears her injuries are more suspect, and some don't match with a fall that morning.'

'Not a stabbing then? One of the rumors.'

'No, her head injuries caused her death. That much we will release to the public.'

'That means you can't tell me much more,' Ariel said. 'Tell me this though. Is it suspicious enough that you're bringing it to that special judge and investigator, the one that sounds like an American district attorney?'

'I have a call into him, and I suspect after I brief him, he is likely to accept the assignment, alas.'

'Did you ever find her carryall, the bag Katherine told you about, that she always had when she went to Katherine's shop to sell something?'

'No, we didn't recover anything from the scene or close by that belonged to her. If she had it – and no one has come forward to say they saw her that morning – then it may have been taken by whoever attacked her.'

Ariel held up one hand. 'About that – the woman who owns

the boulangerie in Noyers thinks she did see Madame before dawn, walking with her dog. Your officers might want to interview her. No,' she added, 'I wasn't investigating. It just came up when I picked up my *gougères*.'

'Just came up, eh?' He looked amused.

Ariel decided it was time to move the conversation along. 'I assume your officers have searched Madame's house? You didn't by chance find her dog cooped up there?'

'Only to see if there were signs of burglary or violence there. No dog. So he hasn't found his way home yet? A pity. Perhaps someone has him and will advertise for his owner in the paper or online. It's not unusual for dogs to wander, and this is a big country to roam in.' He waved his arm in a circle.

Ariel changed the subject. 'She lived in that house for such a long time, I'm told. Wouldn't the place be full of useful information, letters from the relatives, or phone bills, or framed family pictures? You must have looked?'

'Stacks of old newspapers and magazines, bills paid and unpaid, furniture that is far out of fashion and the like. Nothing that rang alarm bells for my officers or gave us clues about possible danger to her, or about her own history. She hardly ever made phone calls, but we're looking into the telephone company's records. Do you have anything more about the old woman you can tell me, anything that might help us find who knocked her on the head?'

'Not really. I catch bits and pieces of what her neighbors say, nothing that seems important. I have heard that she was once part of a larger family, and that they cut her adrift long ago. But one neighbor mentioned they recently re-entered her life and might have been helping her take care of the house. A grandson and his wife, I think.'

'Ah, you would not by chance have a name or phone number?'

'Sorry, the neighbor didn't know their names, only that the man said he was related. He said they aren't local. They will have to claim her body and arrange for burial.'

Allard shook his head. 'Not yet, not until the coroner says it is proper to release the body. The mayor of Noyers agreed to identify the body formally, so at least that is taken care of.'

For a moment, neither of them said anything. Ariel had a

sudden mental image of the old woman on a mortuary slab, even more vulnerable than when she was alive, and it sickened her.

Allard glanced at his watch. They both started to speak at the same moment. 'You first,' she said.

'Apologies. I notice the time, and the food they served at today's meeting was inadequate. I was wondering . . . I mean you are probably busy later, but if not, could I take you to dinner? That is, one with no talk of crime or criminals or missing dogs?'

Ariel felt the blush instantly as it rose to her cheeks. 'I must seem like a pest, or worse, always pumping you for information, or pushing you for more when something suspicious takes place.'

'Maybe.' He smiled, and she noticed his eyes twinkled, probably because she wasn't pressuring him at the moment. 'I realize you are new to my district, and I know very little about you. You might say I have a hidden agenda.'

'Oh.'

'Sorry, that came out wrong. I would like to get to know you better. It would seem you intend to make Noyers your home, or at least semi-permanent home. My favorite restaurant doesn't open for the season until April, but there is a fine, small one tucked away near Montbard. If you are free, I can call to see if they have a table open tonight?'

'That would be lovely. I warn you, there's a lot I don't know about my new environment, so I will probably grill you in return.'

That evening, over a first course of Alsatian onion tart and a Chablis wine, Ariel was more relaxed. The restaurant was a gem really, a small room with dark-red lacquered walls hung with oil paintings of the surrounding low hills. A fireplace warmed the room, and low lamps and quiet piped-in classical music completed the atmosphere. The waiter steered them adroitly to the evening's special entrée, a lentil ragout with Toulouse sausage, and the promise of a red wine from one of the small vineyards in the region.

'Another wonderful restaurant,' Ariel said. 'I've been introduced to several since I arrived, but even informal Tony's café in Noyers is a treat. There are plenty of French chefs in New York, but they're mostly for special evenings.'

'I have never been to the U.S., and I hope I can visit after I retire. Niagara Falls, the Empire State Building, Hollywood, the whole bit.'

She laughed. 'You do realize you've just described what we call a bicoastal perspective?'

He raised his eyebrows as he polished off the last of his wine.

'Sorry, I'm not laughing at your vision, but as an East Coast native, I had to learn myself that there's a lot of America between New York and California.'

'You mean the Grand Canyon, New Orleans, Santa Fe and your great city of Chicago? My daydreams include all of them, but my budget does not.'

'Mine neither,' Ariel said, 'although Dan and I talked about going to so many places.' Her voice trailed away, and she paused. He might not know. 'Dan,' she said, taking a deep breath, 'was my husband, and the reason I'm here.'

Allard said nothing, just looked intently at her, waiting.

'Dan died suddenly. He left me Château de Champs-sur-Serein, you see.'

'Ah, yes, I remember that is how you came to own it, but I wasn't sure if he was deceased or if you were divorced. Pardon me for not realizing. If you are from New York, do you still have a home there?'

'No, I sold my apartment and am here to stay – that is if the French government will have me. For now, I'm in limbo. I got my *carte de séjour*, but as you know, it has to be renewed every year.'

'Do you have children or parents in the States that will require you to be there part of every year?'

'Dan and I were only married for four years, so no children, and my parents are adamant that they'll be fine on their own. And you? Do you have kids?' She wasn't going to ask him if he was married, although she noticed he didn't wear a wedding ring.

He sat back as the waiter cleared their first course and waited as their entrées were set in front of them and the new wine was poured into larger glasses. When they were alone again, he said, 'I was married once, and we had a son who died.' He held his glass up to the soft light for a moment, took a sip and added, 'Something like that can tear apart a marriage. It did mine unfortunately.'

'I'm so sorry.'

'There, you see, we have both been put to the test of life, *oui*? And here we are, fortunate to have interesting lives and to be enjoying a lovely dinner.' His voice made it clear the subject was closed.

The rest of the evening was pleasant but uneventful. Ariel had to restrain herself from asking questions about the investigation into Madame Toussaint's death, while Allard told amusing stories about the life of the area, everything from cattle who routinely showed up in unexpected places to the drunken follies of annual town fêtes and parades that got out of hand. He advised her not to miss the truffle auction in Nitry, or the modest Resistance museum in the Morvan, the forest in which French Resistance fighters hid and from which they attacked the Nazis who occupied Burgundy. 'The Resistance was strong around here, you know? Afterwards, everyone claimed to have been involved, but some were just trying to avoid being ostracized.'

They had taken their separate cars to Montbard and so they said their goodnights outside the restaurant. It was only as she drove home, watching more carefully now for stray cattle on the narrow roads, that Ariel realized she didn't know his first name.

'Stupid,' she said out loud. 'Maybe he told me at some point? Now I have to go on the internet to find out without letting him know I forgot.'

She drove slowly up the drive to her new home, glad to see the welcoming light glowing through the entry-level window. Long ago, she had decided having a light welcoming her back at night was essential for the big mansion to feel like home. Tomorrow it would be another to-do list, but for now she was focused on heat from her pipes, a big duvet to curl into and a good book. Yes, Château de Champs-sur-Serein had become, however unlikely, home.

SEVEN

O ver a first coffee the next morning, she flipped back to her to-do list.

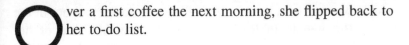

    2. Research some regional French cooking classes and decide how to make hers uniquely appealing.

An hour on her laptop convinced Ariel that she could make a good case online for Regine's particular kind of cooking. She might even persuade the owner of the boulangerie to do a pastry session once or twice a year. The more she thought about making food a particular attraction of her bed and breakfast, the more ideas she had. A trip to the little shop in Avallon that stocked only local cheeses, a talk by the sommelier at Noyers' fanciest restaurant, possibly part of a private wine tasting and dinner. After all, Burgundy was famous for its cuisine and its wines, a gem in France. And the Yonne district was not as well traveled as the west side, which had the great *terroirs* and so the famous wines. If Regine cooked, and she served as the tour guide, starting up a château de cuisine experience wouldn't be that hard. All she had to do was convince Regine, who might feel her skills were too rustic.

She decided she'd put off her visit to Katherine's shop a little longer, until the picture of the old woman lying at the doorstep had faded a little, but she'd invite both of her friends to come for lunch tomorrow, if not today. No time to waste.

A call to Pippa and it was agreed she would pick Katherine up if Michael's new SUV wasn't offered, it being understood that driving even short distances in Katherine's peculiar car was not an option. 'Honestly, I always feel I should be pedaling,' Pippa said, 'and there's the noise.'

Andre wouldn't be back with cost estimates for the new bath-rooms for a few days, Jean-Paul wasn't coming to look at the top floor until tomorrow and Raoul was absorbed in his garden work. She emailed the painter, who sounded charming, but he wasn't coming over for a few more days to size up the job. It was quiet and Ariel was at a loose end. Even her to-do-right-now list was short: grocery shopping, a few more essentials to equip her kitchen, a visit to get her bangs trimmed. She itched to be doing something on Madame's behalf and decided to take a long walk around the outskirts of Reigny to look for her dog. If he was in Noyers, he'd be corralled. Tony had doubtless put out the word. But people in Reigny wouldn't know Madame or her faithful companion, and there were lots of wooded acres and empty fields, plus the Serein's riverbank where he might still be hiding.

The day was good for walking, clouds skudding across the blue sky, pushed along by the winds that translated to a stiff, refreshing breeze at ground level. It was far too early for tourist traffic – the Bellegardes' castle wouldn't be open for visitors for another month, and there wasn't much else for sightseers. The old church was open for Christmas and Easter, and Easter only if a traveling priest was available. Not much to look at, the commune had reluctantly accepted it back from the French government, a century after the French Revolution had confiscated all the churches.

Ariel grabbed her binoculars, a thermos of water and a couple of *gougères* and began her walk at the edge of town, far from Katherine's house, on a path through a forested patch. At one point, she was on high ground and could see Château Bellegarde, Sophie Bellegarde's property in Reigny, from above. It was impressive, and the owners had turned the grounds close to the castle into a handsome if somber garden. No flower beds, no climbing roses, no fruiting trees, no potager that Ariel could see through her binoculars. The scrub woods had closed in around it, and there was no grassy area. Her mansion would be more hospitable, friendlier.

An hour later, having circled the farthest points around the town and the riverbank without success, she tightened her circle to include the village streets. She passed Pippa's house, Madame Pomfort's and the charming farmhouse where the young couple with the baby had taken up residence. According to Katherine, they had dropped out of their business jobs in Paris to begin dairy farming and cheesemaking.

The police tape was gone from the front of Katherine's unnamed shop, but the lights were off, and Ariel resisted the temptation to look in the window. She'd have to step on the very spot where the old woman had died, and she wasn't ready for that.

Madame Pomfort wasn't working in the garden next to the church, so Ariel sat on the church steps to eat her cheesy puffs and gulp down the last of her cool water. The trees across the way rustled, and the engine of a truck coming from the quarry labored noisily under its load. Probably Jean, Jeannette's and the boys' father, hauling the area's pocked stones for an outside wall like her own.

Under that noise, something else tickled Ariel's ears. She got up and looked around. Nothing she could see matched what her brain was suggesting, remembering. No children, no hungry cats, no one humming. So what?

She looked at the thick wooden doors to the church. A sturdy padlock and chain through the iron door handles looked like it had been there forever, but the sound might be coming from there. Of course, there were no convenient windows to look through, the only openings being high up on the face of the building and covered in what looked like poor-quality modern stained glass. Impulsively, she put her ear against the thick door. It was quiet.

Shrugging, she picked up the remains of her picnic and took a few steps when she heard it again, this time without a truck covering the noise. Something inside was making the sound, and she had a sudden flash of intuition – the dog? Madame's dog? Was it possible it had found its way in through a crevice and was now stuck? She pounded her fist on the door and called out.

In answer, a short bark, then silence. It was a dog, and who else's could it be?

'Stay there,' she said to the door in a loud voice, 'I'll get help.'

As she jogged to the *mairie* up the street, she heard herself and agreed with her inner voice that she was an idiot. If the dog had been able to get out, would it have stayed there? The poor thing was probably terrified and starving.

The door to the minuscule town hall was locked, and the sign outside said the office was closed until the roof could be repaired. Delphine's phone number was posted, and Ariel whipped out her phone and dialed. A recording said the mayor was not available and to please leave a message. Ariel wasn't sure her French was going to convey the urgency of her request, but she gave it her best shot and left her own number. 'May I get inside the church right away?'

What now? The Goffs' house was two minutes away, but the gate was locked, and Michael's car was gone. Dimly, Ariel remembered Katherine mentioning she had a toothache and was hoping to get in to see her dentist.

Ariel jogged back down the hill and a couple of blocks past the church to Pippa's house. Pippa answered her knock dressed in an old sweatshirt that read, in faded lettering, 'Quins rule!' *Some time*, Ariel thought, *I will have to ask why.*

'I think Madame Toussaint's dog got into the church and he can't get out. The door's locked and the mayor's out of touch. What do you think we should do?'

Pippa stared at her for a few seconds. 'Come again? Sorry, love, I'm in the middle of a scene. In the book, I mean. The church here? I haven't a clue. Katherine got in to refresh the painting once. Maybe she has a key?'

'She and Michael aren't there. Can you think of anyone else?'

'How about old lady Pomfort? She's the keeper of the garden – maybe she's taken on the role of church guardian too? She lives just next door to me.' Pippa pointed up her driveway.

'Shoo.' An orange tabby was trying to sneak into the house. Pippa said, 'In at night, out in the daytime, that's house rules as this one knows very well.'

Ariel turned and headed up the driveway, worried sick by her vision of a dehydrated, starving and traumatized animal needing rescue.

Pippa's voice followed her. 'I'll just save my doc on the computer and meet you at Pomfort's.'

Madame, confronted a minute later by Ariel, whose voice had begun to shake, insisted she had no key, that the mayor possessed the only other one except for the man who periodically went inside to patch the crumbling walls. 'One day, that place will fall down and then we'll see what will happen to my garden,' she said in a voice that suggested it would be open warfare.

Before Madame Pomfort could get sidetracked with yet another account of her rights to the garden, Ariel said, 'Would that be Jean, your stonecutter? The man who quarries the stone here?'

'Goodness, no. He is useless. It is that other fellow – Descoteaux, you know? He and his wife, poor they are, live up that little lane.' She tipped her head toward a small intersection. 'But why do you want it? You don't even live in this commune. You found that old woman's body the other day.' Even though they had met several times, Madame's black eyes locked on to Ariel's, and her face said Ariel's presence was a harbinger of trouble.

'Madame – the old woman who died – had a dog that ran away, and I think I heard him inside the church. We need to get inside to be sure.'

'Hmph, probably a rat or one of that British woman's stray cats.'

That British woman opened Madame Pomfort's squeaky gate just then, stumbling over a flagstone that rose above the gravel. 'Whoops, sorry, but did you get a key?'

Ariel filled her in as best she could.

'Can you tell me exactly where this caretaker lives?' she asked, turning back to Madame, who showed no sign of inviting them in. The woman stepped out and pointed.

'That's the street Raoul lives on,' Ariel said.

'*Oui*, isn't that what I just said? Raoul Descoteaux. But he is not home. I saw his car leave at least an hour ago. His wife is off at work too.'

'You're right. He's at my house, working on my vegetable garden this morning,' Ariel said and laughed. 'I didn't remember his last name. Thanks, Madame. I'll call him now and ask about the key.'

Madame retreated behind her front door. The lace curtains at her front window twitched as Pippa and Ariel hurried out. Pippa closed the gate too hard, and Ariel, having noticed the curtain's movement, said, 'Watch out, or you'll be in trouble.'

Pippa agreed. 'Funny, though, when you're in real trouble, she comes through. I think she's more bark than bite unless you venture into the church garden. Then all bets are off.'

Ariel was waiting for Raoul to answer his cell phone, but it went to voicemail. She left a message explaining the urgency of getting the dog out of the church then turned back to Pippa. 'I'll wait here until Raoul comes or the mayor shows up. Look, I know you're busy writing this morning, so how about lunch tomorrow at my place – you and Katherine? I know we aren't supposed to snoop about Madame Toussaint's death, but I confess I'm getting impatient to know what really happened. I mean, how did she even get to Reigny so early, and why?'

Pippa scrubbed her already spiky hair, its purpled streak recently augmented by a white one. 'All Philippe would tell me was there was an active investigation. And when I said does that mean there's a case being made for murder, his face gave it away. Yes, the top cop is making a case for an investigative judge to step in.'

'That's what Brigadier Allard told me last night.'

'Last night is it? Brilliant. You're going right to the top to get information.'

'It wasn't quite like that,' Ariel said and then stopped. If it wasn't, what was it?

'That's all he said to me, and I got the message I wasn't supposed to push it further.'

To forestall any more questions, she dialed Raoul again but was once again foiled by voicemail.

She had been easing back toward the church. Pippa cocked her head. 'I don't hear anything.'

Ariel pressed her ear against the door, but it was quiet. She banged on the door. Still silent. 'Maybe he's too weak.'

'How did he get in, I wonder?' Pippa said, and she began walking around to the side that wasn't blocked off by the locked garden gate.

The two women poked around for five minutes but saw nothing that looked like a way in.

'I doubt there's a basement, although I suppose there could be catacombs.'

'Hardly. This was never more than a small village church,' Ariel said. 'It's a mystery, but when someone shows up with a key, we'll get the poor thing out.'

'Maybe we should call the gendarmes to come and break the padlock. If it's Madame Toussaint's dog, it could be evidence.'

Ariel thought about that. 'What if it isn't? I mean, what if it turns out not to be a dog at all but some wild animal that's made a home in there. I'd feel like an idiot. I'll try the mayor.'

'Bugger, there is that. Philippe is spending more time at the barracks these days than with me. It would probably put him off me permanently if word got out I'd called the gendarmes out to rescue a fox.'

'Are you two having problems? I thought you were back together even though you're no longer engaged.'

Pippa tugged on an earring and looked away. 'He says Officer Lannes is amazing, brave, smart. He talks about her all the time.'

'All the time? Any possibility you're exaggerating?'

'Maybe, but they're a team now and so they spend more time together than we do. And she's single.'

Ariel started to tell her she had no reason to worry but realized that might not be true. Best to keep quiet but to observe. She realized suddenly that she was starving. Reigny's tiny café didn't offer anything beyond breakfast breads. 'Are you hungry?'

'No. My dad sent a food package the other day, so I have my favorite crisps and cheddar to snack on.'

'I'm going to drive back to Noyers, pick up Raoul's key if he has it with him, grab lunch at Tony's and head back as fast as I can. Maybe by then, the mayor will already have opened the door, if she got my message.'

Raoul's car was gone. *Lunchtime. Probably as hungry as I am*, she thought and continued around the circle at the head of the driveway and headed straight to Tony's.

'I can't come here every day,' she said to Tony when he waved her to a table. 'You and Regine spoiled me when I first arrived and stayed in the apartment upstairs. I've gotten lazy.'

He waved away her comment. 'This is what my little place is for. If too many people think like that, I will go broke.' His pirate's grin made it clear he had no fears of that happening. In fact, when the summer crowds arrived, it was his practice to keep a few tables open for his year-round customers, which guaranteed their loyalty in the off season. 'Lentil stew with root vegetables or a chicken leg?'

'Whatever's quickest. I need to drive back to Reigny. I think there could be an animal trapped in their old church, but it's locked.'

Tony went to the far end of the bar and called her order out to Regine, who was doubtless assembling plates for the half dozen other hungry customers.

'Here's the thing. It's a long shot, but it could be Madame Toussaint's missing dog.'

Tony whistled. 'That would be something strange – a mystery.'

'Pippa and I think it could have snuck in a gap near the base of the wall, although we didn't see one. One of the neighbors thinks it's probably a rat or something else from the woods. Even so, it would be kind to get it out.'

Tony laughed. 'No one will thank you for letting a rodent back out into their town.' He winked and turned to help a man who had been looking around as he made his way over to the bar. The man didn't look local. He nodded toward the place behind the counter where Tony kept the open bottles of wine and turned with glass in hand to survey the tables.

Ariel had time to notice what must have been an expensive leather jacket, polished boots and a pinkie ring before Regine set the plate of chicken and carrots down and the scent of garlic and herbs distracted her.

'Perfect for today's weather, as usual,' she said, smiling up at the chef.

Regine beamed down at her, her impressive chest almost blocking Ariel's view of her face. 'Nothing special, but I always enjoy chopping and cooking with the herbs, which make the kitchen smell so good,' Regine said then headed back to her fiefdom.

Ariel congratulated herself on the plan to ask Regine to become her guest chef when the château kitchen became a French cooking class.

EIGHT

Thirty minutes later, Ariel was back on the road. When she pulled up in front of the church, the door was open. Delphine, the mayor, was standing on the steps, wrapped in a thick sweater, tapping her foot. 'Ah, there you are, Madame Shepard. I got your message and came over just now, but there's nothing inside. Come look.'

She stood in the open doorway as Ariel looked in every corner and under the rough wooden benches set in rows. There was no sign of any living thing, not even excrement. She looked up at the rafters, in case the sound had been an owl, but they also were clear. 'How odd. I was sure I heard whimpering. I'm so sorry to have bothered you, but at least I won't feel I've ignored something in distress.'

Delphine nodded briskly as she reattached the padlock. 'It's rare that anyone goes in these days, so I guess it could happen. I'll have Monsieur Descoteaux check the stonework this spring. A small animal could burrow underneath, and the hole would be hidden in the grass.'

So, no dog. Seeing the time on her phone reminded her she had been ignoring her château's repair work and she drove back making mental lists. Short term, she decided, she needed to find an appliance repair person who could give her old but impressively large gas stove a good going-over to make sure the gas lines were safe and the oven was ready for use. While she was at it, she needed to buy a few more pots so she could make soups and sauté more than one chop.

Her cell phone rang while she was sweeping the ever-present gravel dust from the entry hall. It was Brigadier Allard. '*Bonjour.* I wonder if you might be able to help us?' The tone of voice made it clear this was solely a professional call.

'Something about the woman who died?'

'Indirectly, yes. We haven't located a relative yet. There's nothing in her house that helps. But we took a more detailed look at her possessions and, well, there's something I'd like your opinion about. You knew her, at least somewhat, and you appear to have liked her.'

'True, although I knew very little about her, understand.'

'My judge has decided from the postmortem that the death is a homicide, but that examination did raise a question. Could you come to the gendarmerie, or may I make an appointment for this afternoon to meet you at your home? I will be in the area.'

'I confess I'm intrigued, although I'm not sure I'll be of any use. It would be best if you could come over here. I'm in the midst of one of dozens of chores. How about in an hour or so?'

'Good. I'll drive over.'

Ariel wondered if the brigadier usually went into the field to interview people. Why not send a junior officer? If he didn't approve of the personal relationships Philippe had with Ariel's friends, maybe Officer Lannes? And why ask her, a relative newcomer, for more perspective on the victim's life? She shrugged and decided she would brush her hair and redo the ponytail; maybe a quick addition of lipstick too. Not that she thought this was anything but business.

Upstairs, she looked out the window to the sweeping view of the land running to the edge of her estate and saw Raoul was back at work, using a rake to smooth out a load of sand he must have gone to fetch earlier. After that, he would lay the bricks, and the basic shape of the small knot garden behind the kitchen garden proper would be set. It would be lovely, a real French herb garden with thyme, tarragon, savory, marjoram, fennel, chives and chervil with a walkway inside. Now all she had to do was learn how to cook with them. Paying guests wouldn't be the only ones taking Regine's classes.

A voice called out from below – the brigadier asking if anyone was home. Ariel ran down the stairs to meet him in the big hallway.

'Let's sit in the kitchen. I haven't got much, but I can make you a coffee, and I treated myself to a half dozen *sablés* from the combined boulangerie and patisserie. She's a great cookie maker.'

He was in civilian clothes today, kind of rumpled, which looked good on him. She filed away the realization that he looked older and less friendly in his full brigadier costume.

When they were settled on her newly re-caned chairs at the big kitchen table, scarred and uneven from a history of serious cooking, he thanked her for agreeing to see him. 'The investigation is proceeding in several directions, and right now the toughest one is learning enough about the deceased to suggest anyone who might have benefitted from her death. I was hoping you might be able to add something to the profile we are trying to develop?' He pulled a piece of paper from his jacket pocket, unfolded it and put it on the table. 'Do you know what this is?'

Ariel peered at two images of the same object. 'A beautifully adorned table implement to stab someone with? I've seen a couple of odd pieces of silver and vermeil at Katherine's flea-market-finds shop but have no idea what you'd do with this one.'

'It does appear something like a scimitar, I agree.' He pointed to the second image, which showed the reverse side. 'Can you make out the engraving?'

'No. Old, I'm sure, and elegant script. Does it connect with Madame Toussaint's murder?'

He made the humming sound she was coming to realize meant he was thinking. 'Right now, we have no idea. I'm told it's a tableware piece from one of the museums that was robbed recently. The thieves didn't take this piece, the Paris detectives said, even though they emptied the rest of the display.'

'Perhaps because they weren't any clearer than we are what one would do with it.'

'The engraving is unique. In fact, I was told it signifies that it was made for royalty, perhaps in the very early 1800s.'

'Wow, that ups the value, doesn't it? Must be worth a lot.'

'It would have to be on the black market, which, sad to say, thrives in many European cities. I wondered if the victim ever made an offhand comment about antiques or trips to Paris?'

'I doubt it. Katherine would have said so. From what my friend told me, she was a woman of few words. I probably know less about her than most of the people who live in Noyers. She dressed in old, worn clothes, and I heard she never let anyone in her house, much less entertained them in high style. She seemed pretty much rooted in her daily walks here. She's supposed to have had relatives who were wealthy at one point, and maybe she traveled to see them.'

'Judging by what we saw in the house, those relatives prob-ably weren't part of her life. No one who visited would let the place get into such a bad state.'

'You really should be talking to Tony and Regine from the café, or the couple who run the hair salon, and one of the neigh-bors. She lived in Noyers for many decades, I understand, and in that same house. He and his wife live right across the street. You can't miss their house. It's as neat and trim as hers is neglected, and they can see her front door from their window.'

Allard nodded. 'Our officers interviewed everyone, but people are suspicious of gendarmes for some reason, and no one had anything much to say. Lived alone, had no visitors, no noises except a bit of barking occasionally.'

'The dog. I don't suppose . . .?'

'Sorry, it has not turned up. I imagine some farmer out there found and has claimed it. Farmers can always use a canine to scare off the foxes or guard the house.'

Ariel was used to the notion of dogs as beloved, pampered extensions of their owners' status, almost like children, and hadn't adjusted to a rural view but guessed the brigadier might be right. The dog would have found its way back to Noyers by now if it were on the loose. 'As long as whoever killed Madame didn't kill the dog too.'

'No, we would have found it – or signs of it. Do not fret any longer. I am confident it is safe somewhere.'

'Well then, if the missing dog isn't a clue, what will you focus on?'

'It is beginning to look like a puzzle we may never solve. My judge asked me to coordinate a fresh look at the little we have, to see if something new might occur to us. Meanwhile, muggers have been hitting the bars and clubs in tourist areas of Burgundy late at night when people are leaving tipsy, and sometimes beating their victims in addition to stealing their backpacks and wallets. I worry this is just a prelude to what they will do as the tourist season heats up.'

'Is this only in Burgundy?'

'No, but our region seems to have been chosen by several gangs recently. Next year, it will be somewhere else. They are quite nimble, these *voleurs*. It is especially sensitive with the public now because there were two museum robberies in Paris in the last year. A night guard was shot and killed in the second – very unusual levels of property crime. Businesses that display jewelry fear the level of violence may spread. I have to deploy my officers all over the region late and on weekends, and my colleagues in Paris are pushing us to look for their gang too.'

She wasn't happy with any of this, his nonchalance about the missing dog or his feeling that the Reigny murder might never be solved, but promised herself she'd stop thinking the worst. She tried to dredge up anything she could recall about Madame Toussaint. 'She knew the work of Jean-Paul Sartre. Quoted him to me one day. Maybe she went to university?'

'Did she have an accent – anything that might help us determine where she was from?'

Ariel laughed. 'You're kidding, right? I'm an American. It's enough that I can speak with a pronounced American accent, but I'm the last person who could say she was born in Paris or Provence, or the Languedoc. For that, you really need to ask any of my neighbors.'

Again, he nodded. She knew he was disappointed, and still thought it was a fool's errand to interview her. She had to wonder if it was his awkward way of staying in touch. The conversation drifted after that, and he said he had to leave.

'Would you like a quick tour of my folly?'

'Thank you. I admit to curiosity, not having much acquaintance with the grand châteaux of the area.'

'Hardly grand, although it must have been something in the nineteenth century when the previous family of owners turned it into a formal mansion.'

She took him up the gracious central staircase and to a window in a room that showed off the back aspects of the estate not visible from the gated entrance. 'See? All the way to the edge of the forest. I have enough on my plate to get the house in shape, but someday I want to restore the glory of those long gardens with their convoluted pathways – sectioned off for roses, my gardener tells me.'

She looked down, closer to the back entrance. 'Raoul is working on creating a small potager and a knot garden right now.' She didn't see him. His irregular presence had lately become a bother, given that he seemed so happy with the garden projects. 'He's actually a stonemason, and you met him last year, but it turns out his passion is gardening. I'm lucky to have his help.'

'We used to have a decent potager,' Allard said, almost to himself. He stared down. 'But,' he added, turning to her with a smile, 'a policeman does not have much time to spend with a trowel and a bag of chicken manure, eh? I really must get back to the office.'

She saw him to his official car, where his driver stood leaning on the hood and scrolling on his phone. '*Au revoir*, Brigadier. I owe you dinner at Tony's, remember.'

'I will take you up on that soon,' he said, bowing slightly.

She stayed on the steps for a moment, looked around. As she suspected, Raoul's car was gone again. A March wind was picking up, the clouds were closing in and the light was beginning to fade. Somehow, it made the thought of Madame Toussaint's unclaimed body lying in the morgue more depressing. What could she do? Should she do anything?

What she realized was she wanted to get into Madame's house. If there was anything there that the police wouldn't recognize as important, a particular piece of bric-a-brac or a book, she felt she and her friends would recognize its meaning quickly. Then, of course, they would turn it over to the brigadier. At the thought of the police chief, she winced. It was quite possible he wouldn't understand, so asking permission to go in seemed foolish.

The brigadier had admitted his force wasn't learning a lot about the victim from people who lived in the area. Madame Toussaint's wrinkled face peering at her, the dark eyes intense, shook her. For the woman's sake and for her own conscience, it was time to call Katherine and Pippa into action. She knew, or strongly suspected, how to get into Madame's house. What would Katherine say if she suggested it? Raoul tended the dead woman's roses. He either had a key or knew where one was hidden. Was it fair to ask him to do something that might annoy the police? She let herself in the big front door and shut it firmly behind her. There was only one way to find out. She had to ask him, but that would have to wait.

NINE

Noyers' little grocery store had bright green bunches of asparagus and bouquets of even brighter green spinach. 'Grown in France, Madame, or imported?' Ariel asked as she put a bunch of each in her basket.

'France. The season has begun. We have strawberries too, although' – she lowered her voice – 'they are not as flavorful as what we will get in April, I think. But good with crème fraiche, yes? Do try the morels. This is their perfect moment.' She pointed to a straw basket heaped with small, dark mushrooms shaped like barrels.

Ariel's lunch menu took shape on the spot. French omelets with diced morels cooked beforehand in butter. Asparagus with lemon and capers, a small spinach salad with slivers of the last of the apples in her refrigerator. Strawberries and cream for dessert. Her basket was filling quickly, but she needed to save room for a fresh baguette, of course, and a bottle of wine from across the street. She hadn't done much real cooking, and her tools were limited, but this she could do for her two friends. She wanted them in a receptive mood when she told them her plan.

She had hardly finished the preparations and laying out plates when the two women arrived together in Pippa's red sports car. As she always did when she was a passenger with the young Brit, Katherine arrived acting as though she had survived a tornado. More than once, she had confessed to Ariel that she believed firmly she would die wrapped around a tree if she accepted every one of Pippa's invitations. Ariel always bit her lip, thinking that it was more likely Katherine would be smashed into by a truck driving on the narrow roads where her little putt-putt would only go twenty-five kilometers an hour.

The three of them strolled through the house as they had done before, making suggestions about what spaces might complete the atmosphere. Katherine had proposed with a sweep of her arm that the big ground-floor room be partitioned by a screen so the far end could hold a grand piano and become a salon for music. 'The part closest to the hall would make a handsome library.'

'But the stairs to my tower are at the far end, and when all the rest is done, I'm determined to restore the tower as my private apartment. I may even rough it up there later this year when it's warmer.'

'It would make a brilliant writer's studio,' Pippa said.

'Um, maybe so. If I need to, I suppose I could rent it out,' Ariel said, feeling a little air escape her fantasy balloon.

'Oh, say, you could rent it out to a famous author and have a weekend retreat, you know?'

'I suppose you mean you?' Katherine said, one finger on her lips as she surveyed the room with its high ceilings and long rectangular floor.

'No, I mean someone really famous. J.K. Rowling perhaps. Now that would get you a crowd.'

'But I don't want a crowd. I can't handle a crowd. More like eight people,' Ariel said, shaking her head and laughing. 'I suggest we keep all these great ideas afloat but, for now, concentrate on our immediate task. I have some ideas about what we can do next for the important business of making sure Madame's killer is found.'

'Super lunch,' Pippa said. 'Sorry I spilled my water on my omelet, but it tasted just fine, really.'

Katherine, happy with her second glass of wine and waving a spoon of strawberries bathed in cream, laughed. 'Pippa, my darling girl, when don't you tip something over? I used to think you moved too quickly. Now I think it's that your arms are too long.'

Ariel wondered if this was an insult, but if it was, Pippa hadn't figured it out. She laughed and raised her water glass in a salute to the older woman. 'My mum used to tell me to stand absolutely still in the kitchen while she was dishing up the food. She said I was as clumsy as I was smart.'

'She'd be so proud of you, Pippa, with one book published and another in the works. How's it going?' If nothing else, it would change the direction of the conversation, Ariel thought.

'Brilliant. Well, maybe not that good. I'm actually having trouble. I can't figure out who the murderer is. I bet I'll get some ideas now that we're investigating.' She beamed.

'Wait, you're not saying you're using Madame Toussaint's death in your story?' Ariel raised a finger. 'I thought you promised not to do that – use our real tragedies for your entertainments.'

'No. I mean the victim is an older woman, but it's set in London, and she doesn't even have a dog. But someone has to have killed her for it to be a mystery novel, right? And that's where I'm stuck. It's hardly over Indian takeout or chips.'

'Madame was killed for what she brought me to sell,' Katherine said, draining her glass and reaching for the wine bottle. 'I'm sure of it. The bag and whatever she was carrying it in are missing, and she always brought her small treasures in it. Have you heard anything new, Ariel?'

Ariel took the plates over to the massive sink that was original to the kitchen and came back to sit down. Absently tearing a piece off the baguette, she said, 'The brigadier was here, and they're not making much progress.' She repeated what he had told her and ended by saying, 'I agree, a big clue is what she was bringing you, Katherine. Where did she get it? Was it part of a collection she owned? Why was she so secretive, and did she have something to hide?'

Ariel didn't like the idea that had begun to form when the brigadier showed her the photo of the old silver. She wanted to see anything Katherine had left before she voiced it to her friends. 'There are things we have time to investigate if it takes more digging. His squad is spread thin working on other crimes. After all, we're neighbors and customers of the shopkeepers, so having us ask around won't be threatening.'

'What do we want to know?' Pippa asked, pulling her cell phone out. 'Notes,' she said when Ariel raised her eyebrows, 'so I don't get the real investigation messed up in my head with the one I'm inventing, promise.'

'If she had the bag with her, which she always did when she came to my shop, I'm guessing it held something she wanted to sell. It never turned up?'

'I saw a line of police walking across the pasture down the

road from my shop with sticks, poking into the grass and under the trees,' Katherine said. 'And a couple more were walking slowly along the side of the road near our house. Made the dogs bark.'

'That suggests one of two things. Either the bag and whatever she had brought to sell isn't in Reigny, or Madame wasn't carrying it that morning – which would hardly make sense. Why else would she come all that way to your shop? My guess is whoever hit her stole it, but unless it contained a queen's crown, it hardly seems worth killing her for.'

Pippa shook her head. 'A third possibility is that your top cop didn't tell you, but they do have it.'

'True, and, Pippa, he's not my cop. I wonder how thoroughly they searched. Regine told me the place was kind of a mess the one time Madame let her in.'

'Would they have recognized it for what it was?' Katherine said. 'It was scruffy, work cotton, and might have looked like a rag. You do realize if the bag is in the house, empty, it means whoever killed her took it back after leaving Reigny with what was in it? That's too creepy.'

'You mean, the killer might have taken the object but brought the bag back to keep the police from finding it? More likely, the bag got filled with more treasures and put into the getaway car, if there were more still in her house – assuming whoever it was could get into her house? So many questions. We need to get into that place and search more carefully – agreed?'

Katherine and Pippa nodded.

'OK then, next question: how do we find the mysterious relatives her neighbor talked about? Allard said so far they haven't found any names by looking at her papers.'

'Does she – did she – have a computer?' Pippa asked. 'That's where I would look first.'

'Allard didn't say anything about a computer, and she didn't seem like someone who would be comfortable with the internet, but you're right. We can't overlook that or a phone. I'll ask him, but meantime let's check the neighbors and see if they have internet service. Mine is good up here on the rise, but I think it's spotty around town. I never saw her on a cell phone when she was out walking. Maybe it's tucked away somewhere the police didn't look. Another reason to get into her house.'

Katherine cleared her throat. 'How do you plan to get us into her house? We're not cat burglars, and if I do anything that gets me arrested, Michael's likely to banish me to the US for the rest of my life, and I like it here.'

'Turns out Raoul tended her roses. He's laying the brickwork for my knot garden, but I'll catch him and ask if he has a key. He's not very forthcoming at the best of times, but I may be able to wangle some information about her from him.'

Pippa raised her hand. 'Should I do a door-to-door check to see if anyone saw people at her house? I'm obviously not a copper, and that might help get people talking.'

'Perhaps, but you – all of us – were portrayed in the newspaper as foreigners interfering with the police last year, remember?' Ariel paused. 'Let me see if I can enlist Tony and Regine to ask around, especially the locals who come to the café. If they find someone, then one of us can have a friendly chat with that person.'

'I like that,' Katherine said, eyeing the almost-empty bottle of wine and upending the last bit into her glass. 'I need this to survive Pippa's race-car driving,' she said parenthetically. 'It will come better from a local person to begin with.'

'Okay, then, the silver. I want to look at it in detail if I can. Allard showed me a photo of a piece that was still at a Paris museum after the rest of the set was stolen. It's pretty distinctive, and I thought it might be similar to the pieces Madame brought you.'

Katherine shook her head. 'The police collected it already, but I took pictures of everything in case I can claim them someday. None of it had been bought, mostly because no one's coming into the shop. I'm pretty sure it wasn't just lying around her house while she ate scraps.'

'I don't know if she was that poor,' Ariel said. 'I know she occasionally bought meat from the butcher and he's expensive.' She laughed. 'Apparently, she did bully the man into giving her the best bones for her dog. I ran into someone who grumbled that she never could get them for her broths because Madame had gotten there first.'

Pippa said, 'The police can do this better than me, but I'm going to do some online research about that surname and see how common it is in Burgundy, and here in the Yonne district.

I may let Philippe know. If he tells me not to bother because the police are doing that, it will tell us something without me being accused of trying to worm it out of him.'

'Which, of course, is what you're doing.' Ariel smiled and shook her head. Pippa would probably have made a better gendarme than her boyfriend, who often let things slip when she pushed him.

Their assignments agreed to, Pippa and Katherine roared off before Ariel remembered she had wanted to make a date to visit the shop and look at the collection of old wallpapers Katherine had. Raoul was probably at his house for a hot lunch. In the warmer weather last summer, when he was rebuilding the low stone wall around the château proper, he had taken his lunch on site, but it was well worth driving home for something hot in this weather – that and another load of bricks to fit in the trunk of his battered old car.

Thinking about lunch brought Ariel back to the dream of holding cooking classes at the château, with Regine wearing the chef's toque. She wondered why Regine never served cassoulet at the café and promised herself to ask the cook. It might be better to hold off sharing her idea of classes until after the funeral. That thought brought her back to the murder investigation. Surely if Madame had relatives, at least one would show up at the funeral, if only to make sure everyone knew the house was spoken for? Another task then. Find out what the status of the funeral was.

Her cell phone rang – Andre, sounding excited. He had some ideas for the new bathroom and for making the other one on that floor more adaptable for two guest rooms. Could she meet with him late this afternoon or tomorrow morning?

'*Absolument*. I'm here the rest of the day, probably headed over to the café for a light dinner afterward, so come when you can.'

Andre's new task was much more fun than his first work for her, when he had spent his time tracing broken sewer lines and marching around in the mud to lay down new drainage pipes. He explained with the help of some sketches and a lot of hand waving what he had in mind. The whole space given to the bathroom that was already there was divided into two rooms as in many nineteenth-century era homes, one with the toilet and a door to the hall. The other opened into one bedroom but could be changed to open into the hall also. The second room, the actual 'bath room', was quite large, with a washstand and an old-fashioned, free-standing tub, which Ariel wanted to preserve in any restoration.

They discussed who could help open up the walls and how much displacement adding new pipes would cause. Enough, he admitted, to mean some cost. Ariel tried not to groan aloud. Of course. The next step was Andre going to his sources, getting bids for everything he couldn't do, then coming back to her with an estimate.

Andre left, whistling as he drove back out of the long driveway, and Ariel made another note to call her financial advisor in New York. She had sold the condo for a shocking amount of money. 'Location, location, location and luxury,' the broker had told her gleefully, and she had brought most of the proceeds with her when she moved to France. The rest she had left to be invested and, fortunately, those funds had grown over the past year. At this rate, she'd have to cash out what she first thought would be her nest egg in case Château de Champs-sur-Serein didn't work out.

'It will succeed,' she muttered as she threw on a parka and locked the door. 'It damn well has to.'

TEN

The café's last customers had gone, the neon sign outside was turned off and Regine's helper had finished the kitchen cleanup when Ariel sat down with Tony and his beloved Regine, she with sweat glistening her forehead and he massaging the small of his back. 'I stand for twelve hours,' he said.

'Pffft, I cook and serve for twelve hours. Don't complain, you big baby.' She cuffed him gently, and he mock groaned.

'That's why I brought you Marc de Bourgogne,' Ariel said, nodding toward the expensive bottle of Burgundy's famous brandy, 'to salute you both for your hard work, without which I'm sure I would have starved by now.' She poured the brandy into the fat-stemmed glasses Tony had brought over with him from the bar.

The three were silent for a moment, enjoying the peace and quiet, then Ariel asked, 'Regine, whatever happened about a funeral for Madame?'

'No one has claimed her, so the cops and the rectory in Avallon which has say about this church said we can go ahead. Not sure if you know, but there's a small group here who get together to sing choral music, just for fun, and they have offered to provide music. The bookstore has a copy machine, and if we can get someone to write a bit about her, he says he'll make programs. Of course, we're none of us sure what to say, she was so private.'

'I understand the police aren't having any more luck. The brigadier asked me, of all people, if I recognized a regional accent that might be a starting place. The only regional accents I would pick up are Boston and Brooklyn, but what about you?'

Tony thought for a minute. 'She barely spoke to me beyond "un espresso", so I can't say I heard anything. You?' He turned to Regine.

'She's from the Yonne, but I don't know that from an accent. She said something to that effect a couple of years ago when I brought her a tart to celebrate VE Day. I can't remember exactly but something like: "We beat them right here where we lived, the bastards, even if we lost some of our own."'

'Did she say anything else?' Ariel asked. 'This is the most significant detail I've heard.'

'No – slammed the door in my face in fact.' Regine shook her head. 'Took the tart though. A tough woman.'

Tony raised his glass. 'To a tough woman – one after my own heart.'

Regine gave him a side eye. 'You're saying I'm tough?'

'Absolutely. Look how you saved Ariel last year. I'd pity any Nazis who might have come your way if you'd been around during the Occupation.'

'Agreed,' said Ariel. 'You're the best kind of tough, Regine.'

The door to the café opened, and the man Ariel had seen there briefly entered, wearing the same fashionable leather jacket. 'Pardon, I forgot to take the other key to get in the separate entrance. All right if I go up this way?'

Tony waved him in. 'The reason we have so many locks now is my friend here, Madame Shepard. She once rented the apartment and there was a break-in. Can't happen now.' He waved his glass. 'Care to join us?'

'No, better not. I have an early day tomorrow – house hunting.'

He trotted up the stairs, using it, Ariel thought, as exercise. His physique suggested a man who kept fit.

'I should get back to my shabby little château. Actually, it's coming along nicely. I wish you two would come over sometime to see it.'

'I wish it too, but I don't have anyone to take over the bar, and we're open every day except for the two weeks in early March when we go to the Mediterranean.'

Regine scolded him. 'I've told you many times, you need to hire a worker who could take on a bit of the load once tourists start coming. Then we could have at least part of August for the traditional holiday.'

He shrugged. 'I agree, but I can't think who.'

The conversation trailed off because none of them had a suggestion, and Ariel said her goodnights and drove home. The warm light from the lamp in a window of the great hall welcomed her as it did every evening. She took a mug of hot water up to her temporary bedroom, fluffed up her duvet and repeated her bedtime mantra. 'Thank you, my darling husband, for giving me a new home, a great adventure and the courage to tackle it.'

ELEVEN

Raoul was already at work the next day when Ariel wandered
out the kitchen door with her morning coffee. She was
pleased to see him. These days, he seemed to come and
go without any reason. 'From upstairs, I can see the shape of
the knot garden now. I'm sorry you're having to make so many
trips to bring back the bricks for trimming it. Should we hire
Jean to fill his truck and save you time?'

Raoul looked up at her from where he kneeled in the vegetable
garden, spade in hand. Ariel thought he looked tired, even stressed,
and worried he had taken too much on at the château.

'It's fine.'

'It's just that you're coming and going on your trips so often,
and I'm sure it's hard on your car. It might be cheaper to pay
Jean for one big trip.'

'I don't charge you for the times I'm gone,' he said.

'That's not it. You do look a bit tired is all. I hope you aren't
having to take care of that dog again?'

'The dog?'

'Your sister-in-law's dog – the one who was barking so much
when I came by the other day.'

'Ah, no, it's back with her.'

'I thought I heard a dog barking inside Reigny's old church,
but when the mayor opened the building up, there was no sign
of one. That wouldn't have been your sister-in-law's dog, would
it?'

Raoul looked up and harrumphed. 'Was there a dog? I told
you she took back her mutt. You were mistaken.'

He bent his head again and went on with his spading. Ariel
could see that he was carving straight lines in the soil, which
consisted of red clay and lighter sandy stuff. He had explained
that he was amending the soil, which would be excellent for

vegetables, but which needed additions first because it had not been tilled before.

'I understand you used to take care of Madame Toussaint's roses. Did you know her well?'

'Well enough,' he said without looking up.

'I walked by recently and didn't see a gate from the street into the garden. Did she give you a key so you could get into the garden through the house?'

He nodded but said nothing.

'What will happen to the roses? Can you get in to feed them now that the growing season is beginning?'

He sat back on his heels and looked up at her. 'I don't think the *flics* would let me. The roses are all right for now. The house is vacant, and who knows when someone will occupy it again.' He paused. 'That big chief of police visited you.' How Raoul knew that she had no idea. 'Maybe he knows something?'

'Not much unfortunately. No relatives have stepped forward, and the police aren't sure where she was from, so they haven't got much to go on. It's a pity really. She must have some history.'

Raoul stood up, grunting a bit from the effort. He knocked the spade against his work boot then dropped it into a bucket of small tools. 'Everyone has history; some of it important. Pardon, but I have to leave for a small while. I will be back in an hour.'

'Of course, but keep in mind my offer to hire Jean and save you some trips.'

He nodded but didn't say anything. Lately, she thought, watching his back as he walked to his old car, he seemed to have regressed to the grumpy version of himself that she first knew. She hoped he wasn't sick but didn't know his wife, and there was no way to inquire politely.

Pippa supplied a possible answer to the dilemma of getting into the victim's house later that day while they waited for Katherine to walk over and open the shop in Reigny. 'You can talk to your— I mean the brigadier and explain Raoul has to get into the garden to get it ready for spring. I heard that the city requires the houses and gardens to look pretty, since Noyers is one of France's special towns.'

'That would help us how?' Ariel said, sitting on the unkempt grass across from the shop. No way was she going to park herself on the very step where a murder took place.

Pippa paced in the empty road, waving her arms as she explained. 'While he's there, we go in, saying he needs our help. You can get him to say that to the gendarmes. While he putters outside, we search.'

'Not if there's a gendarme on duty the whole time, and I don't want to ask the chief of police. He'd just say no. But it's an interesting idea. If we're seen carrying in bags of fertilizer or tools, I bet one or two of us could peel off now and then. I'm not sure I can get Raoul to agree to create alibis for us, but it's worth a try.' She decided to stop by his house after choosing wallpapers.

'*Bonjour*,' Katherine's treble-warbling voice said as she came down the street. Today, she was dressed in a red-and-blue flowered cotton dress from the 1930s that reached her knees and was almost covered by a knitted brown cape of some undetermined style and era. Her boots were black and buttoned up the front. It was, Ariel had to admit, not a particularly attractive outfit and, knowing how much attention Katherine usually paid to her outfits, Ariel thought she must be in some state of shock or confusion.

'I'm on my own today. Michael has gone into a frenzy about putting down these vocals. His producer has decided he wants them immediately so they can be ready for when my husband arrives in Memphis to do whatever it is they do there.' She pulled a large key ring out of a pocket hidden under the cape and stepped gingerly on the shop's top step.

'Should I make a sign to memorialize Madame?' she asked her friends as she turned on the lights, and the colors and patterns in the shop burst forth. 'A painting of her perhaps?'

'It might put off customers,' Pippa said, 'but it would be a way to start conversations.'

'I wasn't going to say anything like the plaques on village walls all around the Yonne, you know – "Here so-and-so was shot and killed by les Boches."'

'Yes, well that would be disquieting,' Ariel said. 'A portrait with no explanation, perhaps attached to the wall or here in the window, would be much nicer, but it would mean finding a photograph of her. Maybe we'll find one in her house. I'm sure the neighbors organizing her funeral would like one too.'

'Hmmm,' Katherine said, looking up at the ceiling and squinting. 'I shall think about that. Now' – she turned to Ariel with a flourish – 'let's look at the picture of Madame's treasures.'

Laid out on part of a table once she'd pushed some other things aside, collectively, they were evidence of something far grander than Ariel would have imagined. 'What gorgeous old repoussé serving spoons. You took pictures of the backs and the grapevines continue all the way up, and there's a monogram with what looks like a coat of arms too.'

Katherine picked up a picture of a small bowl with large, curved handles. 'This has the same design and I wondered if it was a crown, not a coat of arms. She only said it was old and she didn't need it in her house. But here's a piece I forgot about when the gendarmes came. I had put it in a display in the corner.'

Pippa picked up the odd-looking piece that had a large vermeil handle and squared tines, covered with vines dripping grapes. 'What on earth is this? You could fork hay with it.'

Katherine shook her head. 'I've been meaning to do some research. If you look carefully with a magnifier, there's a date under each of those images, so curvy that I'm not sure if I'm looking at a one or a seven.' She made a sound. 'I need an expert, but I can't begin to afford one. Who knows?'

'Uh oh,' Ariel said suddenly. 'This has been bothering me. What if this is from the set stolen from a museum in Paris? The brigadier showed me a photograph of a piece that was oddly shaped and had elaborate markings but didn't say if he suspected it was exactly like the missing treasures. Is it possible Madame was fencing stolen merchandise through your shop?'

'Little old lady as super criminal? That would be quite a turn-up for the books.' Pippa looked thoughtful.

Katherine picked up the strangely shaped tool and waved it over her head. 'This odd one isn't for sale. If I get to keep it in the end, maybe someone will wander in and exclaim because it's a rare giant pickle gatherer like the one their grandmother had. Now, look at the other treasures I have – wallpapers that you'll never see again.'

While Ariel and Katherine unrolled the flowered papers, Pippa wandered around, picking up one small object after another, trying on a slightly bent hat, poking through stacks of books with foxed and musty pages.

Twenty minutes later, Ariel had decided to take all of the wallpapers Katherine had collected. 'I'll have to do some patch-work where the amount of paper isn't large enough for a whole wall, but you'll help me, right? Your creativity and flair are much more suited to this than my timid decisions would be.'

'Of course. We'll create a bricolage, and I bet you become quite creative as we go along.'

'What's that when it's at home?' Pippa asked, looking up from a book she was thumbing through.

'A bricolage is what you make when you combine many things that don't seem to get along. In America, a crazy quilt is one that comes out well. Our wallpapering will be another. The restaurant Michael's producer took us to in Los Angeles when I went there with him last year served the most expensive and ridiculous bricolage – a paper-thin slice of raw beef centered on two crisscrossed, nearly raw green beans, with some kind of fishy foam on top and two tiny croutons supposedly flavored with herbs on the side. Really, too ghastly.'

Ariel burst into laughter. 'Good thing they didn't hire you to write the menu description.'

'Give me a good veal chop and parsnips any day,' Katherine said as she made her way to the desk in a back corner.

Ariel had a basket full of wallpapers, which Katherine looked at for a moment before naming a price that Ariel suspected was quite a bit lower than if these were at a *brocanteur* – a real antique store.

Pippa brought over a magazine with curled edges. 'I think this might be good research material,' she said, handing it to Katherine.

'*Le Monde*, and from 1945? I thought your mysteries were set in the present?'

'Yes, but the present is built on the past, isn't it? Anyway, I'll use it to practice my reading skills.'

Ariel looked over her shoulder. 'There's an article I'd like to read when you're finished. The stories of the French Resistance fascinate me, and this looks like a story about some of the women who fought side by side with the men.'

Pippa flipped to the story. 'Some of them look like girls. Where did they find the courage?'

'You must visit the Museum of the Resistance in the Morvan,' Katherine said with a loud sigh. 'It's so moving to see the old photos, the radios and code machines the brigades used to track and surprise Nazi troops. Many young people died for their efforts, including English fighters parachuted into the Morvan forest. Local housewives risked everything to bring food and messages in to their husbands and sons, and relay plans out. Even children were active. A lot of the action took place in this part of the Yonne. In fact,' she said, waving away the euros Pippa held out, 'you only have to scratch the surface around here to find the sons and daughters of the Resistance fighters. There was a memorial event in Avallon about ten years ago, before we moved here, and several old people in Reigny attended.'

'They've probably all died by now. Pity,' Pippa said.

'Not all. There's an old man Michael and I bumped into at the farmers market in Noyers last summer. Ancient really, and so frail. The mayor, himself a war veteran from the second war, was with him, holding his arm and treating him like royalty. We were introduced, and he told us in a whispery voice that two of his Resistance comrades still lived in the area. Michael was awestruck, I think.'

Pippa tucked the magazine under her arm, then she and Ariel lugged the heavy basket of wallpapers out to Ariel's car while Katherine locked the shop door.

Ariel said, 'I'll see if Raoul is home and ask him about help getting into Madame's house. I'd better do it alone. He's a bit of a loner, and if he sees three of us at his door, he may get nervous.'

But Raoul's car wasn't there, and Ariel figured she might have as much luck back at the château.

Traffic was light, as it always was, on the narrow road that cut through newly planted rapeseed fields. There was little room to pass, but at least drivers could see cars and small trucks – seemingly the equivalent of America's pickup trucks – as they drew closer. Drivers who used these little roads were accustomed to the challenge, but Ariel was still getting used to it. Seeing a car behind her today was a bit different, at least before summer's onslaught of tourists. It came close, and Ariel wondered if it might pass. Surely the driver didn't expect her to pull on to the narrow verge, which might be a problem since there was a drainage ditch next to it?

She couldn't see much of the driver's face, only that he was wearing a cap pulled down low. Suddenly, he pulled out and shot past her, rocking into the ditch opposite before barreling away at a higher speed than anyone from around these villages would drive. It was gone before she turned into her own drive. She hoped she wouldn't read about an accident or a hit-and-run in tomorrow's paper.

Raoul's car was there, and there was a little sunlight warming the far side of the building when she walked around the perimeter.

'I'm glad to catch you,' she said, smiling to show this wasn't a complaint. 'Can I bring you a coffee or some tea?'

He shook his head and went back to trickling some earthy material into the rows he had set earlier in one part of the garden.

'Fertilizer?' Ariel asked. 'What should we plant there?'

'Compost, from my yard.' Goaded into speech, he described the best vegetables for this spot and when the seeds needed to be planted. Soon, it turned out, and he offered a sheet of paper, folded and stained, with a list of the seeds he recommended she buy soon. 'You can use that fancy seed company, but my wife and I usually buy from around here. Cheaper.'

'How about I go to the local place with you? My French might not be good enough to understand the details, and I'd like to see what's available in the local market.'

Again, he nodded but didn't say anything. She wasn't sure his nod was in agreement or avoidance, and wondered if she'd find one day that he was already planting what he thought she should have. In a way, it was all right. She had so much else on her plate. She did hope to make some of the decisions and, as time permitted, get her hands dirty.

Right now, she had to turn the conversation to the business of getting into Madame's house. She took a deep breath. 'Raoul, I've been thinking. The police haven't gotten anywhere in learning about Madame's family. They haven't found the bag she was probably carrying when she went to Madame Goff's shop. I know they did some kind of search in her house, but I'm not sure they were as thorough as . . . well, as I would be.'

He stood up, wiping his hands on his work pants. 'You want to search her house?'

'Yes, and I know it sounds bad, but we think the police might not have known what to look for.'

'We?'

'My friends Katherine and Pippa. You must know them? They live very near you. We all care about her, and with the funeral coming up, we'd like to see if there's more about her history, maybe a picture somewhere, that could go into the program.'

He looked hard at her. 'That is all you want?'

Ariel felt her cheeks getting hot. 'Almost. She must have some nice things in the house because she was bringing them a little at a time to Katherine, wanting to sell them. We think maybe that was why she was killed.'

He didn't speak for a minute then said, glaring at her, 'You want me to let you poke around looking for things you can sell?'

'No, no, we would tell the police that she had things, antique sterling silver and items like the sugar caster that she sold to Katherine. They're worth money. A robber could have known somehow.'

'Why do you think I could get you in?'

'Because you have a key, so you could get to the enclosed garden, maybe store gardening supplies in the small shed I saw out back when I walked past the house.'

Raoul shook his head slowly. 'I do not know. I need to think about it. I do not want trouble with the police, and I do not like the idea of people rooting around in her possessions either. She had dignity and was an honorable woman.'

'You knew her properly then? I didn't realize. She lived in Noyers. Did she live in Reigny at some point?'

He shook his head. 'Never in Reigny but elsewhere in the Yonne. Long ago.' He looked around. 'It is late, and I have an errand I must do for my wife. I will come back tomorrow and get the rest of the soil prepared. It may rain soon, and I want the added material to soak into the ground before planting.'

She nodded. 'Good, but will you let me know tomorrow if you'll help us look in Madame's house? It's really important, and I assure you we have no intention of robbing her estate of anything there. By the way, your neighbor thinks you have a key to the old church. Is that right?'

He turned to squint at the sky and shrugged. 'I guess I do somewhere. No call to use it much.'

They left it like that. Raoul put his tools in the little lean-to he had set up near the back door and walked away, brushing dirt off his pants. Ariel wasn't sure what she could do except wait and hope he said yes. It was interesting that he respected Madame. It seemed he knew more about the old woman, but it was clear he had no intention of sharing whatever it was.

She shook off her curiosity and went inside to consult her list. Jean-Paul – she needed to get on his schedule for the former servants' quarters. He had the skills and the artistry to reclaim the windows and could probably do some small carpentry jobs up there. The space needed a new door to the utilitarian 'water closet', a replacement for the top steps of the narrow back stair-case the servants would have used, and the repair to a mysterious hole in the wood plank floor in what was probably the luggage room, a low-ceilinged space that ran along the length of the back wall under the roof. She had time to think about what the space would be used for. An apartment for herself, at least until her fantasy tower was realized? A rentable room? She had no plans for live-in help, but maybe the second room would be where everything she might want someday could be stored. After all, that's where she'd found a jumble of chairs and small tables. She looked forward to having Jean-Paul's cheerful presence in the house again, and the sound of his boom box and French pop music.

His voicemail informed her he was on a short job in Beaune. She and Dan had stopped there on their honeymoon. Ariel remembered the historic town with cobbled streets and beautiful buildings, and that it was set in the heart of Burgundy's Côte d'Or, a region with superb *terroirs*, parcels of land perfect for raising the grapes that turned into famous wines. She could only hope, selfishly, that Jean-Paul wasn't working on a restoration project that might take him into the summer months.

Looking at her cell phone, she realized she had enough time to load her laundry to take to the modest business in Noyers.

Not everyone had a washing machine, and fewer people had dryers. Here, clotheslines were normal, even in the winter, and more than once while visiting Katherine, her host had jumped up and deftly unpinned and gathered sheets, blouses and underwear and dashed back inside as the first drops of rain fell. Where would one put something as pedestrian as a clothesline on the grounds of a château, she wondered? A problem for later. Right now, wallpaper, paint, furniture and modern bathrooms took precedence.

Ariel decided an omelet would have to do for dinner, along with the remains of the onion tart she had picked up at the boulangerie. Even though Tony and Regine charged her less than other customers (*'Tu es famille'*), Jean-Paul's services didn't come cheap, and she saw euro signs in her daydreams along with images of the luxe bathrooms.

After dinner, she picked out a book from the crate that had arrived with her clothes and furniture, a biography of the French author Colette she had purchased long before she knew she would be coming to live in the Yonne, where Colette was born.

Taking her hot tisane upstairs after locking all the doors, Ariel had another of the moments when Dan seemed especially close. 'You couldn't have known what buying this château would entail, my darling, but thank you. I love it, and you are always a part of it in my heart.'

TWELVE

Tony was busy at his noisy espresso machine when Ariel came in the next morning with a bag from the boulangerie that held three chocolate croissants. The lodger she'd seen before was waiting for his hot drink, and he and Tony were talking.

When he saw her, Tony beckoned her over. 'Monsieur Tremblay, this is Ariel Shepard, who owns the château down the road. Monsieur is looking for a house to buy.'

'Not a château,' the man said, turning to her. '*Enchanté*, Madame. Noyers is such a lovely town that I thought it might be a good place to look, but there's not much.' He smiled, but the smile stopped before it reached his eyes.

Ariel slid her gaze toward Tony. Had he mentioned that the old woman's house might go on the market? If the police couldn't find her relatives, what then?

As if he read her glance, Tony said, 'I mentioned Madame Toussaint's house, which is fairly large. Nothing will happen until after the funeral and the police have completed their investigation.'

'Your friend here told me she didn't die naturally. Do you know if they have a person in custody yet? It's only that I would love to see the property as soon as it's appropriate.'

Vulture, Ariel thought, but said, 'I don't know much, but I'm sure the police would have announced it to the public if they arrested the despicable person who did this.'

Monsieur Tremblay's lips twitched. 'Indeed.'

'Anyway, she has relatives, I'm told, and they will doubtless show up to claim the property soon.'

'Ah, yes? I would like to speak with them. You have their contact information?'

'No, not even their names, although one neighbor spoke briefly to them once. He thinks the man is Madame's grandson.'

'Interesting,' Tremblay said, nodding. He drained his espresso in a single gulp, fished some coins out of his jeans pocket and set them on the counter. 'I hope we will meet again, Madame,' he said and left the café jingling car keys.

'He's a little cold,' Ariel said as Tony pumped the machine again for her drink. 'Is he originally from around here? Did he tell you why he wants to move to Noyers?'

Tony shook his head. 'He says almost nothing, and when I asked if he knew Noyers well, he said this was his first time here. Maybe he's a real-estate speculator. I mentioned the empty house up the hill near the ruins, but that didn't seem to interest him. He's only taken the apartment for a few more days, so I expect he'll head to another town anyway.'

'I almost forgot.' Ariel held up the bag. 'I want one – you and Regine get the others.'

Tony peeked in. 'Regine has decided she and I need to go on a diet.' He looked around. 'She's at the shops in Avallon, so if you don't tell, I will have one anyway.'

Ariel laughed. 'Have both. Just make sure you don't have chocolate on your face when she comes back.'

She stood up. 'I suppose you haven't heard about a stray dog?'

'No, although at this point, every time a dog barks, someone comes to tell me. You'd think I offered a reward.'

'That's not too helpful. I'm sorry if I started something that's a nuisance. The brigadier told me the dog's probably been adopted by a farmer by now, so it's time to accept that he's gone from Noyers.'

Today was shopping day, and the pleasure of it would distract her from her growing impatience to be doing something more active on Madame Toussaint's behalf. Ariel had decided soon after arriving in Burgundy to avoid the large, impersonal super-market in Avallon with its prepackaged and branded foods and assorted household necessities. There was a huge indoor food market, and it was a treat to browse scores of individual stalls with a large basket under her arm. There were cheeses, meat, charcuterie, fish, produce, flowers, dairy and eggs, wines, and every stall bustled all day long.

She had learned to be decisive. The vendors had little patience for customers who held up the line and potentially interfered with sales, but if Regine took château guests on a shopping trip one day as part of her program, Ariel bet she'd get a better welcome.

She had a headache and an empty wallet when she was done, but she had enough food to be able to invite her friends to a dinner party. Tony and Regine – she would pry them from the café somehow – the Goffs, Pippa and perhaps her on-again, off-again gendarme boyfriend, and, if she could surmount his reluctance, Raoul and his wife. *Are you dreaming? This isn't going to happen soon*, she scolded herself. She had to curb her enthusiasm at the market. By the time she could round the guests up, the vegetables would be limp or worse. Some other time, then, and she'd have to ask Regine for some tips on how to use all this bounty.

She pulled into the château's forecourt and was pleased to see Raoul's battered old car there. There was another she didn't recognize – a spotless, black Peugeot SUV with tinted windows and someone barely visible sitting in it. It looked like Michael's new car, minus the dust and pollen her friends' car gathered sitting in their uncovered driveway. She walked over, and Monsieur Tremblay opened the door and stepped out.

'Hello again,' she said, puzzled. He'd said he didn't want to buy a château, and if he'd had any curiosity, Tony would have set him straight.

'Please excuse me for barging over without an appointment, but my landlord's description made the place easy to find, and I had no other way of reaching you.'

'Can I help you? I'm a relative newcomer myself so don't have much to share about properties or possible sellers.'

'I understand. Correct me if I'm wrong, but I have the sense you might know a bit about the house owned by the deceased woman in Noyers?'

Ariel shrugged. 'Very little, but if you'll help me carry in my grocery bags, we can talk while I put things away.'

Ten minutes later, he was sitting at the antique wooden kitchen table, and Ariel was putting the last of her shopping treasures in the refrigerator. She didn't want to offer him anything but knew it would be considered rude not to, so she held up a paper-wrapped slab of young Comté cheese. 'I have a fresh baguette, if you'd like?'

He shook his head. 'Good of you, but I won't take more of your time. I've talked to a few neighbors, but they seem a tight-lipped bunch, and no one claimed to have met the grandson. The house is locked up tight and none of her close neighbors has a key. I doubt the *flics* – I mean, the gendarmes – would lend me whatever keys they might have found among her things, so I'm trying to get a sense of the condition of the place in less obvious ways. Have you ever been in the house?'

'Sorry, no. She kept to herself most of the time.' She had no intention of volunteering that she was hoping to get in herself. 'I think Tony's girlfriend, who is the wonderful chef at the café, was in once, but only for a few minutes and only in the kitchen and living area near it.'

'Good to know. I will check with her this evening. I thought there might be a caretaker when I walked by last evening. I thought I heard someone moving around inside.'

The hair on Ariel's neck stood up. 'That can't be. She had a dog though. It's been missing since the day she died, and every-one's been looking for it. The police did a search, and they would have found it had it been locked in before she went to Reigny. I worry it might have been hiding there, but I can't believe the police could have missed it.'

'If the gendarmes have already been through the place, I'm sure you're right. The wind in the trees probably fooled me. Actually, I thought it might be the relatives. If they inherit, it would be good to know if they had an interest in selling the place. But no one answered when I knocked.'

Could that be? Ariel wondered. Wouldn't someone have noticed?

The man's voice jarred her from her thoughts. 'She was in that little crossroads town to see a shopkeeper, isn't that right?'

A thud and a throat clearing made Ariel jump.

'Why is he asking?' Raoul stood just inside the door, knocking his work boots on the old boot scraper Andre had unearthed in the boiler room last year. He fixed the stranger with a suspicious glare.

'Raoul, come in. Would you like something to drink? This is Monsieur Tremblay, who is asking me about Madame Toussaint's house. Raoul is the stonemason and expert gardener who is helping me redo the château. Not sure what I'd do without him.'

Tremblay got up and walked over, holding out his hand. Raoul waved it away, indicating with a gesture that it was too dirt-covered to be suitable.

'I'd like to see the inside,' Tremblay said, smiling. 'I might want to buy it when the old lady is resting in the ground, God willing.'

Raoul growled and turned it into a cough. 'The house is sealed up. No snoopers allowed. And she's not in the ground yet.'

Turning to Ariel, he said, 'Just came in to use the working toilet if that's all right.'

'Of course. You know the way.'

Turning to Tremblay, she said, 'There is one downstairs, but my plumber isn't totally convinced it's been set up correctly. To drain, you know.' Why was she discussing sewage with a total stranger?

Raoul took off his boots, brushed past Tremblay and padded up the stairs.

When he was out of hearing range, Tremblay laughed. 'Noyers isn't exactly opening its doors to a potential resident. I hope you got a better reception.'

'She might have been a recluse, but I do think the people around here cared about her. Anyway, Raoul lives in a different village, Reigny-sur-Canne. He's done some yard work for her.'

Tremblay nodded and smiled at her again. 'I see. Well, I'll be off. Thanks for letting me interrupt your day.'

'No problem,' Ariel said as they ascended the stairs to the front hall. 'Good luck with your house hunting.'

When he had driven off, Ariel walked back to the kitchen. She'd had time to process what Raoul had said and was sure his response to her was going to be no – he would offer no help getting into Madame's house to see what the police might have overlooked in their search for answers.

'You haven't been inside Madame's house yourself?' she asked when Raoul plodded down the stairs into the kitchen. 'This guy said he might have heard someone. I hope it wasn't like the big rat that was inside this fireplace.' She shuddered at the recollection. 'Another reason to let some people who respected her inside, don't you think?'

Raoul muttered something too low for her to hear then cleared his throat. '*D'accord*, but just for a little while. And nothing leaves the house.'

'Agreed.' Ariel was surprised but pleased. 'You can be there too. Tonight, early evening when neighbors will be busy at their dinner tables?'

'No, tomorrow evening after work we will go together, you and your friend – the one with the musician husband. I have some chores to do at home tonight.'

Ariel decided not to bargain for Pippa too. It might be best to convince Pippa to stay away, given that Philippe would be furious and, given his tendency to let things slip, might wind up tipping the gendarmes off before their mission was complete.

'Thanks, Raoul. We'll be discreet. I'm glad you'll be there too, so you can be assured we mean no harm.'

When he had left for lunch, Ariel called Katherine and told her the news. 'We need to be careful, so no nosy neighbors call the sheriff. The power might be off, so we need to bring flashlights.'

Katherine cackled. 'Is there time to get hold of a couple of balaclavas? Really, I think we should just waltz in as if we have approval. It would be less likely to raise suspicion.'

Ariel's vision of being a cat burglar faded. 'You're probably right. After all, Raoul has every right to be there, and we'll hold our heads high, at least until we're inside.

'Changing the subject to something less exciting, I've sorted the wallpapers into batches that would look good together. My next chore is deciding which go where and how far these rolls will take me. Any suggestions?'

'Be bold, but don't start pasting until you're sure you can finish a whole wall. Your painter should finish painting, I think. You can wallpaper over paint better than he can paint around wallpaper.'

Ariel made a mental note to make contact with the painter soon.

'Get a tall ladder since your ceilings are high. We can go looking for more wallpaper this summer when the flea markets start up, so don't fret if a room you want to paper is bare when you're done with this lot.'

Ariel spent the next hour playing with ideas for papering some rooms. If she wallpapered one of the vast bedrooms, should she paper them all? Maybe the floral patterns that looked so charming on the rolls would be too fussy if they surrounded the guests? Paper one wall? Truth was, she couldn't visualize the effect and wished fervently she knew an interior designer.

She reminded herself as she moved rolls from one pile to another that she had fallen in love with Katherine's hodgepodge living room. Was that something that made sense for a dignified château? The headache that had begun when she had been forced to choose her cheese selections quickly or annoy the woman behind the counter came back. So many decisions, and she wasn't equipped to make them all on her own. One she could make – a glass of wine with the cheese and bread Tremblay had refused.

She popped the last dried apricot in her mouth just as her cell phone rang.

'*Bonjour, Madame.* Jean-Paul here. I am back for a few days only, but I hear our project needs me again, yes?'

Back to work on matters I can handle, Ariel thought as she arranged to have the master carpenter come over the next morning to look at her top floor.

'Servants quarters, eh? You are sure I am the man for it? I am working on an elegant old mansion in Beaune's oldest district at the moment.'

Ariel assured him that restoring the windows on the top floor needed to be to the same high standards as the rest of his work. 'If you decide the other projects are beneath you, you can help me find someone else, yes?'

Jean-Paul didn't hear the gentle sarcasm and replied earnestly that he would look at them and let her know. 'Tomorrow then. Will I see the rest of your crew? I miss their company – well most of them.' He half-laughed, half-growled.

'Only Raoul now. Andre will be back soon to add a bathroom, but the roof's complete and Pippa's London friends finished the electric updates a long time ago. I haven't got anything for them to do. I miss them too. Lucas drops by now and then. He and Regine have become friends, I think, and he's always looking for work.'

She didn't add that Lucas was like a puppy wanting to please, bringing her his homemade cookies and offering to do odd chores. Ariel had an idea that he somehow felt responsible for his roofing partner's actions last year. But he was at loose ends and her attempts to interest Pippa in Lucas as an alternative to Philippe when Pippa and her gendarme boyfriend had broken up had not taken hold. So far Pippa was still attached to the young policeman, although her role as an overeager amateur sleuth and Philippe's as an untested officer in the gendarmerie provoked awkward moments.

Ariel liked being busy. With no house-related meetings until the next morning, and the search of Madame's house postponed until tomorrow evening, she was at a loose end and on her own inside the château. She decided it was time to make lists of what she wanted in the way of furniture, lighting and floor coverings. In all her planning, she had left the large public rooms on the ground floor as question marks. Who needed a ballroom, and if it wasn't that, what on earth could it be? A library for books she didn't have? An office for running the building, or would that break the mood she was trying to create? She grimaced.

The ancient stone staircase at the far corner of the long, gallery-like room connected to the romantic tower that was, sadly, far down on the priority list. A thick wood door with iron hinges kept the cold from the tower from leaking into the big room.

On the other side of the sweeping central staircase was what must once have been a room for eating, huge for a dining room, and far too formal in size to be practical. So, she thought, pacing around the space, her footsteps echoing in the emptiness, what would it be in the future? She'd lived in city apartments and college dorms for so long that her imagination couldn't cope with a large open space big enough to fill with a New York apartment.

What if Katherine relocated her shop here, much closer to the tourist village of Noyers? Would that even be possible? Her eyes widened and she turned in a circle. Here, there would be room for furniture to sell, arranged in settings that would inspire buyers. Yes, it could work. She added it to the list of exploratory conversations she needed to have for the next stage of the château's rehabilitation.

The sun was setting beyond the trees on the back side of the mansion. She looked for Raoul's car, but it was gone. Flicking on the lamp in front of one of the ground-floor windows, now so beautiful with the wavy glass panes Jean-Paul had salvaged when he reframed the windows, Ariel promised herself a pork chop, boiled potatoes with local butter and parsley, and charred carrots for dinner, then an expansive evening with the mystery novel she had rooted out of her unpacked cartons. Things were falling into place and, just at this moment, she was happy.

THIRTEEN

March 24

Jean-Paul was his usual cheerful self, bestowing the traditional kisses on either cheek when she answered his brisk knock the next morning. His red hair was still in a ponytail, but he looked more put together, albeit still gangly, than when she had last seen him, maybe because he wasn't covered in sawdust and wood chips. He was as curious as she was about the hole in the servants'-quarter room as she had been but decided there must have been a small fire, perhaps from a candle. 'See, there's just the hint of blackened wood here and here? Someone chiseled out the ruined wood, probably not someone who understood you can't plop a new piece in over the hole.' He grinned. 'Don't worry, I'll find a way, but I can't start for a couple of weeks. Will that do?'

Ariel said it would and begged him to block off the time before someone else took it. She didn't dare ask how much money his work on the top floor might cost. One could hardly live in a space with a hole in the floor, or windows as they were now, rattling and letting in every stray gust of wind. And some rain, he pointed out.

'Like below, see? Do not worry. I will do exactly what I did on the lower floors, and I know I can find a replacement for that one small pane of glass at an antique store, and it will be perfect, I guarantee.'

She waved at him as he took off on his motorcycle. Not for the first time, she wished Raoul was in the habit of answering his cell phone. He was absent again. They hadn't decided where or exactly when to meet beyond 'after work', and now he wasn't in the garden.

As the day went on, she realized she was getting nervous. On one level, it was perfectly reasonable to look for Madame's biography for the funeral service. On another, not so reasonable to be digging through her belongings in the belief there was a clue as to her death buried in her house when the police had already done that with professional skill.

While she was still asking herself questions she couldn't answer, Katherine called her and added more to the list. 'We can't pull up like a motorcade. Should we meet in the *mairie* parking lot in Noyers, which is close by? I know you promised Raoul you wouldn't take anything, but there might be documents we don't dare leave unattended. Would that be all right? Oh, and by the way, Pippa is coming too.'

'What? Raoul said you and me, not someone else.'

'She promised me she would be as quiet as a mouse, and what could I say?'

'How did she even know?'

There was a brief silence. 'I may have let it slip. Michael's in Paris and when I mentioned that, she suggested the three of us meet at Tony's, and I . . .'

The renewed phone silence was broken by the deep woofs of Gracie, the bear-sized dog in the Goff household.

'Wait, someone's coming. It's Pippa, and she appears to have donned a disguise. Catwoman, if I'm reading it right.'

Ariel groaned. 'This could easily turn into a circus. Raoul will be mad. He might even call the whole evening off. If you can't get her to stay out of this by reminding her if our search goes wrong, she could be arrested, then at least read her the riot act about how this is not a game and definitely not a chance to create a scene for her new book.'

'I will, and if she drives, it makes everything easier, doesn't it?'

With that, Katherine signed off and Ariel's nerves ratcheted up a few levels.

Her stomach was too knotted to eat an early supper, and when Raoul's car crunched over the gravel and stopped at the bottom of the steps, Ariel's breathing sped up. It was too late to call off the plan. Part of her wanted Raoul to say he had decided against it, but the look on his face when she answered the door said he was, however unwillingly, ready.

'Do you want me to drive?' she asked, shrugging on her quilted coat.

'I'm the one supposed to be working and my tools are in my car. You better be with me. Less noticeable.'

'Okay, but Katherine will be arriving on her own.' Ariel paused then added, wincing, 'With Pippa.'

Before Raoul could protest, she said, 'Katherine doesn't have a dependable car, you see.'

Raoul's laugh was more like a bark. 'That little thing? It's like a child's toy and as loud as a two-stroke motorcycle. Everyone in Reigny knows immediately when she putters off in it. Just as well she gets a ride. I hope no one in Noyers recognizes the bright red of that young woman's car though. In Reigny, all know it immediately.'

He hadn't cancelled the meeting. Ariel checked her pockets – keys to her house, small water bottle because her throat was already dry, flashlight because they might be poking around in dark corners. To show Raoul she wasn't going to remove anything, she had decided not to bring a bag, which might prove to be a problem if she did decide to take something like a document or an old photo, for the funeral program. She assured herself she was following the spirit if not the literal promise she had made to the old man.

Raoul's car smelled like stone dust and something she couldn't name. Maybe the remains of a sandwich? If there were springs in the chassis, they had long since given up. The covering on the passenger-side seat was tattered, but she agreed that this car would raise less curiosity than having several parked outside.

'I should have asked Pippa to park a couple of blocks away, but Katherine must have.'

Raoul only grunted, his gnarled hands fastened to the steering wheel, his body hunched forward as if he expected a rhinoceros to charge into the road at any moment. They were at Madame's house in a few minutes.

He pulled into the little driveway area to one side of her house and switched off the engine. It was late in the day, and though it had clouded over some time ago, there was still some daylight left.

'No sign of my friends,' Ariel said, peering through the windshield. 'Do you want to go in right away to start the garden work?'

Raoul nodded. 'I need to pull up the weeds and old plants so they don't crowd the roses. She loved her roses.'

He got out of the car and opened his trunk, pulling out a tarp and a bag of fertilizer. After closing the trunk carefully – 'Do not want attention' – he unlocked the door and motioned Ariel in with his head.

She stood in the gloomy entryway, and he moved around her and opened a door on the far side of the big room, heaving his supplies on to a small brick patio, beyond which the winter remains of the garden waited. Her first impression of the space was that it was crowded and messy.

Behind her, a sharp knock made her jump.

'It's only us,' Katherine said in a whisper, edging inside, almost pushed by the tall young woman who had chosen a thick black sweater and a knit cap pulled down over her distinctive hair.

'Close the door,' Katherine hissed, and Pippa did, although she managed to knock over a tin jug on the little table closest to the door, which made a racket as it bounced on the tile floor.

Raoul poked his head in from the back door. 'What the hell? If you cannot be quiet, you had better leave this instant.'

'Nothing broke. We're all a bit nervous,' Ariel said. 'Sorry, Raoul. We promise to be careful and quiet. Come on, you two – no time to lose. Katherine, you take this area. Pippa and I will go upstairs for a look around. Regine had noticed some boxes stacked up down here, but I don't see them, so maybe they're in an unused room.'

'What exactly are we looking for?' Pippa was already on the narrow wooden stairs, one hand on the wall for balance.

'I'm not sure,' Ariel said slowly. 'In general, anything that might be a reason Madame was attacked. Valuable objects, papers that might point to financial gain for someone if she died, something that looks like it might be a secret she was holding.'

'I'm ready to say it's not likely there are gold coins hidden in the dirty dishes over there,' Katherine said, 'but I'll shake out the blankets on the chaise that looks like it might have been her bed. But something's already bothering me.'

'Me too,' Ariel said. 'She may have been a recluse, but not this bad.' She pointed to open drawers and overturned cushions and an upside-down wastepaper basket. 'I guess the gendarmes did this, but it seems cruel or lazy to leave it in such a state.'

Katherine edged into the kitchen area and looked down.

'Ugh, sugar on the floor. Interesting. The sugar container's here too.' She bent down and picked it up. 'A glass jar still with its soup label. If she had silver serving dishes like what she sold me, she wasn't using them here at home.' She looked around. 'The silverware drawer's open and there's nothing but some tarnished silverplate, nothing I'd look at twice in the *vide greniers*.'

'Fast first look for each of us, then meet to figure out what's next.'

Through the open back door, Ariel saw Raoul raking the neglected garden. He looked their way at that moment, a worried frown pulling his bushy eyebrows and the corners of his mouth downward. He wasn't sold on them being here, so they'd better move quickly in case he changed his mind.

Pippa had already clambered up the rest of the staircase. When Ariel got to the top, she saw that there were rooms on either side that opened directly to the stairs.

'I'm in here,' Pippa's muffled voice said, and Ariel turned into one room that led directly into a second.

In the farthest one, Pippa was shining her flashlight into a beat-up armoire with a door that swung open at an angle. 'Just junk,' she said, tugging at a yellowed lace cloth.

'Feel around to see if there's anything hidden in the fabrics or anything under the pile. If we have time, we may have to take everything out and put it back.'

'Judging by the way it's crammed in, I think the gendarmes beat us to it and tried to make it neat. It's jumbled up not folded.' She looked around. 'This might have been a bedroom once. There's a couple of lamps, a bed that looks like it would ruin your back if you lay down in it, and some other stuff.'

'Take a quick look. Remember, we're searching for anything that might explain why she was killed.'

Ariel left her there and backtracked into the room she had passed through. It was empty of furniture except for a desk. When Ariel went over to look through it, she realized it had the signs of being a genuine antique, with graceful lines and delicate legs. The top was covered with dust.

'No, not quite,' she said out loud. Near the front edge and the edge of a shallow drawer that was halfway open, there was a handprint. She reminded herself they were on a hunt for clues, and if fingerprints were as important as they were in the TV detective shows she had turned to in the bleak months after Dan's death, she didn't want to mess this up.

She bent down and shined her flashlight into the drawer. At first, it looked empty, but the flashlight picked up the edge of a piece of paper that seemed to have been jammed behind the drawer. She held on to the delicate metal pull on the drawer, easing the drawer farther out, and tugged at the paper, hoping she wasn't adding her own prints to the scene. It came out slowly, but she was finally able to pinch the packet between her fingers and pull it out. She stood upright and would have opened it, but Pippa charged in, holding something like a prize.

'Look at this – the same magazine Katherine had at the shop. The same issue she gave me. There's a coincidence.'

Ariel shoved her rescued packet into her jacket pocket and peered over Pippa's shoulder. 'Have you had time to read the copy you got? Is there anything that might explain why Madame would have this?'

Pippa made a face. 'My French is still pretty basic. I read some captions and I'm working through the article about the Resistance heroes, but slowly. Should I leave this here?'

Ariel started to say yes, but something stopped her. 'Let's take it – if Raoul doesn't object. I don't know what's significant. Obviously the police didn't think so, unless it was hidden?'

'Not really. It was on top of that old armoire, along with a dozen other old magazines and some newspapers. They were just lying there.'

'Then hang on to it. Later, we should look at that stack of papers. It might mean something that we figure out when we see all of them. For now, let's look at the room across the landing.'

It was dark now, and they had to use their flashlights.

As they crossed the top of the stairs, Ariel called down. 'Katherine, find anything interesting?'

'It looks like the police scooped everything from the desk. The drawers are mostly empty, and what's left is random slips of paper – receipts and things. I'm not sure what to look for, and Raoul is putting his tools away. It's too dark for him to work outside. He wants us to leave.'

'We'll be right down. We haven't seen the boxes Regine described, so we're just going to take a quick look in one more room.'

She stopped in the doorway of the new room. 'Phew, what's that smell?'

Pippa looked around. 'Dog doo,' she said and pointed to a dried mess in one corner. 'There's a blanket on the floor that must be where it slept, and a couple of dishes.'

Ariel peered into the dark room. 'Weird. She walked that dog constantly, so an indoor mess must mean it was sick, poor thing. See any boxes?'

The two women shined their flashlights into every corner and along the walls. 'No need to go in – there's nothing here. Let's—'

A door crashed against the wall downstairs. Katherine screamed. Multiple voices began yelling, 'Don't move! Hands up now!' At least that's what Ariel, frozen at the top of the stairs guessed they were saying, because it had to be gendarmes, and she and her friends had to have been caught in the act of rummaging through a dead woman's house.

Almost immediately, there was another loud noise that sounded like it was coming from the garden, a clatter that sounded like garden tools falling or being hurled.

Pippa spun around into the dog room, put her finger to her lips and jerked her head in Ariel's direction, but it was too late. A head she could only see in outline peered up, a large, blindingly bright flashlight focused on Ariel's face.

'Come down immediately.'

Ariel glanced in the direction of the dog room. She couldn't see Pippa.

'Come on, Pippa,' she said quietly in English. 'It's no use hiding. It's the police. The next thing is they're going to come up here and search, and you'll just make things worse if they think you're trying to escape. Remember, we're not here to commit a crime. We'll be all right.'

Pippa emerged slowly, her eyes round, her mouth open in an O. She was patting the front of her sweater. 'Magazine,' she mouthed and motioned Ariel to go first.

Ariel stepped out of the flashlight's beam and moved the packet she had picked up from her jacket pocket to under the back waistband of her stretchy jeans. 'We're coming,' she called down the stairs.

The scene below was alarming. Katherine was standing stiffly next to the kitchen sink, a woman in full uniform holding her arm. Raoul, thrashing and cursing, was being held by two grim-faced policemen, and a third stood behind him, arms akimbo. Two more police officers stood at the bottom of the stairs, waiting for Ariel and Pippa. Flashing blue lights illuminated the scene, filtered by the curtains at the front window.

Ariel started to explain when they entered the room. 'We're not doing anything wrong. We were friends of Madame Toussaint and we wanted to find some material for her funeral program because no one knew what to say about her.' She heard herself and realized that the excuse that had sounded so reasonable when she and Katherine planned this little outing was flimsy at best when spoken out loud to a room full of policemen – well, five men and one woman – in the dark of night. Proof of that was in the faces that stared back at her without expression – and the tight grip on her upper arm that didn't loosen an iota after her attempt to shrug off the situation.

Another car arrived, its siren on, and a car door slammed. Of course, Ariel thought, and her face flushed with heat as Brigadier Allard stomped in, his jaw thrust out and his eyes darting around at the crowd in the room. They stopped when he noticed Ariel and his eyebrows shot up.

'What is this? Do not tell me you blundered into my stakeout, Madame Shepard.' He didn't wait for an answer but turned to the men holding Raoul. 'Is this the suspect? Who are you and what do you have to say for yourself, monsieur?'

Raoul twisted his shoulders and kicked out at the man closest to him. When the officer pulled him upright, he pushed his neck forward and spat out a reply that Ariel guessed was only French curses.

'Wait,' she said, 'I can explain why he's here and why we are. There's nothing criminal going on, I promise.'

The chief of police turned to stare at her, but he didn't back away from Raoul. 'You will definitely explain to me, Madame, and in detail.'

Turning back to the officers holding Raoul, he said, 'Take him to the gendarmerie. And you,' he said to the female gendarme and the one holding Ariel, 'outside and do a thorough search of the garden and that shed. After that, his car. Immediately.'

It was clear Raoul had no intention of going quietly, and his exit from the room was something of a wrestling match. For a single instant, he snapped his head to look at her and it looked like he was trying to say something, but the police holding him jerked him forward.

Ariel attempted to call out to him to let him know she would straighten things out right away, but she wasn't sure he heard her or was even listening as he was hauled roughly through the door.

'He has a wife in Reigny, you know. You must inform her,' she said to the brigadier. Her voice caught. What had she done? Stupid, stupid, and now that innocent man was in trouble.

Allard ignored her and walked over to stand in front of Katherine. 'Madame, we have met, I think. You are American also?'

'I live in Reigny, have for years. I consider myself almost French.' Katherine had adopted an aristocratic tone, and despite being five-foot three, she somehow managed to look down her nose at the six-foot-tall uniformed police chief.

Ariel had to stifle an inappropriate giggle. *Nerves*, she chided herself. *Laughing right now would not be a good idea*. The giggle died in her throat.

'And now I know who you are,' Allard said, pivoting to look at Pippa. 'You are with them.'

'Ariel invited me,' she said, dipping her head in Ariel's direction. The black watch cap she had chosen to wear with skinny black pants, a black sweater and – Ariel noticed for the first time – black gloves holding a small flashlight did make her look a bit like a cat burglar, not the best presentation at this moment.

'Please, Brigadier Allard, let me explain. It's not what you think, and Raoul has a right to be here. He has taken care of Madame Toussaint's garden for a long time.'

'In the dark?'

'It wasn't dark when we got here.'

'So you came with the gardener? Is he the same man who works at your château?'

'Yes.' What to say next that would help?

'I recognize him of course. He gave evidence against the criminals in the case last year. You must feel you owe him a great deal. He helped you then.'

'Of course. If it hadn't been for him—'

'So naturally you wish to help him now when he is arrested, but you cannot interfere with a police investigation. All three of you will come with us to the gendarmerie, where you will explain why you are here in the night, in the house of a woman who was recently murdered, someone you knew and someone' – he turned back to Katherine – 'you did business with.'

'You can't just take us. My husband will be worried.'

Ariel thought that was rather an understatement. Michael would be livid once he returned from Paris, and not only at the gendarmes for holding his wife.

Ariel decided this wasn't the moment to focus on that. 'Brigadier Allard, I'm really sorry I made a mess out of what was supposed to be a quick look for anything that might help the people planning her funeral. Could I please explain it to you here, rather than having to haul us all to Avallon and the station? We were only trying to help.'

'I know you well enough to believe you were trying to solve the case, you and your fellow sleuths.' He sighed, paused and looked around. 'Did you make this mess?' He indicated the spilled sugar in the kitchen area.

'Of course not. We noticed it right away and wondered if the gendarmes had done it if they were here right after she was killed. Her desk was a mess, and her clothing drawers opened and stuff tossed around. I think a mattress upstairs had been moved, but I was only up there for a few minutes and didn't look around.'

'Why would the police do that? There was no reason to suspect her of a crime.'

'That must mean someone else was here after your officers?' Ariel's thoughts were as jumbled as the contents of Madame's wardrobe, but this had to mean she was right. There was, or at least had been, something here for which the woman was killed. But what?

Brigadier Allard stood for a moment, chewing his lip. 'I need to hear from all of you about what you noticed and what you looked at, but not here. My officers need to begin a search and look for fingerprints and other evidence. I don't want you in this house, and fairly soon I need to be on hand to question the suspect, but I'm willing to escort you all to your house, Madame Shepard, and question you there. Will that be suitable in lieu of the gendarmerie this evening? We will need your fingerprints tomorrow.'

Ariel noticed that she was now 'Madame Shepard', no longer 'Ariel'. Pity, she had been warming to him. 'Yes, if Katherine and Pippa agree?'

Nods from her co-conspirators confirmed the plan.

Katherine said, 'My husband will be home in an hour. Will I be able to get back by then?'

'*Ça dépend*,' the police chief said, echoing a phrase Ariel had learned early in her restoration project from the workmen who were unwilling to commit to a certain time for starting their tasks, and waved the women toward the exit.

Ariel led the way out the door. 'I'll have to ride with my friends because Raoul and I came in his car.'

'I think you shall come with me,' Allard said. His driver opened the rear door before Ariel could argue, and she slid in.

'You two' – he raised his voice to Pippa and Katherine as they were about to turn the corner on foot – 'wait right there. My driver will follow you to your car, and you will drive straight to your friend's house with no foolishness. Otherwise, there will be consequences.'

The situation was humiliating enough, but Ariel slid lower in the seat when she noticed the neighbor she had met days earlier standing in front of his tidy house, staring at her. He had been skeptical when she had first poked around the exterior of the house, and his worst suspicions had just been vindicated. She wondered if he had called the gendarmes but remembered with a start that the brigadier had said something about her interfering with a stakeout. Had Allard discovered someone else, maybe the person who had upended the sugar bowl and dug through Madame's belongings? Could that unknown thief already have stolen the boxes Regine saw, and, if so, would anyone ever know what was in them? She needed to get Allard to share what his team had been looking for tonight.

She looked around and saw a small group of people clustered

together well away from the activity, soaking up the action – housewives in aprons, men in overalls or jackets, even the visitor looking for real estate, probably writing off this house as a bad risk.

Finally, the police chief came back. He sat in the front seat as the driver slowly followed the pair of women marching to Pippa's red sports car. Allard didn't say anything until the little cavalcade was on the road to the château.

'I am disappointed that you did not accept my assurances about this investigation, Madame. It is, or was, proceeding well until you decided to enter the victim's house without permission. May I ask what specifically you were looking for?'

'First, we didn't enter illegally. We were invited by the gardener, who goes there regularly to tend her roses. And how is it the police showed up?'

'I will come back to that later. Continue.'

'As I told you, the people who knew her at least somewhat feel kindly toward her. She never argued or caused an uproar, just went her own way. They intend to honor her at a church service, but someone mentioned to me it was a shame there was so little they could say about her on the funeral program.'

Allard sighed, a loud and melodramatic sound. 'You insult me, Madame. It is not necessary to break into someone's home to find birth and death information.'

'I keep telling you, we didn't break in. Raoul had a key, and when I told him what we were looking for, he agreed to let us in as long as he could be there too. In fact, he made me promise not to take anything.' The packet digging into the back of her waistband reminded her she was going to have a lot more to explain if it fell out – or if she was searched later at the gendarmerie.

'We will continue this at your home,' was all he said, and he lapsed into silence for the remainder of the short ride.

Twenty minutes later, glad to be home and caught between being a host and a suspect, Ariel offered hot drinks as the others stood around the big kitchen table. 'I have some cookies too,' she said, but a glance from Brigadier Allard stopped her from further attempts at hospitality. The women sat, and the police chief stood at the head of the table.

'First,' he said, looking at Pippa, 'I would ask you to remove whatever you have hidden under your sweater.'

'Me?' Pippa said, raising her eyebrows almost to her hairline. She looked, Ariel thought, like the kid caught with her hand in the cookie jar.

Allard nodded.

Slowly, her face turning bright enough to compete with the streak in her spiky hair, she tugged the magazine downward. 'I only put it in my jumper so my hands would be free. It's nothing really – an old magazine.' She put it on the table and slid it a bit toward Allard.

'That is all you stole from the victim's house? And why did you decide to take it?'

'I didn't steal it, not exactly. I mean, it's an old magazine and I . . . collect them.' She looked up with wide eyes.

'It's *Le Monde*. It is in French. Do you read French, mademoiselle?'

'I'm learning and I use things like this to practice.' She flapped a hand at the evidence.

Pippa obviously felt on firmer ground and was beginning to sound like herself, Ariel thought, which could turn into a problem if she said more.

Allard was silent for a moment, looking hard at the young woman. 'Perhaps you need to read the penal codes next,' was all he said. 'And you, Madame Goff, you have nothing from the house?'

Katherine grimaced and pulled an old cloth sack from her own bag. 'She always carried a bag like this when she came to my shop, and I thought this might be it, which would be important, wouldn't it, since you never found her bag? I figured that would mean he was able to get into her house. But it's not the same at all. It's blue, now that I see it in the light, and hers was black – faded but definitely black.'

Ariel began to panic. He'd ask her next, and she had no idea if the packet she had picked up was something the police should have. It must have been important to Madame, who had tucked it away securely. She doubted it had anything to do with the murder. It was probably a deeply personal memory.

'And you? You have a souvenir to show me?'

Ariel willed her expression not to give her away. 'No, there wasn't time. I was distracted by a beautiful desk, perhaps eighteenth century, upstairs, wondering how she came to possess it. Then Pippa and I walked into a room that smelled of dog, and immediately your officers shouted for us to come down. So, no, I didn't even have time to search for a photograph of her or anything that would tell us a bit about her. Sadly, she remains a mystery, as I guess her death does.'

The brigadier looked from one woman to the other. He walked a few steps away from them then pivoted back, his index finger held up in front of him. 'If at any time I discover you have done anything more than this, I cannot promise that you will not be arrested as accomplices, or at least for breaking and entering.'

As Ariel opened her mouth to protest, he held the finger up again. 'I know you say you did not break into the house, but that is playing with words. You had no legal right to be there, were not invited by the victim, nor are you her relatives. You surreptitiously took things that belonged to the victim. I assure you, I can present that to the judge in such a way that you can be arrested. Have I made myself clear, *mesdames*?'

There was nothing to do except to say yes, and they each did.

'Very well. There will be no more "investigating" on your part. As it is, you may have cost us the opportunity to catch the thief. Someone reported lights on in that house several nights ago. Now, anyone watching knows we are aware. They will not return. Investigations are the job of the gendarmerie and the national police. Madame,' he said, turning to Katherine with a grim expression and lowered eyebrows, 'I suggest you think carefully about anything else of hers you have in your possession. I can see myself out.'

After he left, the three women were quiet. Ariel made herbal tea and got out the cookies. Katherine played with the cloth sack and Pippa flipped the pages of the magazine dejectedly. Ariel wasn't sure she should produce the packet right now. It would show her up as a liar, which might upset her friends, who had confessed and been threatened while she had stayed silent.

She had crumbled a cookie into a pile before Katherine said, 'Okay, what gives? Something's bothering you, and you've taken it out on that hazelnut *sablé* long enough.'

Pippa looked up. 'Wait, you know something you haven't told us? I was upstairs with you and there was hardly any time to search. Did you find something other than a pretty desk?'

Ariel pushed back her chair and stood up. 'It goes no further than us, agreed? I'm not even sure what it is.' She reached around and tugged the packet from her jeans. Carefully, she placed it on the table and unfolded the bundle of paper to reveal a photo.

'I found this pushed into the back of a shallow drawer of that old desk, but I didn't have time to look at it. For all I know, it's not important, but I wanted to be sure.'

The others scooted their chairs closer to look at the contents.

'The writing on the page is in longhand and not too neat. I'll translate it later when I have my glasses. Who's this, I wonder?' Ariel turned the black-and-white photograph to face her friends.

'It's old, that's for sure,' Pippa said. 'It looks like the ones in the old magazines – the hairdo, the clothes and a gun.'

'Do you see Madame's name?' Ariel asked, peering over her friend's shoulder at the paper.

'Not so far. I'm only seeing first names – Pierre, Marie, Roland and what might be the name of a small town.' She sat back. 'Combined with that old picture, this may well be about the partisans who hid in the Morvan and the other forested areas nearby and fought against the Nazis. I want to translate it carefully, and I'm too tired and distracted because Michael will be home and worried.'

'Why not invite him to meet us at Tony's for dinner if it's not too late?' Ariel said. 'Want to give him a call?'

Katherine patted her pockets and ducked her head into her bag. 'Damn it, no phone. When will I learn that the point is it's portable and you're supposed to take it everywhere?'

'Use mine,' Pippa said, holding out what Ariel recognized as a new model.

Katherine took it gingerly. 'I'm not sure how you turn it on or dial.'

'Dial? What's that?' Pippa said with a snort. 'Here, I'll do it – you're on speed dial anyway. Your home phone too.' She punched a button and handed the phone to Katherine.

Michael seemed to like the idea.

'He was wondering where I was. He'll meet us there after he's walked the dogs. Lately, they've been especially barky, probably because I'm not as diligent as my husband when it comes to going out in wet, windy weather. I'll do the translation tomorrow and we can meet and figure out what might be important. One thing – don't tell Michael about tonight.'

Ariel agreed and pointed out that their stated mission has been to learn something for the funeral program, and maybe this would help. 'Do you think it could be a picture of her?'

The three leaned in and looked at the photo again.

'She looks so young. Madame is – was – so old, and what I see in my head is a small, bent woman with the face of a dried apple,' Ariel said.

Katherine said, 'Pippa, could I borrow the *Le Monde* you found? It might help me understand what the writer of this paper was saying.'

'Sure,' Pippa said with a shrug. 'I have the same issue anyway. I'm thinking Madame Toussaint was a collector of war records, like I try to pull together research for my books. The bunch of papers on the high shelf upstairs may be more of the same stuff. Madame would have been a kid during the war, but maybe someone in her family was part of the partisan group, and this is her way of researching family history.'

'I like that idea. If her family was from the Yonne or any occupied territory in France, she might have kept records of what happened. Such terrible times.'

Ariel stopped. She had already seen that for the French, the German occupation, and the presence elsewhere in Burgundy of France's Vichy administration, had left deep and permanent scars. More than once she had stopped her car at some minor crossroads to get out and read a dusty bronze plaque memorializing a spot where Nazi soldiers had shot a local man or boy.

Pippa's phone jarred her out of her thoughts, playing a thumping beat that Ariel was pretty sure was music, although it could have been pistons, if people actually recorded pistons punching down and uploaded the result for use as a ringtone. *Yes, I am getting old*, she pointed out to herself, even if she was unwilling to say it out loud.

'Michael says he's on the way,' Pippa said, 'and I'm starved. Come on, Katherine. We'll meet you at the café, Ariel.'

FOURTEEN

When Ariel got to Tony's, there was a small group standing outside, peering at the window. Feeling certain that a movie star or a famous rap musician hadn't dropped in for dinner, she sidled up to the window and saw a poster. 'Have you seen any of these individuals? Wanted on suspicion of robbery, burglary and assault. Please call your gendarmerie with information.' Unflattering black-and-white photographs of four glaring men made the point.

A few people murmured their disgust at these criminals' behavior (*Alleged behavior*, chided Ariel's inner voice), and one man in overalls loudly proclaimed his intent to shoot them with his hunting rifle if they dared to come to his house. The group drifted apart, a couple of people heading into the café.

Ariel followed them in and said to Tony, who was pulling the lever on his hissing espresso machine, 'So what's that about?'

He shrugged. 'The gendarmes say they're asking merchants and cafés to post these all over the Yonne. They told me the attacks have not stopped and that the national police are getting involved.'

'Has anyone been hurt?'

'So far, nothing serious. But the *flics* said the gangs are getting bolder and it is only a matter of time. This *bande de voleurs* - gang of robbers, you know?' he tilted his head toward the poster – 'have done this kind of thing before, which is why they've been chosen as the poster boys.' He set several espresso cups on the bar, and the man who had threatened to shoot any crooks on his property came up and took two back to the table he and his stern-faced wife occupied.

'But no one in Noyers has been robbed, have they? And you're the only place in town where people might hang out.' She swallowed a bracing mouthful of the rich brew.

Tony jerked his head to the back end of the zinc bar. 'I keep my phone there, and if I see anything, I am ready to call for help. But thieves here would stand out, if we are truthful. Other than summer tourists, the community is made up of middle-aged people, and they recognize each other even if they are not friends.'

Ariel thought for a moment and downed the rest of her little cup of espresso. 'You'll have to watch carefully when the tourists arrive, which they will soon. I see the Belgian jewelers are back and decorating their shop window, getting ready for business.'

Tony nodded. 'That is the most vulnerable place for a burglary or even a daytime robbery. I can see their front door from here, and I will make sure they are alerted.'

Ariel took a deep breath. 'Don't tell anyone, but I think I may have been followed once when driving back from Reigny. It's probably just my imagination and my own feeling of anxiety after Madame's death, but I've promised myself to be careful.'

Tony had stopped wiping the bar and stood, bar cloth in hand. 'But what is this? You have told the brigadier, yes? You are perceived as wealthy, because how else could you afford a château? You must be careful.'

'I wouldn't have anything to report really, just a car that seemed to be following me. Anyway, it passed me after tailgating me for a while, so I'm sure it was nothing.'

Tony shook his head vigorously. 'You saw those men on the poster? You read what they have done. You live alone. Please call the gendarmes. Perhaps they will pay closer attention to your situation.'

Ariel nodded but made no promises. Her vague apprehension would probably only annoy an overstretched Avallon police department.

Braised leeks stuffed with diced mushrooms, thin slices of chicken breasts poached in white wine and tarragon, and little potatoes kept the foursome quiet for a while. After, over espresso and lemon tarts, Michael regaled them with funny stories about having to find his way around Paris with the most rudimentary French.

'I'd say "*bonjour*" and they'd switch to English or shake their heads and disappear. I was trying to be polite.' He had made his way to a studio that had a sound engineer he'd been told about. 'The guy's a genius. I've been trying out the idea of doing my own harmony on a couple of songs, but I just couldn't get it. He pulled everything together in a day and sent the producer and me copies, so I hope I'm free for a few weeks now.'

'Weeks? How lovely. Maybe we can have a real vacation. Morocco? Portugal? Venice?' Katherine said.

'Can you leave the shop for that long?' Ariel asked.

'I've only opened it once, for a half hour after we looked at the wallpaper. A woman tourist was peering in the window and was interested in small things she could give as gifts, so I let her in with her silly little dog. I have to say, she was rather unpleasant and turned her nose up at my lovely dinner plates and old lace curtains. She bought a silver-plated salad tong set, nothing special. Still, the most business I've done since last summer. If I'm back by the middle of April, that will be fine. Now, what about Morocco, my darling?' she said, fluttering her eyelashes at her husband.

'If we can drive. The dogs have to come too.'

'Drive to Morocco? You can't be serious? They're dogs. What would they do in a souk or on a beach or a gondola?'

Michael chuckled. 'Kay, better ask what I'd do with all of that. Crowds, boats, not my thing. I get seasick, and I begin to itch in the middle of a crowd. If we drive, we can go to Normandy, or up into the Alps, or down to that region, the one with all the prehistoric caves. Now that would interest me.'

'Funny,' Pippa said, 'not liking crowds. Now that you're famous, you play in front of crowds every night.'

'Not famous and not every night. I've only done two tours, both as the warm-up act for the Leopards. Believe me, that isn't fame. The biggest difference is I'm in front of the audience, not in the middle.

'Ariel, you look tired – or distracted. What's up? More workers who need to open up more holes in your plaster walls?'

Ariel started at the sound of her name. Michael tipped his chair back on to two legs and took out one of his little brown cigarettes. Knowing there was no smoking inside, he just rolled it around in his mouth, his eyes crinkling as he smiled. *He looks so relaxed*, she thought. *It's a good thing he doesn't know the trouble we got in.* 'Oh, just processing something I heard. Not important.'

Pippa eyed her, but she didn't say anything. Ariel had been

replaying the last chaotic moments in Madame's house, with Raoul being muscled out the door. Had he been trying to tell her something? He had looked so intensely at her, and it seemed like he was signaling something, mouthing it without saying it. What was it? She needed to think harder, and Tony's bustling café wasn't the place.

'I'm exhausted for some reason,' she said, standing up. 'Here's my share for dinner. It was such a treat, especially catching up with you, Michael, but I have a busy morning to look forward to. Managing a house this size is never-ending.'

After exchanging kisses with everyone in the group and waving to Regine and Tony, she headed the short distance to the château and its welcoming lamplight. Briefly on the way, she had wondered if the car that had pulled out of a parking place and was headed in the same direction as she was might be following her.

'Enough drama,' she said out loud. 'Next thing I know, I'll be seeing ghosts.'

The car turned toward Reigny where the road did, and she laughed. She had a feeling that sleep wouldn't come easily.

FIFTEEN

Ariel was buttering her fat slice of bread the next morning when the idea came to her. Had Raoul been trying to tell her something about the church, and if so, the one in Noyers where the funeral would be held or the locked building in Reigny? When she closed her eyes, she could picture something that might have been *l'église*, the church, and a sharp nod. It also might have been a cursed version of 'I told you so' – the effect of being manhandled. But she didn't have much else to go on and she was sure he was trying to give her a message, so she would plan a visit to both churches as soon as her meeting with Andre was over.

Andre had two bids for the bathroom expansion and the new one, and she trusted he would not tilt his proposal toward cronies. He might be hoping to expand his business beyond repairing sewers and leaking pipes, which she could understand. However, tempting though it might be, she couldn't afford to begin paying a middleman. She also couldn't afford to lose the hard-working man who had waded around in the mud, climbed into icky places to replace old ceramic waste pipes and deal with inspectors on her behalf.

'Nothing here is simple,' she said to the empty kitchen then remembered nothing was simple in the States either.

She reached for her handy French–English dictionary for the right term. '*Chef-d'équipe*, huh?' She had a feeling crew chief was what Andre had in mind.

Andre brought a dark-haired man in his late thirties with him, Théo, and explained that Théo had recently worked on a much larger château in Burgundy, near the Loire region. 'He was trained as an architect, but, alas, there is small work.'

Théo smiled as he pulled out his cell phone. 'It is exceedingly rare for a new architect to get a whole house to create. My father-in-law promises that he will hire me to design his retirement home in the suburbs of Nice. But not yet, so I am happy to help clients create new spaces within old buildings.' He turned the phone toward Ariel and swiped through some photographs of his recent work.

The three of them toured the first floor together, the men knocking on walls, pacing floor spaces and peering into corners. Théo said he would be pleased to write up a quote for a design and include a rough sketch and recommendations for the finish materials so she would have a better idea of the actual cost to carry out a version of his design. Ariel agreed, and thanked Andre for the introduction, but her attention was elsewhere.

As soon she they had driven off, she checked that her phone was charged and ready, locked up the house and drove to the church in Noyers. If Raoul had hidden something in either church, she needed to find it.

A balding man wearing overalls was unlocking the church door when she arrived. 'Just cleaning up,' he said, looking over his shoulder at her. 'The place gets dusty, you know, between baptisms and funerals.'

'The church isn't open every day?' Ariel asked as she stepped into the dark, cavernous space.

'Not these days. This is not a parish, so the building is only opened for special events. There will be a funeral here soon. Are you visiting?'

'I live here – well, just outside of Noyers – but I came here once for a concert, and it was lovely. I do know about the funeral. Madame Toussaint?'

'May she rest in peace,' he said but sniffed. 'Although I do not know how, since she was beaten to death.'

'Did you know her?'

'Not at all, but everyone around here has heard about this. So now you are perhaps organizing an event? You need to ask permission. I can give you the phone number of the rectory that manages this church.'

'That would be lovely, thanks.' Ariel wasn't sure what else to say. 'Perhaps you'll let me look around while you work?'

He nodded his approval, and Ariel wandered off, scanning the seats and under the legs of the spindly wooden chairs lined up in rows that substituted for pews. She went into the corners but didn't pull out her flashlight. It would be difficult to explain to the caretaker that checking out a venue for a concert required scooting around on her hands and knees in the darkest places. She looked hard at the sills under the regular windows. This had always been a poor church, she was sure, and the only stained-glass window was near the high ceiling – a rose window and a restoration or new artwork from the late nineteenth century – pretty but hardly profound or awe-inspiring.

If there was something Raoul wanted her to find here, she was striking out. 'Excuse me, but there's no choir loft, I see. Are there any other spaces in the building?'

The caretaker looked up from his kneeling position next to the wood pulpit, which rose well above the seats for the congregation that wasn't. 'Mice,' he said, 'always mice.'

'I beg your pardon?'

'Sorry, Madame, I clean several churches and there is always evidence of mice. I have no idea why since there is nothing for them to eat. But,' he said, pushing himself up to standing and swiping his pants legs, 'that is not what you asked. Other spaces? A small sacristy behind the altar, a simple washroom and I cannot think of another space. There is no basement or catacomb here.'

For a few moments, Ariel's hopes rose, but when she followed his pointing finger into the sacristy, she was disappointed. It had been stripped of whatever cupboards or closets it might have had for the priest's sacramental clothing. A single shelf ran along one wall, and the only objects on it were the chewed remains of a Bible that helped explain what the mice were eating and an empty plastic Badoit bottle, covered in so much dust that it could not have been left there recently.

She thanked the caretaker for the scribbled phone number of the rectory and gave up hope of finding anything in that church. Brushing a cobweb from her hair, she set off for Reigny's even less used church.

Ariel decided not to invite Katherine or Pippa to join her. She had gotten them into enough trouble less than twenty-four hours ago, and she didn't want to add to their problems if this search turned embarrassing – or worse.

She parked at the *mairie* and lucked out. Delphine, the mayor, was just unwrapping her baguette sandwich when Ariel knocked on the open door of her office.

'Come in, Madame,' she said, smiling as she stood up. 'Are you still disquieted by the shock of discovering that poor woman dead? It has hit our little village hard.'

'It was terrible, and my heart goes out to her. The Goffs and Pippa Hathaway are good friends, which is the only reason I happened to be here that morning. Reigny is a charming town and I always enjoy visiting. Violence must be rare here.'

'*Bien sûr*, of course, and how may I be of help today?'

'I own Château de Champs-sur-Serein, and when I have guests, I'd like to be able to point them to places they can explore.'

'I have a little brochure around here somewhere about a tiny but quite amusing museum of art, not quite in town but in the commune.' She rotated her upper body, looking at several shelves and a plain square table all piled with papers, and at a battered file cabinet that must have dated from the years immediately after the war.

'Thank you, but I came to see if I might look inside your old church for my research.' Ariel blinked and wondered if it was a lie if you actually thought you might do it?

Delphine laughed so hard that her printed housedress jiggled. 'You will have your work cut out for you regarding Reigny-sur-Canne. I was born and raised here. My grandparents were farmers, my parents were farmers, and my husband and I still hold fifty hectares in rapeseed and winter wheat, but, bless me, that's not much to interest the kind of people who stay at a château. Sadly, our little church isn't much either, only a relic from long ago. Your friend Katherine Goff gave us the gift of repainting our Madonna and Child fresco and the little paintings at the stations of the cross, and our neighbor Raoul keeps the place from falling down. His wife does the flowers when we have our rare baptism Sundays and Christmas program. Madame Goff told me we should have an art historian examine the carved pieces set high at all four corners, but I don't have the budget to hire someone.'

Ariel took the opening Delphine had offered. 'Actually, Raoul was going to open the church for me, so I could look around. I do want to see Katherine's painting, of course, and get a sense of how a small church functioned before the Revolution.'

Delphine made a face of apology. Waving her hand at her lunch, she said, 'I regret I am not free to give you a tour today. I am only waiting for the man who has offered to fix the leak in the ceiling, and then I must go to Avallon. My teeth. It is always something at my age – teeth, knees, hearing. What can I do?' She smiled and held her hands palms upward. 'If you don't mind being on your own, I can give you the key? You must be careful. Raoul thinks there might be an owl or a rat trapped inside, so he suggested I stay out. He promises to come today, but he's not here yet. You can leave the key with him if you see him.'

Ariel took this as a sign that the universe was on her side. 'Thank you,' she said, 'that's a good idea, and I'll make sure the key gets back to you without fail.'

The mayor hadn't yet heard about Raoul. Going beyond what the gendarmes had the initiative or the capacity to do in their investigation was the right thing to do. This way, she could peer into corners, poke around the pulpit and generally search the place fully, as long as a wild animal didn't scare her out.

A loud knock on her open office door startled Delphine, who burst out laughing. 'Well, my savior has arrived, no? Madame, this is René, who has kindly offered his services to fix our roof. He is a farmer here for how many generations, René?'

René admitted his family's property went back so far he couldn't remember, but as a member of the commune, he liked to help the local government when he could.

'We must get on with our inspection,' Delphine said and held out the big key. 'I hope you find something of interest.'

Ariel made noises of appreciation and drove down the hill to the church. No one was around, and there were no cars parked nearby. A good time for a quiet search. After, she would go to Raoul's house. If his wife was there, she would apologize for her role in his detainment and hope to hear that he was released or about to be.

Flashlight in her hand, cell phone in her pocket, she turned the key in the rusty lock. The noise it made seemed to come from inside the building. Odd. She stepped in and closed the door behind her. It was gloomy but not dark. Windows up high let in enough light to show dancing dust motes in the air, which had a smell not unlike the upstairs room in Madame Toussaint's house. A low sound from the farthest corner made the hair on her neck rise. There was an animal trapped in here.

Standing near enough to the door to make a quick exit, she shone the flashlight around. Whatever it was seemed to rise and move toward her – dark, not small, not a rat and certainly not an owl.

Backing into the door, Ariel wished she had brought a stick. The light wavered but picked up something familiar. She moved the light higher and gasped. 'Oh my God. It's a dog. Wait, it's Madame's dog.'

The animal was taking slow steps toward her, looking at her with caution in its posture.

'You poor thing,' she said. 'Come here – I won't hurt you.' She held out her hand, hoping it wasn't going to lunge at her, but it seemed to relax a bit and its tail began to wag. Ariel had never heard Madame use a name for it, so all she could say was, 'It's OK, dog,' and hope the tone of her voice was reaching it.

A few more steps and it was standing in front of her, looking up with liquid brown eyes.

'You must be starving,' she said and aimed her flashlight to the place where it had been lying.

She walked in that direction, the dog walking at her side, and saw there was an empty metal bowl and a large bucket of water. Of course, she realized suddenly. Raoul had told the mayor to stay out. It hit her that Raoul's mysterious absences had to have been his hiding the dog and moving it from place to place. He must have kept the dog here, for how long and why she didn't know, but that had to have been the message he was trying to give her. He wanted her to take care of Madame's dog, make sure it had food and water, until he could get back.

The dog had a worn leather collar, and Ariel spent the next five minutes looking until she found a coiled rope, obviously recently used, on one of the few wooden chairs set into two small rows. When she uncoiled it, the dog loped to the door, looking over its shoulder at her. It knew what the improvised leash meant.

'All right, dog, but stealth, OK? A quick pee and then we're getting in my car and driving as fast as we can to my house.'

Ariel didn't know why Raoul hadn't turned the dog over to

the police, and she didn't like the suspicion forcing itself on her, but she owed him a chance to explain. It could implicate him in Madame's murder, although she couldn't come up with a reason he would kill the old woman. Had they quarreled about his work for her? Had she refused to pay him? Had he cheated her or at least caused her to think he had? Was it possible he had stolen a few things he saw in her house when he was there to work, and she had threatened to turn him in? Finding the dog raised a lot of questions, and as Ariel locked the door and Madame's dog lifted its leg to pee on the grass next to the steps, she realized that the investigation had suddenly become more complicated.

'Do you like cheese? Leftover pasta?'

The dog looked up at her attentively. Having scoped out the kitchen as soon as she undid the rope leash, it now sat beside her expectantly.

Ariel had never owned a dog, although she liked them well enough. Cats were much easier, especially when it was raining or sleeting and they needed to pee. Her last cat, before she moved to New York to take the teaching job, had been an orange tabby who pointedly ignored her unless it was hungry and seemed to prefer the neighbor who had adopted her.

She knew Madame's dog was used to multiple long walks, rain, shine or freezing temperatures, and Ariel thought it must be having a hard time. 'Do you miss her?'

Its beautiful brown eyes didn't answer directly, but Ariel thought she saw sadness and confusion in them.

She filled a bowl with water, and put some Époisses cheese and a bit of pasta on a plate. No sooner had she set them down than the dog stood up and rushed to the food.

'OK, you're hungry. As soon as I can talk to Raoul, I'll make a plan. No point in turning you over to the gendarmes since you can't tell them who killed your mistress, right?'

Talk to Raoul? That might be hard. She had no idea why the gendarmes were questioning him or if they had actually arrested him last night. By now, his wife must have been notified. Should she approach the woman, someone she didn't even know, with her concerns? What if they were holding him in custody for good reason?

She needed caffeine, and after pressing the ground beans through her cafetière, she sat at the table watching the dog bolt down the food. She needed to marshal the facts she had. Raoul had taken possession of Madame's dog, after her death, but when and for how long she didn't know. He had a key to Madame's house and could come and go with the understanding he was tending her tiny garden. The dog had obviously been kept in Madame's house, maybe by her routinely but perhaps after her death.

She remembered the barking at his house shortly after Madame was killed that he' had dismissed as his sister-in-law's visiting dog. Could that possibly mean Raoul was somehow related to the dead woman? If so, why had he concealed it? In any case, Ariel had to believe it was this dog, which would mean Raoul had either found it nearby or had taken it away directly from the site of Madame's murder. The thought made her shiver.

The previous night, as she and her friends had looked for evidence in Madame's house, it wasn't so much what they found as what wasn't there. Regine's description of a lot of boxes stacked up downstairs, and the quick search upstairs that didn't show many boxes, meant someone had taken them away. Raoul? The relatives Monsieur Legrand had mentioned? There weren't any boxes in Reigny's church – or at least none immediately visible. She'd been so startled about the noise and the dog that she hadn't looked. Maybe she needed to go back while she still had the key.

'What do you think, dog? Would you take a nap here if I go out for a while? What if I promise to stop at the grocery store and buy real dog food?'

Seemingly in answer, the handsome creature turned around a few times and settled into a spot under the table, letting its head rest on its paws.

'OK then, we're agreed.' She fastened the rope on its collar and tied the other end to a table leg. The table had to weigh ten times more than it did, so she knew it would be safe.

She locked the front door, deciding as she drove away that she would indeed revisit the church in Reigny in case she had missed something in the need to get the dog out quickly. She'd detour on the way back to the *supermarché* in Avallon where no one would be likely to see her buying dog food. If the brigadier heard that she was harboring the missing dog, any deference he might have shown before would vanish. As it was, he doubtless saw her as a nuisance, arrogant enough to think she was smarter than the gendarmes, and stupid enough to think she could throw her weight around and force a workman to let her invade the victim's house. The heat rose in her face. Best not to imagine what he thought of her. She knew she was on the right track, and hoped she would prove it by bringing him something important to share with the investigating judge.

What if she and her friends turned up real evidence that implicated the stonemason she had come to know since arriving in Noyers?

As she approached Reigny, she tried to see him the way the gendarmes might – a rough character, given to arguing, ready to fight with the police that night, sullen, uncommunicative, generally suspicious. All that resonated with Ariel, but it still didn't explain what could have made him angry enough to hit Madame over the head that fatal morning, if that was a reluctant thesis.

Still fretting, she saw that Madame Pomfort, alas, was hard at work in the church garden when she pulled up to park. Ariel decided to brave the sharp questions she'd get for opening the church door. She only had a short time to do this search, and she couldn't waste it.

'*Bonjour, Madame,*' she said, smiling and nodding as she approached the church. 'You're busy already. Getting ready to plant?'

Reigny's one-woman security force and collector of gossip straightened up, a hand on the small of her back. 'Too early for anything but cabbage and potatoes, and who knows how they will do in this soil.' She looked around at her plot – not actually hers, if Reigny's other residents were asked – with a frown. 'Rabbits will be after the cabbage unless there are foxes to keep them under control.'

For an instant, Ariel imagined little foxes with shepherds' staffs herding fluffy bunnies. But that vision was replaced by what she had seen in real life – a small fox trotting through the underbrush, a limp rabbit in its mouth.

'Your roses look healthy. No buds yet?'

'Any day now. Some warm days with more sun and they will become showpieces, I can assure you.' She squinted and frowned at the sky for not supplying her with adequate sunshine. 'But what brings you here today, Madame Shepard? Meeting our Katherine again? She's already walked her dogs, out with that handsome husband of hers. Frankly, I do not know what she sees in them – the dogs, I mean. Always with burr-tangled fur, sloppy-looking things.'

'You don't have a dog, Madame?'

The older woman sniffed. 'I did, once, when I was first married. A sweet little thing it was – Pekinese, you know, with the charming little nose? Never fussed about anything and did its business in the same spot every day. It died a year after my husband – of a broken heart, I said.'

Ariel didn't know how to respond to this unexpected burst of personal information. While she was still searching for the right thing to say, Madame Pomfort pointed her garden fork at the church. 'Do you know, I thought I heard something making noise over there a couple of days ago. Quite strange, and impossible unless it was an owl. Do you know if an owl could be said to make a sound other than a hoot?'

'There are so many kinds of owls, aren't there? I'm going in there now to look at the stone sculptures Delphine said might be valuable. I'll take a look for an owl.'

'Shall I come with you?'

Ariel hesitated. 'Best not. What if it's some other animal – something like a rat?'

Madame Pomfort frowned. 'Rats are silent unless they are chewing on your rafters or your pipes.'

Ariel realized keeping this person out of the church would be impossible, so she simply nodded and smiled as she used the big key to open the church door, glad that she had whisked the dog away before the woman had turned up with her garden fork – and her curiosity – at the ready.

With the door open and the sun higher in the sky, there was more natural light to help her scan the obvious places. Spindly wooden chairs like those in Noyers' church, but fewer of them and scattered around rather than set in rows. Alcoves on either side of a raised platform and an altar with a modest pulpit. There were no doors to suggest a robing area for priests, but there was a deep space underneath the altar shelf.

Ariel heard Madame Pomfort's footsteps behind her as she stood and looked around. 'Hmph, as I thought. No owl. You know, we only clean the church once a year, before Christmas, unless someone asks for a priest to come and do a baptism or a funeral.'

'Yes, the mayor told me. Do you have many of those?'

Madame sniffed. 'No. We're a town of old people, mostly. The Catholics generally go to the big church in Avallon, which is well maintained and has its own parish. We don't always get a priest at Christmas even. There are too few, and everyone wants them at that time of year.' She took another look around and turned to leave. 'You might as well take a look at those figures.' She pointed up to the carvings. 'If they really are medieval, perhaps the *mairie* can sell them and put the funds to good use.'

Ariel nodded and waited until she heard the gate squeak, signaling that the woman was back at her gardening. The alcoves were shallow, and she saw that the dog's bowl and an old blanket were still there. She bundled them together, hoping she could smuggle them out when she left. Nothing else, not so much as a scrap of paper. Nothing along the walls or on the ledges under the windows and Katherine's repainted panels. She did a double take at the Virgin and Child fresco. The mother's face looked suspiciously like the ethereal Jeannette, although the smile was more sly than serene.

It wasn't until she got down on her knees at the altar and used the flashlight that her heart began to race. 'Eureka,' she said in a whisper.

Shoved far back at one end and almost invisible in the low light was a box. She leaned in and with one hand began tugging it closer. It wasn't cardboard like the ones Regine had described but looked like thin plywood, gray with age. When she had it completely out, she leaned back on her knees to look at it. It wasn't dust covered, so she was sure it was something that had been hidden there recently. It was nailed shut, and the nail heads were still shiny.

Who else but Raoul could have brought it into the church? Mayor Delphine would hardly have given Ariel her key if she was trying to hide something there. Ariel would ask Katherine if someone had lent her a key to do the paintings. But there was so little interest in or use of the building that Ariel couldn't think who else other than the mason and handyman and the commune's mayor would have any use for a key after the annual Christmas gathering. Delphine had explained that the other small town in the commune had its own disused church building. 'Churches were everywhere. It's a wonder people had time to breathe, much less tend to their animals and crops.' That and the presence of Madame Toussaint's poor dog pointed clearly to Raoul.

Ariel heard the gate squeak again and shoved the box under the altar shelf, but when she went to the door, she saw Madame Pomfort latching her own gate behind her and opening her front door. Lunchtime.

Looking around, she saw the street was empty except for a man driving a dusty tractor slowly across the intersection near Katherine's shop. She hurried out, laid the box and the bundle next to her driver's-side door and was opening the back door when the sound of a car approaching fast made her look up.

It was Pippa in her bright red sports car, and she braked hard when she saw Ariel and shouted out of her car window. 'Hey, Ariel, what're you doing here, and what's that you've got? Not stealing the church statues, I hope.'

Ariel cringed. 'Shhh, Pippa,' she said in a low hiss, leaning toward Pippa's car window. 'It's about the murder, but you've probably got the neighbor across the way so excited she'll be here in a minute, and she can't know about any of this.' She opened her trunk, shoved the box and bundle in fast, and closed it just in time to hide the contents from Madame Pomfort, who appeared on her doorstep, soup spoon in hand, a napkin tucked under her chin.

Pippa glanced at the older woman, turned to wink at Ariel and sang out, 'Brilliant. You picked up those mystery books I asked you to get from the shop. I'm chuffed, thanks. Did not have time before my trip tomorrow.

'Follow me to my house and we can unload them, then maybe you'll stay for lunch,' she said in normal speaking volume, carefully not looking across the street.

As she pulled away, Ariel looked sideways in time to see

Madame Pomfort retreat into her house, spoon held high. Something the neighbor had said was pinging her memory, but she lost her hold on the thought as she drove.

Pippa headed down the hill to her own driveway at a leisurely pace then eased in, Ariel right behind her, both of them glancing around to make sure none of Pippa's cat colony were in their path.

Pippa unlocked her front door and stood aside, allowing Ariel and three cats to enter. 'Shoo,' she said. 'Not you, these cheeky guys.' None of the cats paid the least attention and she shook her head. 'Ignore them. Want to bring in the loot?' she asked.

'Not really. I'll tell you what I found, but you have to swear on your cats' lives not to tell a soul. I will tell Katherine.'

'I swear on the lives of seven, or maybe it's eight, furry beasts' existences. It must be important.'

Ariel raised her hands, palms up. 'As to the box, I haven't opened it and won't until I get home. But it definitely was hidden in the church – and recently. The bundle, well, that's a real clue. It's a dog's bed and a food bowl.'

Pippa spun around from the sink where she was pouring kibble into an old ceramic cup. It splashed across the tile counter. 'Bother,' she said. 'Oh well, animals, come and get it,' she added as a ginger cat with white paws leaped up. 'Madame's dog was there, right? I wonder where it is now.'

Ariel swallowed. 'At my house.'

There was silence for a full minute. 'Say that again?'

'I recognized it. It was in the church.'

'Bollocks! You checked before.'

'Yes, but it was there just now.'

'And now it's at the château? This changes everything, don't you see? I know you and Katherine like Raoul, but, seriously, you can't think he isn't the most likely suspect now?'

As much as she wanted to resist that conclusion, which seemed to imply that Raoul was a thief as well as a killer, Ariel was having trouble explaining away his possession of an animal everyone said was Madame's constant companion, day or night. She admitted to herself that she had never seen the old woman without the dog either.

'I don't have any special loyalty to Raoul. I hardly know him outside of his work at the château. But I have no idea why he would hit her over the head, even if he didn't mean to kill her. Surely not for some silver spoons? We need to approach this carefully and not jump to conclusions.'

Pippa ran her hands through her hair, lifting its spikiness to new heights. 'I need a cuppa.'

'And I need to get proper dog food.'

Pippa nodded. 'A meeting and lunch at your house? Let's see if Katherine is around, and then I'll pick up a quiche. Do they have dog food in Noyers?'

Ariel explained the need for discretion but promised to get to the *supermarché* and back quickly.

Pippa called Katherine, who demurred about lunch because she was at 'an interesting moment' in her current painting until Pippa told her it was an urgent meeting about 'the case', at which point Katherine said she would finish the sky, clean her brushes and be over soon. She had to deliver some flea-market finds she had squirreled away in her house to the closed-up shop. 'I have to get over my dread of walking up the steps.'

Ariel left Pippa after reminding her she was not to talk about the dog or, for that matter, anything to do with the situation to anyone. 'Most of all, if you see Philippe, nothing.'

She knew Regine never shopped at the modern grocery store where the meat was not only pre-cut but slapped into plastic-covered trays and allowed to sit in its leaking juices for what the local butcher considered a shameful time. She was unlikely to run into anyone else she knew, particularly since she knew relatively few people, but she prepared a story anyway.

Once in the huge space with its sterile lighting and aisle after aisle of packaged food she used to buy without a second thought, she had to search a long time before finding the pet food. She piled a dozen cans and a big sack of kibble in her basket and wheeled it toward the cashier. Joining the line, she fretted that someone might see her after all. She was unprepared for the voice behind her.

'Ah, you have a dog, Madame?'

Stifling an impulse to abandon the cart, she turned. 'Oh, it's you. I'm sorry, I've forgotten your name. My apologies.'

The man in the leather jacket, the one who had been sniffing around Madame Toussaint's house, smiled. 'Tremblay, but why should you remember it? I am not offended. I have my own big dog at home, and I buy this brand also. Not here of course,' he said, holding up a pre-made sandwich. 'What kind of dog do you have?'

'It's not for me. I don't have a dog. My friend has two, and she asked me to pick up something because she's so busy today.' Ariel sent a silent message of gratitude to Katherine's two brutes.

'I see,' he said, smiling and looking straight into her eyes. 'Perhaps someday you will come to have one of your own.'

The cashier cleared her throat, and Ariel was relieved to end the uncomfortable exchange and get out of the store and in the car before the man, too curious for her comfort, could engage her in any more talk about dogs.

When she got home, Katherine's little clown car was in the circular drive. The artist was wrapped in a fringed shawl, tossed crookedly over her shoulder. She rushed over to Ariel's car, waving one arm wildly. 'I've been robbed,' she said in a high voice when Ariel opened the car door. 'Someone broke the little window in the back and climbed in.'

Ariel's heart skipped a beat. 'They didn't get Madame's small trove, did they? Hadn't the gendarmes come for them yet?'

'Yes, I mean no, the police have everything. Well, except that peculiar piece with the vermeil handle that we looked at together. I set it on a table in one corner and whoever broke in didn't see it. What shall we do? Call your policeman? I'm so frazzled I can't think straight, and I have no intention of telling Michael. He'll decide it's too dangerous to reopen the place. I need to sit down, I'm so upset. Let's go in.'

'I need you to be prepared. There is a . . . dog in my house.'

Katherine froze and after a moment's silence said, 'A dog or *the* dog?'

'The latter,' Ariel said through tensed jaws. 'I'll explain.' She winced at the sound of a revved-up engine and turned in time to see Pippa's car skid to a halt in the forecourt next to Katherine's.

Pippa slammed her car door and trotted up the steps, almost tripping on them, swinging a plastic bag. 'I've got lunch. Katherine, have you heard? Isn't it amazing?' It was all said in a rush.

'That's not all,' Ariel said and let Katherine break the newest news to Pippa.

'What if whoever's behind this knows we got into Madame's house? I bet they'll come after us for whatever they think we have,' Pippa said with a gasp.

Ariel looked at Pippa. *Why is everything a drama with her?* 'Inside, everyone, and don't upset the dog. It's probably scared half to death already.'

If Madame's long-lost and oft-hidden animal was scared, it didn't show. Ariel dumped an opened can into the bowl she'd recovered from Reigny's church, and the animal concentrated on that to the complete exclusion of the three humans. She set the blanket in the back corner of the kitchen, and after it ate and drank, it walked over and plopped down, resting its head on its paws and looking up at them. Ariel couldn't help smiling. It looked as though it was ready to hear the next chapter of the investigation.

'I don't know its name,' she said.

'Him,' Katherine said.

When Ariel raised her eyebrows, Katherine said, 'You didn't notice?'

Pippa took a bite then pointed her ham-and-brie baguette in Ariel's direction. 'Never mind that. What did you find and how did you know where to look? Did the brigadier tell you – or Raoul? Have you opened the box?'

Katherine's 'What box?' and Ariel's first attempt to answer collided, and Ariel held up her hand.

'Eat while I tell you everything that's happened. We'll open the box together as soon as we've eaten, and then we need to decide what – not if – we check out next, because this whole business is getting complicated, and if Raoul isn't the killer, he's in big trouble. And the theft of Madame's treasures has to be connected, so there's that to factor in.'

After lunch and a break while Katherine took the dog for a necessary but quick walk out back, the three sat looking at the wooden, nailed-shut box.

'I'm almost afraid to open it,' Ariel said. 'It has to be significant – I'm sure it was Raoul who hid it at the same time he hid the dog, and it can't be good. What if there's more silverware inside? That makes me nervous.'

'So get a hammer or something. The sooner we see what's there, the sooner we'll know.' Pippa jumped up and looked around, as if there might be a hammer lying around.

Ariel went to a shelf near the back entrance and held something up in each hand. 'A hammer and a screwdriver. Pippa, will you start taking a video the minute I touch the box? I want to be able to show the gendarmes exactly how we found it and what was in it when we turn it over, which you know we'll have to do at some point.'

'Righto, that's brilliant.'

Katherine held up her hand. 'What if we find something we don't want to share with the police?'

'Like what?' Pippa asked.

'Well, I don't know until I see it, but if there's something that implicates that harmless old lady, I'm not sure I want everyone to know, now that she's dead and can't defend herself.'

Pippa snorted. 'If she's part of a gang or something, she's not exactly a harmless person, is she?'

Ariel said, 'If she did something illegal that led to her death, it's part of solving the crime to know that, and we have to pass it along. Are we going to do this or not?' She stood at the end of the table, hammer raised.

'I'm in,' Pippa said and pulled her cell phone out.

'I'm in,' Katherine said more slowly. 'I hope we don't regret this.'

Five minutes later, Ariel said, 'I'm not the best with tools. This box does not want to be opened.'

'Here, let me,' Katherine said and grabbed the hammer. 'Didn't you ever have to use the claw end before?'

'I didn't know that was what you called it,' Ariel said, grinning in spite of the seriousness of the moment. 'With me, it's always cardboard boxes for a reason.'

The nails squealed as Katherine pulled, and she lifted the top off and set it on the table.

'Were you recording?' Ariel asked, peering at Pippa.

'Bugger all, I forgot, I was so excited. Here, put it back on and I'll video it.'

'Forget it – just take a photo of the inside and outside of the lid. At this rate, the video would be long enough for a feature film. But please try to take the pictures,' Ariel said. 'If you don't, we may be in as much trouble one day as the killer is.'

Katherine was peering into the box. 'Papers mostly. No fancy silver on top at any rate, no visible money, something bulky in cloth underneath. We're taking out one thing at a time, right?' She held up a piece of paper, obviously old and dry, with a list in columns.

After Pippa photographed it, she held it toward the window's soft light. 'The first column is obviously names, some of which have red lines drawn through them. The second column I don't understand – seems like names too. The third is abbreviations, I guess, because there are period marks at the end of each word, only they're not words I recognize. The last column is partly blank, but there are dates against some names.'

Ariel took it from her and set it aside. 'We'll see what we can make of it later. What's next?'

'A letter so water stained I can't make it out. ". . . make you proud . . . he is fine but so thin . . ."'

'Signed?' Ariel asked.

'Well, it's odd. Could be *petit chien*, but I guess that must be a nickname since dogs can't write.'

Pippa recorded it and the three looked for the next bit of treasure. It was an old brown envelope, and inside were five black-and-white photos.

Katherine described them as she held them up, one after another. 'Two pre-teen boys laughing, a line of young men standing awkwardly in front of some trees, a stern-looking mother-and-son portrait, and a girl hugging a dog. Kind of like this one,' Katherine added, nodding toward Madame's dog, who was sound asleep.

Pippa lined them up, took a photo then turned them over. 'Nothing on the back, but clearly from a long time ago. Look at the woman's clothing and hairstyle – probably the same era as the magazine.'

The next items appeared to be shorter lists, a street address and sets of numbers.

'More detective work,' Ariel said, 'but so far these are all suggesting life around the time of the war. Do you see Madame's name anywhere?'

'Not so far,' Katherine said. 'Here's another snapshot of a man, blurry and from the side, but it seems recent, given it's in color.' She turned it over. 'Again, nothing on the back. I don't recognize him. I wonder who it is?'

Ariel and Pippa peered at it, but neither of them recognized the subject.

'Definitely not Raoul,' Ariel said, shaking her head. 'This man has dark hair and he's not stooped over.'

'Here's a book, small and with cheap paper, *L'éranger*. Pretty beat up.'

'Hey, that's Albert Camus's early masterpiece,' Ariel said and came around to look over Katherine's shoulder. 'It must be Madame's. I'm positive she read the existentialists, although this book isn't exactly philosophy. Now, how did that wind up in this box? Does it give the publication date?'

Katherine waited until Pippa had taken a snapshot, then opened it. 'It's from 1942.'

'Wow, then it must be a first edition. Worth something today.'

'OK, all that's left is this bundle, an old rag, but there's something bulky . . .' Katherine trailed off, and when she spoke again, Ariel could hear the fear in her voice.

'A gun.'

SIXTEEN

Pippa peered into the nest Katherine had made around the gun. 'What kind of gun? It doesn't look like anything I've ever seen. It looks like a toy, and it's covered with dirt. Obviously ancient.'

'Not a toy, a pistol,' Ariel said, 'although that's all I know. I agree, it's so old I doubt it could be fired.'

'A theory we won't test,' Katherine said. 'I'm going to guess it's a souvenir, a memory of something from the same time as the rest of what's in the box. War memorabilia. Whose box is this? Madame's or Raoul's – or someone else's? Who are the people in the photos and on the list, and who owns this?'

Ariel stood up and walked over to the sink. 'You know what? We've stumbled into two mysteries with no way of knowing if and how they might be connected. Someone killed an old woman last week and the three of us believe it had to be because of the treasures she had in her house and tried to sell. Now, there's another mystery and it concerns mementos from a war that ended almost eighty years ago, bits and pieces either Madame or Raoul cared enough about to hide. Are they important, and why hide them?'

Pippa snapped her fingers. 'Maybe the old lady killed someone in the war and stole their silver. Maybe Raoul helped her. What if his father wasn't a hero? What if he was a Vichy agent or something? I saw a movie about that – a thriller.'

'Hardly,' Ariel said. 'Raoul wasn't even born then.'

Katherine said, 'Madame was only a child then, and even if a relative of hers stole silverware in the mid-1940s, that generation is all but gone, and the few who remain are hardly able to walk, much less chase down and kill a person in cold blood over some forks and spoons.'

'If I'm right that Raoul put the box in Reigny's church, then I have to wonder if it's his and why he had to hide it,' Ariel said.

'If it isn't her stuff,' Pippa said, 'it's totally irrelevant and gets us off the track of the real problem, which is solving her murder.'

The women were quiet, and Ariel realized they were all staring at the box and the gun as if waiting for some oracle to emerge. 'I need sugar,' she said, 'or coffee, or possibly both. Anything to help me think.'

'Tea would set me up nicely,' Pippa said and sat back in her chair abruptly.

'Teabags are all I've got. Katherine?' Ariel asked, opening a cupboard.

'Do not offer me wine. I'll say yes, and that will be the end of clear thinking. What I really wish I had is a paintbrush. That's when my mind is sharpest and most creative. But if you have coffee with milk, that will do.'

She stood up and started pacing. 'Raoul has lived in Reigny a lot longer than I have. His wife is pleasant, but she never shares anything important about him or their lives. I know you said he was too young, but is it possible Raoul's older than we think and was a Resistance fighter?'

Ariel did the math out loud. 'He'd have to be in his late nineties. The man can still carry bricks and drive a car, so I'm thinking not. More likely his father.'

Katherine nodded. 'You're right. I told you about the time Michael and I met the war veteran a few years ago. He was tethered to a walker. So let's say these are Raoul's father's mementos. Then I'm guessing his father was in the communist party's resistance group.'

Ariel brought a mug with a teabag string hanging out to Pippa and a big cup with milky coffee to her artist friend, then returned with a black coffee and a plate of almond cookies. 'All this is interesting, but we need to find out if these belong to Raoul or to Madame Toussaint, because if they weren't hers, I agree they aren't going to bring us or the gendarmes closer to catching her killer.' She took a big bite of a cookie.

'Here's the question that really disturbs me: Raoul was desperate to hide the dog – why? Was it to cover up the truth that he ambushed her?'

Katherine said, 'Isn't that what the police are investigating? For me, a question is do we have to tell them about the dog?'

All three looked over at the sleeping animal.

'What if I talk to Madame Pomfort? She's a collector of gossip and other people's business, so if anyone knows Raoul's history, she will. What she doesn't know isn't worth knowing. I've been wanting to paint her, and she won't be able to resist sharing decades of old gossip while she's sitting for me.'

'Brilliant.' Pippa waved a cookie at her. It promptly crumbled, parts landing in the mysterious box.

Something more to explain to the brigadier when we hand the box over, Ariel thought.

'Can you set it up soon?' she asked. 'You have to be sure you don't mention anything about the box of stuff, so it'll all be vague.'

Katherine started to speak but was interrupted by a voice with a strong French accent coming from the hall upstairs.

'*Bonjour*, is anyone at home?'

Ariel jumped up. 'Stay put – it may be that strange man looking for property. I'll be right back.'

A youngish man stood inside the big door. 'I hope I am not disturbing you,' he said, smiling. 'I am Sebastian Oualalou, the painter.'

'Of course. I didn't realize you might come by today. I'm so sorry. I have a couple of guests and we're having lunch. Could we reschedule?'

He nodded. 'Of course, although I begin a job tomorrow so it will have to be perhaps a week. And my kids have a few days off school after that. My wife has asked me to be responsible for them, so perhaps in two weeks?' He looked around the unfinished space. 'I am not sure how ready you are for the painting.'

'Upstairs, the first floor, that's about ready, but you're right. Do you have a cell phone?'

'But of course,' he said, pulling it out of his jacket pocket.

Ariel gave him her number and said she'd be much readier in two weeks. 'Forgive me for not being prepared. I know you're an excellent painter, so please come back when you can.'

As she headed back down to the kitchen, Ariel thought he looked too upscale for her simple project, standing there in his sports jacket and polished shoes. A far cry from disheveled Jean-Paul in skinny jeans or Andre in coveralls.

'Another workman, a painter, but I'm not quite ready to set him loose upstairs.'

'From around here?' Katherine asked, putting her empty cup on the table.

'Sebastian Oualalou – know him?'

'Sebastian? I do. He's a painter – I mean an artist who paints, mostly brilliantly colored abstracts. Didn't know he painted walls too, but it's hard to be an artist and make rent money. His wife, Geraldine, is an artist too, a weaver. I met them at a vernissage in Vézelay, the opening of her exhibition of large abstract yarn structures – rather somber but beautiful.'

Pippa stood up and pointed to the little gun. 'I'm good at research, so while you pump my neighbor, I'm going online to dig up more about how the war was fought around here. I'll see what I can find out about that gun too, because it's rather peculiar. The women in the magazine photos are holding what look like machine guns. I didn't notice anything like this chunky little pistol.'

Ariel spoke slowly. 'I think I have to talk with Raoul, and I don't know if he's home or in jail. Who knows? He might turn up at my house with packets of vegetable seeds tomorrow. But he will want to know the dog's safe, so Raoul's my assignment.'

After she saw them off, Ariel wandered through her house, her mind switching back and forth between the mystery of the old woman's death and the long and always growing list of tasks that had to be completed before the château would be able to earn money. Some days, the path seemed straightforward, but today everything was jumbled and uncertain. She needed to concentrate on getting the bathrooms on the first floor done, and the windows on the highest floor made good again. The painter couldn't come in until all the replastering was done. The replastering couldn't be done until the pipes were added. The pipes couldn't be redone until the architect had given them a design for the bathrooms and the corridor. Her brain refused to track backward further.

As for the dog, she had no plan. Food, walks and secrecy? Did Raoul want the dog, was the dog evidence of his guilt, or had he just found it on the street and parked it in the church while he decided what to do with it?

She walked back down to the kitchen and found it sitting up, looking at her with hope in its eyes. Dogs expressions, she realized, were almost human.

Shrugging on her windbreaker, she smiled. 'Hello, dog. Shall we take a walk? I have no idea how often you need to pee, but I need fresh air, so let's do it, OK?'

It scrambled to its feet, toes clicking on the tiles, tail wagging.

'You understand English? Or are you signaling something, hoping I can translate Dog?'

She grabbed the end of the leash, which she had hooked over the back door knob. She decided on the back way where no one could see her, out to the long path that might someday be an elegant sweep to a rose garden or perhaps a maze in the French style.

'In your dreams,' she muttered and followed the eager animal.

Dinner that evening was at Tony and Regine's. Spring peas, the cook told her, had inspired her to make a herb-enhanced risotto, each portion topped with shredded duck meat that appeared to have been roasted in citrus juice. A sprinkling of the bright-green harbingers of spring accompanied each serving.

'What's in the wonderful sauce?' Ariel asked after cleaning her plate with a slice of baguette. 'It ties everything together.'

Regine grinned. 'That's a secret outside the family. Pomegranate juice, but I don't want those people down the street to copy it.'

'Those people' were a lovely couple from further south whose specialty was vegetarian dishes. They had lots of business during the tourist season but hadn't yet opened this year. Ariel had eaten there a couple of times in the name of neighborly relationships, and admitted to herself that their aubergine tian – soft roasted eggplant bathed in tomato sauce and covered with semi-soft cheese – was special.

'Unless it's vegetarian, I doubt you have to worry.'

Regine merely winked and took away the empty plate.

It was quiet in the café, so Tony took a break and came over to sit with her. 'You know that your stonemason was picked up for Madame Toussaint's murder? He doesn't even live in Noyers, so how did he know her?'

'Tony,' Ariel said, 'you make it sound like the two places are a hundred miles distant. Reigny is ten minutes away by car and

Reigny has no stores, so I bet everyone comes here for their bread and groceries.'

He did the dramatic Gallic shrug she had come to realize was a favorite gesture. 'So, if he saw her around, then he must have seen her when she went to Reigny that morning.'

'Then what? Honestly, Tony, I'm trying to figure out why he could have been mad enough to bash her head and leave her there. If you have any ideas, I'd like to hear them. So would the gendarmes, I'm sure.'

'Love or money – it's always love or money.'

'Let's put love aside and think about money. If she had any, it wasn't visible in the part of her life we saw. If the police found a horde under the mattress, they aren't saying.'

'But if she did have money under the mattress,' Tony said, 'the person who killed her probably found it, right?'

Ariel bit her lip. She wanted to tell Tony that the house looked like someone had searched it more brazenly than the gendarmes, which would mean there were two searches before her crew had tried and failed. Did he know about their aborted effort?

Tony cocked his head and raised his eyebrows. 'You didn't happen to find it when you went in?'

Ariel felt that familiar heat rise from her neck to her cheeks. 'How did you know?'

'You're not the only regular diners, you know, and a few even come over from Reigny.'

'We were there to, er, help Raoul with the gardening.'

The pirate's gap-toothed smile was his answer. 'So money, jewels, stacks of dog-food cans? You must have seen something before the *flics* arrived.'

Ariel lowered her voice. 'Regine had said there were boxes inside the front door when she visited. They weren't anywhere. We found some war pictures and mementos, but if there was something significant there, the gendarmes must have taken it into custody, and no one's talking.'

Tony squinted at the ceiling. 'I heard she has some nosy neighbors, nice-enough people but with nothing to occupy themselves with in retirement but to twitch the lace curtains, if you know what I mean. If some other person got in before the cops and before you, they might have taken the boxes and anything else of value. But it would have been tricky. Three in the morning perhaps, or in the guise of a service truck? Assuming it wasn't your stonemason of course.'

A man at another table called out to him and asked for wine, so Tony left her then.

Ariel sat tapping her teeth and trying on Tony's theories. She didn't remember the brigadier mentioning evidence of anyone being at Madame's before the police came. Could that third entry have been after the gendarmes? No, because the brigadier would have mentioned all the boxes. Or would he?

An idea struck her. Maybe the relatives, the professional-looking woman and her husband, had taken the boxes before Madame was killed, invited in by her. If that was the case, then the mystery of the stack of boxes wasn't important, just normal family activity.

The tiny meringue in the saucer next to her espresso didn't result in a sudden surge of clarity. Tony was chatting with a couple of regulars – a rosy-complexioned man with high cheek-bones and his silver-haired wife – and Ariel decided she would just pay her bill and call it a night. But then Regine appeared with plates for them, and Ariel beckoned her over when she was done. 'Has the funeral date been set yet?'

'Yes, day after tomorrow. We're rehearsing a lovely hymn, and the church is swept and ready. We'll skip a program but have cards with an appropriate quotation about long lives lived well and her name.'

Thinking of the anonymous photos, Ariel was sad. 'I don't think she was religious, but no harm. Have the relatives contacted you?'

'I got a note addressed to the café today. I was waiting for a free moment to tell you. They want to host a small reception here before the funeral.'

'Not after?'

'I know, seems a little strange, but she said they have to leave immediately after the service. It won't bother me. She said they'd pay well, and I'll arrange for quiches and a meat platter, and we'll make sure we have plenty of Badoit water. Don't want our townspeople to turn up tipsy for the funeral.' She chuckled.

'I wonder if that man who wants to buy the place knows that they'll be here.'

'Tony told him at lunch, and he says he hopes he can come.'

The dog had a quick last trip out when she got home, but she stopped as she was about to tie it up near the kitchen door. 'Oh, why not?'

She led it up to her bedroom, where it settled down on a small rug between her bed and the wall with a sigh and a snuffle.

'Much better than the cold floor and all alone in that old church, right, boy?'

He had already settled his muzzle on his front paws but gave her what Ariel chose to believe was a grateful glance before closing his eyes. When all this was over, what would become of him? Was there a humane society somewhere near? She told herself that was a problem for another day and turned off the light.

SEVENTEEN

March 26

'I'm calling Brigadier Allard please. This is Madame Shepard.' While she waited with her second large cup of *café crème* the next morning to see if he would take her call, Ariel rehearsed for the third time what she would say that wouldn't give away anything she and her companions had learned. When the time was right, they would explain the box and the gun, but this wasn't the moment.

'Hello, Madame. Have you recovered your good spirits after the confusion of the other night?' He chuckled, and Ariel was distracted by the warm voice.

'Good morning. Quite recovered, thank you. We appreciated your understanding.'

'And you have abandoned your heroics?'

'Yes.' His definition of heroics and hers might be different. But that was a bit of semantics she'd save in case she needed it later. 'I'm worried about Raoul though. Can you tell me what his status is – if he's in jail or under arrest?'

'Ah, you need to read the Avallon newspaper more often. We are conducting a full investigation, and he is suspected of the crime, but he has not been arrested yet. He is still in custody.'

'May I see him?'

'No. He has talked to his wife on the phone, but no one may visit him at this time.'

Ariel paused. 'Well, may I talk to him by phone?'

'Only his wife may speak with him at this time. Sorry. I am curious. What is so important that you feel the need to speak with him?'

'Nothing urgent,' Ariel said, trying to keep stress from her voice. 'I feel responsible for this mess, and I don't want him to think I've abandoned him after asking him to let me accompany him into her house. Really, it's a terrible mistake, nothing more.'

'If it is, our investigation will uncover that, I assure you. Now, I really must go.'

Ariel had to let Raoul know the dog was OK and that she was doing what she could to argue for his release. That meant, if she understood the gendarme's rules, sending the message through Raoul's wife, Madame Descoteaux. The stumbling block was that she had no idea if the stonemason's wife knew Raoul had found the dog or, worse, that he might have taken the dog after having some kind of dispute with Madame Toussaint that ended in her death. That last thought stopped her racing mind and brought her back to the biggest dilemma. What if Raoul had killed the old woman? There might be a secret, a lifelong animosity attached to those photos and documents, one she couldn't unravel. Even if it was an accident, should she be inserting herself in the business by advocating for his release? Maybe advocating for his release was putting the wrong task first. Coming up with a more likely suspect first would be ideal, but it was hardly something one could blithely add to a to-do list.

The dog in question was lying on his improvised bed looking bored. Ariel thought a bite of the croissant she was only nibbling might cheer him up.

'If you could talk, you might be able to solve this whole mess,' she said. He glanced up at her but concentrated on the treat. 'Did Raoul's wife know about you?'

That gave her an idea. She'd bring the dog on a visit without comment and see how Raoul's wife reacted. That might be a way to get her to carry a message, maybe on her own if Raoul had talked about the dog. Since the woman worked part-time and Ariel didn't know her schedule, she'd have to visit in the evening. This evening, in fact.

Restless again, she wandered up to the guest suites on the first floor and told herself to focus on them. She was letting the work slide, and she needed to set herself a goal, maybe a calendar deadline or as close to one as she could get given the '*ça dépend*' nature of busy renovation workers. It was almost April, and Château de Champs-sur-Serein wasn't on the map for the region's upcoming tourist season. She had almost a year to complete the four guest rooms and bathrooms, finish the kitchen so she could offer a special Burgundian food event, add young trees to the formal entrance and drive, and do something interesting with the large entry-level rooms. Raoul, if he was innocent, would deliver a vibrant kitchen garden and a planted knot garden. If he couldn't create the small vegetable garden near the back entrance, she could do that job herself. In fact, it might be fun.

She stood at a high double window facing the drive. Jean-Paul had done an impeccable job saving the old glass panes, fashioning new wood casements and sills where the old ones had dry rot, and reinstalling the original, tall Crémone Bolt mechanisms that allowed the double windows to open easily but be locked securely against wind and rain. She looked out at the long drive from the pillars that marked the entrance to Château de Champs-sur-Serein up to the courtyard. A new layer of fine gravel, perhaps twenty young linden trees? Surely not that expensive.

What she'd love to create was something special for the circular space in the forecourt. There must have been a statue or a fountain there at one point. Unlike the restored lintel with its medieval motto, *Fatum manet* – 'destiny awaits' – the forecourt was built later for horse-drawn carriages and then cars. It occurred to her that she could climb up and investigate that island in the middle. Maybe she'd find an old water pipe, or the remnants of a base for an artwork. That she could add to her to-do list. If she were rich, she might commission a bronze sculpture, or a large stone fountain like one she had seen in a John Singer Sargent painting.

'If, if . . .' she said, turning away from the window. She looked back, noticing for the first time a big car of some sort that was idling next to the entrance gates. Maybe an early tourist admiring the château. It made her realize she had to order a sign for the entrance even before it was ready to receive guests. Another item on the to-do list.

She and Katherine had tentatively chosen two walls for the artist's frescos – one at the end of the wide corridor on the ground floor facing the back of the property, the other in the largest guest room. An alcove in one other room would be wallpapered, as would the large portion of the bathroom that Andre had suggested be divided into two parts. There was enough wallpaper from Katherine's flea-market rolls for both. Katherine would be sure to find a place where any leftovers could add a bit of brightness and whimsy. *This will never be a cozy cottage*, she reminded herself. Even a small château required a degree of formality. What she needed was an interior designer. What she could not afford was an interior designer.

Her cell phone jingled.

'Thought you'd want to know. A blue-and-white is parked in front of Raoul's house. I didn't see the gendarmes who went in, only that Philippe wasn't one of them. One guy was new to me, haven't seen him around.'

Pippa stopped to take a breath and Ariel jumped in. 'I met a young officer in training, a Frenchman whose family is Algerian, when I went to see the brigadier to pump him for information, however unsuccessfully. I guess you're hovering somewhere close. Did Raoul's wife let them in?'

'Don't know. I only saw the police car when I started to drive away. I parked near Katherine's and walked back. Oh, hang on, here comes another car and Philippe's driving. I can't stand around.'

This complicated Ariel's plan to drop by Raoul's house later. One police car might suggest a short visit to talk with her. Two cars suggested a search. Not the best time to show up with the missing dog.

Pippa rang off, and Ariel waited fifteen minutes before calling back for further news bulletins.

Pippa sounded out of breath. 'Katherine had this brilliant idea. We're walking the dogs. Whoa there. I have the big one who weighs more than I do and doesn't respond to stop, sit or slow down until he decides to do his business.'

'Can you see anything? Do you think they're doing a search?'

'Not so far. I think they bring this other car, more like a van, when they do searches, or at least that's what Philippe told me once. No hazmat suits in evidence, and they didn't have sirens going.'

There was rustling and indistinct muttering, then Katherine came on the phone. 'Advice. If you ever get a dog, don't ask Pippa to walk it. She has gotten herself completely tangled in Gracie's leash, and now Fideaux has jumped in. It'll be a miracle if our friend stays on her feet, and a bigger miracle if her boyfriend doesn't notice her waving her arms and wobbling all over the grass.'

'Listen, if you can manage to loiter, see if they come out with any boxes. Remember, we still don't know what happened to the big stack of boxes Regine saw in Madame's house while she was alive. If there isn't a simple answer, I think whoever killed her must have wanted what was in those boxes.'

'We have an excuse. Our charming but remarkably awkward friend is sitting, untangling herself from long leashes but says she may have twisted her ankle. We'll call you back.'

Ariel swore as she retraced her steps downstairs to the main floor and then farther down to the kitchen. She wasn't getting anywhere and was feeling paralyzed – and not just by obstacles like not getting to see Raoul's wife's reaction to the dog. She was feeling an internal battle between her loyalty to the workman she'd met last year who had never harmed her and the proud old woman who could quote Sartre.

She ran through the meager clues she and her friends had identified to see what they might have missed. The elegant silver, the stack of boxes, the missing dog who was no longer missing, the disappearance of the cloth bag Madame might have had with her when she was attacked and whatever was in it. The letters she had stolen – no, borrowed – in her search, and maybe the box of war mementos and the old pistol.

She wanted the villain to be a stranger, one of those crooks the brigadier talked about.

She was about to sit down with a fresh cup of coffee and a madeleine when a quiet 'woof' reminded her she was cooking for two.

'Sorry, boy, kibble coming.'

Looking at the handsome animal, who didn't show signs of trauma or mistreatment, Ariel came up with the idea of trying to enact a scenario that might include a way to answer the question that the dog couldn't.

'Food first,' she said out loud as she shook a large helping of kibble into his bowl.

She had eaten two of the pastries when her cell phone rang. As usual, Pippa started talking in a rush. She never identified herself, which was fine since she was the only woman with a strong British accent Ariel knew, so Ariel didn't even have to depend on the phone identifying her. The gist of Pippa's report was that the gendarmes came out with a bulky computer 'way out of date' but nothing else and that Philippe, seeing her rubbing her ankle, had come over and offered to drive her in the patrol car to the clinic in Avallon which was close to the police station.

'Clinic? Then your ankle is really hurt?'

'Oh no,' Pippa said with a giggle. 'His partner looked at me like she thought I was a right fool, but I told him ice would do. It was rather brilliant though, having it happen right then and there. Honestly, it barely hurts. I told Katherine I'm not equipped to handle her dogs. They have no manners.'

'So no boxes with old silver or whatever in Raoul's house. That's good to know. Where's Katherine now?'

'Off home for the day – she had things to do apparently. She walked me home but left right away, after insisting I couldn't say a word about our investigation or the break-in around Michael.'

'I have an idea. Are you busy? Do you have plans?'

Pippa snorted. 'I never have plans unless Philippe gets an evening off, which isn't happening with all the attention on these local muggings. No one has any leave. I miss the boys, Mick and Pete. When they were here, we'd head into town to the pubs. I suppose you don't have any more electrical work for them?' She sounded wistful.

Ariel sometimes forgot that Pippa was young, stuck in an isolated hamlet populated almost exclusively with old people. She laughed. 'I miss them too, but no, not now. Maybe when it gets to the point of hanging fancy chandeliers in the public rooms. That would be fun. But here's why I'm asking.' She told Pippa about her idea of acting out a likely scenario of Madame's killing. 'It would work better if there were two of us to think it through. I could come over now if you're willing.'

'It's brilliant, but can we do it later? If I don't write at least a thousand words today, I will have to kill myself. I've been so distracted by all of this, I've lost sight of my own story.'

EIGHTEEN

The sun had set a short time before, and the street near Katherine's shop was getting dark when the two women finally met. There was only one dim streetlight on the far side of the small crossroads. Ariel realized she was nervous and was glad her car was close at hand. Several houses were dark. Katherine had explained there were properties whose owners had passed away. The buildings were owned by relatives who weren't sure what to do with them but had no desire to move to 'this creaky little town. Fact is, not even squatters are attracted. They'd be noticed and run out by the few people who've made a life here,' Katherine had said.

Pippa's upstairs window showed a sliver of light through the trees. As she eased around the curve to the houses at the intersection, she passed Madame Pomfort's house and saw the garishly colored, flickering lights of a TV screen. The *mairie* at the top of the hill was dark, the *pétanque* court and parking lot next to it unlit and empty. The café had long since closed for the day.

Ariel took the small flashlight from her glove compartment and the cloth tote bag with a whisk in it from her kitchen that represented the missing bag and possible treasure that had been stolen by Madame Toussaint's killer. She stepped out of the car, closing the door quietly. A car came through the intersection and headed away but didn't slow down, its headlights marking its exit from the village.

'Pssst,' a voice said, making her jump.

'Pippa, you scared me,' she said, turning to see the younger woman dressed as a cat burglar again.

'Sorry. I didn't want old Pomfort to come running.'

'She has her TV on, so she probably can't hear a thing.'

'Hah, you have no idea. I think she has microphones posted outside her house and a second pair of eyes on that suspicious head of hers. Mind you, there have been times when I've been awfully glad of her extrasensory powers. Now,' she said in a low voice, 'what are we doing?'

'This may sound crazy, but I've been trying to picture what happened in the moment. It might tell us who it was, for one thing. Did someone she knew meet her? Could a stranger have crept up behind her without her realizing the danger? Would someone have run away with the loot in his hands rather than dumping or hiding it? It would make a difference if she was arguing with someone who then hit her, wouldn't it? Would she have given the person whatever was in the bag?'

'If I was the killer,' Pippa said, looking around, 'where would I run to make sure no one heard anything and came out to look?'

'Yes, and if the dog was here too, would you have taken it? That seems unlikely unless . . .?'

'Unless you knew she loved it and couldn't stand the thought of it maybe being run over.' Pippa looked sideways at Ariel.

'All right then. Let's start here – the road that leads to Noyers. Assuming she was walking, she'd come from here.'

The two women walked past two dark houses to the intersection.

'She gets to here, with the dog and the bag, and she looks around. From here, we can see to the spot uphill that curves. Madame Pomfort's house isn't visible, but it's right after the bend. What else can she see, and are there any residents who could see her?'

Pippa stared. 'If I were standing in my bedroom window looking out, which I never would be before daybreak, or pretty much anytime, I might – just might – see something through the trees. But the streetlight doesn't reach the shop, so no.'

'Raoul's house is down that side street beyond the intersection, but I can't even see the street from here, so he couldn't have seen her.'

'But what if his wife had to leave early for her shift at the *supermarché*? She'd drive at least to the intersection before she turned toward Avallon,' Pippa said.

'Remember, it was probably right before daybreak, still murky, and we know Madame was wearing black, and she is – was – short and kind of bent over. It would be easy to miss her. Look, there's a car doing the same thing and its headlights barely reached us before it made the same turn.'

Pippa followed the taillights until they disappeared. 'I see what you mean. Not likely.'

'Who else might be driving by, Pippa? The delivery van for the café's morning bread? Some regular traffic? I'd like to think the gendarmes have already contacted every possible driver.'

'If it were high summer, I'd think about the farmers, who get out early with their tractors. They go through here to the fields in both directions in the middle of the season, but March?' Pippa said, chewing her lip.

Ariel pulled her shoulders back. 'Let's go look at the scene from the old lady's perspective, on the steps.' She shuddered slightly. 'I'm her. I have the bag with whatever I want to sell. My dog leash is in one hand, the bag maybe over my shoulder. The steps are a little uneven. Could she have fallen?'

'Don't think so,' Pippa said, standing off to one side. 'She was lying on her side but kind of curled up on the top step. Remember, Pomfort thought she was sleeping? She didn't look like she'd fallen. A fall would have knocked her down to the pavement.'

'I think you're right. If someone was holding her when he hit her, he could have laid her down deliberately so it wouldn't attract attention from the first car or walker who passed by. Good thinking.'

Again, a vehicle came toward the intersection, not toward the Noyers road this time but to the smaller one that led from Reigny to another hamlet and the open fields above the Goffs' house. It was darker now, and the driver's lights swept over them briefly as the car continued up the hill toward the curve, the dark café and the *mairie*. Ariel looked up but only long enough to get the lights in her eyes. She hadn't realized there was this much traffic on the tiny back roads.

When her vision was back to normal, she took the last step up and turned to gaze all around her.

'OK, it was dark most likely, possibly a hint of light in the sky like right now. To my – her – left, the street before the curve, one empty house, a vacant space, trees. No sidewalk of course, so anyone walking would either hug the verge and the shadows or walk right in the street. In front of me is the house across the street that Katherine said is unoccupied. To my right, the crossroads. Someone could come from any direction, but she'd likely see them even in the weak light of the lamp post, once they were within a few hundred feet.'

Pippa strode over to the intersection and back. 'A minute, no more, for someone in good shape to get from there to here.'

'So I'm standing here. In one scenario, I recognize and I'm not afraid of the person. I stand here until he gets to me, then maybe he's trying to grab my bag and I'm resisting.'

'The dog would bark when she's getting assaulted, right?'

'I don't know. What if the dog knows the person?' *Not a good theory for Raoul's sake*, Ariel thought. 'Stick with this for a minute. He knows her, she doesn't want him to take what she's brought, he grabs it, maybe hits her with something he's carrying and runs away. Where?'

'Why do you think he's on foot?' Pippa asked. 'He might have jumped into a waiting car with the bag, which would explain why the police didn't find it.'

'And take the dog?'

'Probably just shooed the dog away from the car.'

'I don't buy that. If her dog was left here, he would have been right by her side when we found her. I already see that he's loyal and people-focused, not easily scared.'

They were silent for a moment. It was full dark now, there was a growing breeze that rustled the leaves and clouds covered the moon. Frogs sounded from the nearby stream, and a particularly large fish splashed.

'I wish Philippe weren't so close-mouthed these days,' Pippa said. 'I'm sure the police have asked for witnesses who saw a car on any of the roads, although I suspect most people, even if they were awake, were making breakfast in their kitchens and not looking out their front windows to the road.'

'Let's try the other idea. The assailant is unknown, deliberately stalking her because he somehow knows she has something of value. He hides, maybe in those trees, maybe along the side of that house or even in the bushes behind the shop and springs on her, bashes her, grabs the bag and takes off. Pippa, would you go along the side of the shop and see if there's a place close enough so you can hear me – I'll mumble – and then come out as fast as you can and tap me?'

Pippa played the role with enthusiasm, and when she'd touched Ariel's arm, she stopped. 'I'm not convinced. The ground's uneven, and there's a tree root or something I almost tripped on.'

'I heard you breathing hard. If her hearing was good, she would have turned.'

'The dog would have growled,' Pippa said.

'OK, so less likely. Funny, we keep coming back to the dog. He was her constant companion, and he's a good size. If he barked, he might scare the thief away. Why wouldn't he bark?'

Pippa said, looking over at Ariel, 'Sorry, love, but we're agreed Raoul hid the dog and took care of it properly. Your reenactment only makes me think more that Raoul had to be the guy who approached her.'

Ariel didn't have an answer, although she wasn't convinced. Raoul – grumpy, strong physically, interested enough in Madame's history to have saved some of her war mementos. That is, if they were hers. Another tangle to unravel. 'Thanks for indulging me. It's getting chilly. Let's call it a night. I'll head home. I want to sleep on what we learned. If it was Raoul, more fool me, I guess.'

Pippa nodded. 'All good then. I have to drive over to Avallon early tomorrow, but I'll call you when I get back.'

Not quite French, she hugged Ariel briefly rather than bestowing the traditional *bis*, turned her flashlight on and walked up the street to her driveway, which sloped down into the hollow where she and her cat brigade lived.

Ariel stood for another minute, wondering if she had missed something. She had assumed it must have been a quiet attack if the always alert Madame Pomfort hadn't heard it, but that flickering TV screen might negate that if she was up early watching the news, for example. The victim probably didn't have time to put up a fight, and there was no place she could have run to without the attacker seeing her. On the other hand, an attacker would also have been under pressure to run or hide, if he had been on foot. The police would have found some evidence of him if they had searched the bushes and the damp earth at the stream's edge.

She walked slowly back to her car. Thinking out loud, she said, 'He must have had a car, something quiet or known to everyone and so ignored. Still, why didn't the dog bark?'

A sound – a sudden breeze moving the tall shrubbery? She strained to see, reluctant to turn on the flashlight in her bag for fear of attracting the nosy neighbor's attention, however remote the possibility was.

A slight crunching sound, a bit farther away. An animal, but what? Wild boars were not uncommon, and she knew they were dangerous, but it didn't seem likely.

She stood still for a full minute but heard nothing else. Probably her imagination.

Shaking her head at her own skittishness, she unlocked her car door and pulled away from the verge, still trying to answer her own question as she headed back toward Noyers. Behind her, in the distance, a car's headlights appeared.

Reigny disappeared behind her, and the sky was matte black, clouds having descended while she and Pippa were at the inter-section. Not for the first time, she marveled at the total absence of light, so different from the Manhattan apartment, its floor-to-ceiling windows pulling in the light from a thousand other windows and streetlamps winding through Central Park. Tonight there was only that other car on the road, probably coming from the hamlet on the far side of Reigny, on its way to Noyers or the A6 throughway.

For a few moments, the car seemed to be closing the gap between their two vehicles, its light growing brighter, although passing on these narrow roads was dicey. At night, you'd see a car coming in the opposite direction, but you'd never see the deer you hit. The driver must have had the same thought and dropped back.

She signaled as she approached the long driveway to her château and was relieved the other driver slowed down too so there was no chance of an accident. She parked in the forecourt and had the same moment of pleasure she always had at seeing the warm light on in the window of the ground floor.

Locking the door behind her, she smiled at the sound of clicking toenails as her four-legged visitor came up from the kitchen to greet her.

'Hello, boy, have you been napping or sitting next to your food bowl all this time?'

The dog stood quietly in front of her, looking up as if to say thanks for not being left alone again.

Flipping on lights as she went downstairs, Ariel reminded herself that she hadn't eaten recently.

'You first, fella, then I need to prowl around and see what I can put together for dinner.'

While the dog gobbled up a can of food, she put water on the stove to boil for pasta. Then she ran upstairs to her cozy room to get a sweater and set her cell phone on the charger and paused at the front window of the first floor, looking to see if the clouds had lifted.

The view was still black until, for a moment, it wasn't. A weak light shone briefly at the end of the drive, and for an instant, she saw movement. The light went out, but in that brief glimpse, she thought she saw a vehicle. She stood still, waiting for something more. But there was nothing.

Ariel made her way down the big staircase to the ground floor. Did someone have car trouble – a flat tire, or maybe they'd run out of gas? Most people had working cell phones, and the reception was usually OK at that spot. If not, would someone be knocking, maybe banging since the door was so thick, in a few minutes to ask to use her phone? She was uneasy at the thought. Usually, being alone in this big place didn't bother her, but thinking so much about criminals was making her jumpy. Nevertheless, she checked the door lock on the way back down to the kitchen. The windows with their traditional locking systems were fine, thanks to Jean-Paul's meticulous restorations.

Steam was rising from the big pot, and Ariel hurried to slip in some *coquillettes*, a popular pasta shape in France that looked exactly like what Americans called elbow macaroni. And just like at home, Ariel tossed it with a sharp cheese, fresh herbs and crème fraiche. She poured a glass of red wine and sat at the table. Raising it in the dog's direction, she said, 'Here's to us, and to your mistress.'

Suddenly the dog stood up stiffly from its bed, its ears upright and rigid, its head cocked. It took a few steps toward the back door and froze.

Ariel put down a forkful of pasta and felt the hair on her neck tingle. It was probably a fox, but the dog sensed something, and now she was straining to hear any sound.

There weren't any outside light fixtures yet for either the front or the back doors, although Mick and Pete had put in the wiring. She had a flashlight for the times when she went out at night. Researching and ordering lights that would complement a nineteenth-century mansion took time she hadn't found. Surely anyone with a car problem seeking help would come to the front door. Coming around the house would mean picking their way along the low wall Raoul had reset then edging around the traditional potager and over the rough walkway, which had low piles of bricks scattered around.

The dog took a few steps toward the back entrance, which was at the bottom of a couple of shallow steps, and began to growl low in his throat.

'Easy, boy.' She realized she was whispering. Maybe what she should be doing was shouting, either to let a stranded motorist know she was here or to scare away someone who hoped the place was empty and ripe for burglarizing.

She opened her mouth but couldn't do it. If she advertised her presence and it wasn't someone innocently asking her help, what then?

She stood, paralyzed and irresolute, and the dog stood, stiff legged and battle ready.

A furtive rattling of the door that led to the garden behind the house made her heart jump. Had she locked the kitchen door after taking the dog for a quick walk when she got home? It was such an ordinary part of her routine that, even though she could picture it, she wasn't sure whether she was remembering tonight's act or some other night's.

She waited for another sound. When it came, it was in the form of a scraping noise and a soft curse. Something metal scratched at the door for a minute that seemed like an eternity, then nothing.

Ariel had no idea how long she and the dog stood there, or what changed, but the animal's posture eventually relaxed, and it went back to its bed and lay down, head raised, still not completely relaxed, but no longer ready to attack whatever it had sensed beyond the door. Ariel tiptoed to the door and saw the bolt was in place but was still nervous. She sat back down to cold pasta and decided a second glass of wine was necessary.

As she played with her food, she wondered. Raoul, out of

detention, coming to steal back the box he had figured out she now had? No, the dog wouldn't have growled like that. Raoul had obviously been caring for him, and he might have barked if he recognized Raoul. The driver of the car stuck at the end of the drive? She had manufactured that driver and story entirely, hadn't she? Nothing else made sense unless it wasn't someone whose car broke down. Her indoor lights were on, her car was in the forecourt – anyone could see the place was occupied. A burglar wouldn't try something stupid like breaking and entering when the owner was there.

What if it was someone who wanted to get into the château without her knowing, someone who realized she was there and wanted to confront her? She scraped her half-eaten pasta into the garbage and promised herself no more wine this evening.

Calling the dog, she climbed the stairs to the entrance level and then the wooden ones to the first floor. She turned off the hallway light so she could look out of the window facing the drive without being seen. There was nothing but the solid darkness of a moonless night in the depths of the countryside. No more suggestion of a light or movement, only the sound of an owl making its questioning hoot as it sat somewhere high on a branch, hunting. She shivered.

Turning the hall light on again, she retreated to her temporary bedroom. She brushed her teeth, the dog at her side, and forced herself to focus on something positive, imagining a wallpapered space with more lights, a dressing table and a soaking tub.

Wrapping herself in a robe, she picked up the French novel she was reading and slipped under the duvet she had brought from New York.

'Nope,' she said, shaking her head at the dog, which had followed her. 'You're a great companion, but not on the bed.'

It looked mildly hurt but turned in a circle several times and plopped down on the floor next to her with a loud sigh.

The book must not have captured her interest completely because she realized she had slipped into a half-sleep that was broken abruptly. It was still quiet, but had there been a noise? The dog was standing up, ears cocked, tense again. She was trying so hard to hear that her ears were registering her own pulse and the kind of pitched hum that was only audible when nothing else was.

'What is it, boy?' she whispered.

Then she heard it – a slight *thunk*, not close by, in fact not inside the château.

She eased out of bed and with the dog next to her crept down the hall to the window that overlooked the long drive. A weak light seemed to be bobbing away from the house, faster and faster, and while she looked, it shone on a vehicle's door. The door opened, and someone climbed in.

Ariel held her breath until she heard an engine start and, a second later, the vehicle's headlights shot rays into the darkness as it pulled out of the grass and on to the road, one taillight showing red. In a moment, every trace of light from the road was gone. When she turned her head though, she saw a soft glow near her front entrance.

'If you think I'm going to open the front door, you're mistaken,' she said to the dog, but it had already begun to trot down the staircase. Whoever had been prowling around must have given up. The heavy French locks had held.

She shined her flashlight on the entry-floor windows, but their casings were all in place, and there was nothing to suggest anyone had tried to pry open or break one. She saw the soft light through a window and edged closer, turning off her flashlight. Without drapes, there would be no hiding if someone were peering in. The dog, however, didn't seem anxious, more curious than scared.

She peeked out from one corner of the window. 'What? My car door's open?' Still inside, she used her flashlight's beam to survey the steps, the forecourt, the portions of the low stone wall Raoul had restored and a few dormant rose bushes under the windows.

Nothing.

The owl hooted again, reminding her how late it was. The dog stood at the door, turning its head toward her, its thin tail waving back and forth.

'Well, whatever or whoever, you aren't afraid, so I guess I can't be either.'

Slowly, she turned the big bolt and pulled the massive wooden door open. Her car sat where she had parked it, the passenger door open and no sign of anyone inside or near it.

The dog had bounded out, lifted its leg on the side of the

circular shape at the center of the forecourt and now stood looking expectantly at her.

Ariel used the flashlight's beam like a lightsaber, taking small steps toward the car. When she got there, she peered in. The glove compartment had been opened and everything in it scattered on the floor or front seat. The empty bags she used for groceries had been thrown around on the back seat.

Someone had obviously been looking for something. It had to be important and relatively small, and the search seemed targeted not random. Items from the box she had recovered from Reigny's church? The gun perhaps?

The owl hooted again, and possibly because it sounded spooky, she suddenly had images from movies and TV shows of people opening the trunks of their cars and finding bodies.

'It couldn't be,' she said to the dog but waited until he had trotted to her side before lifting the latch.

Nothing. No bodies anyway. She exhaled sharply. An empty picture frame Katherine had insisted she take for later decorating and a pair of rubber boots in case she needed to tromp around in muddy terrain.

Calling the dog in, Ariel locked up, detoured to the kitchen for a mug of hot water for herself and a fresh bowl of cold water for the dog, then walked up the grand central staircase and to bed. Tomorrow was Madame's funeral.

NINETEEN

Tony had set out more espresso cups than usual, and the café was already busy by the time Ariel arrived for her morning caffeine on this unusual day.

'*Bonjour*, Ariel,' Regine sang out as she walked past, carrying a plastic-covered tray of what looked like charcuterie. 'There are fresh croissants on that table. Please help yourself. Everything is paid for today by Madame's relatives, Madame and Monsieur Gaudet.'

Clearly, everyone else knew that, because almost every table was occupied and almost every hand held a flaky pastry in the process of being dipped in a coffee cup. It may have been for a funeral, but the air was positively cheerful, less than two weeks after Madame's death.

'Quite a crowd,' Ariel said to Tony as she picked up her *café crème* and turned to survey the room. 'At least we know Madame Toussaint's grandson and his wife by name now.'

He grinned. 'Half these people never met her, to be sure, and most never even spoke to her. But I myself do not mind. What is it to her if others can enjoy an espresso in her honor?'

Ariel smiled. 'I can imagine her being quite grumpy actually, stomping off and muttering.'

'Yes, but if it were someone else's funeral, she would be sure she got her free coffee and croissant first, right?'

Regine stopped her rushed coming and going for a minute and said, 'My adored one, while you stand there and do nothing, your Regine is dying of thirst. An espresso right now, if you please.'

Tony opened his mouth, and Ariel thought he was about to defend himself until she saw his lady friend's face.

Regine winked at Ariel and leaned over the zinc counter to give Tony a playful slap. 'I am glad we are not asked to put on special parties often. Everyone is helping, but it's a lot of work for such a stubborn, unfriendly old woman. Have you seen the church?' she asked, not pausing for breath. 'The woman doing the flowers complained there was nothing in bloom, but it's like a miracle. She found wild irises up in the park near the old fort and cut some young branches from her own yard.'

'It's lovely to see everyone pitching in. Is there something I can do?'

'Nothing, thank you. Jeannette and those boys have already set up chairs on the square for overflow seating, and I heard they helped with the chairs in the church too. Hey, Tony, the butcher's assistant is coming with the last trays, and you need to set some of these tables together and clear off the bar for food. The relatives are due shortly.'

Ariel decided the best thing she could do was to get out of the way. She wandered toward the church, checking her watch. The service would begin in an hour, plenty of time for Noyers' residents to stop by Tony's for the reception and to offer condolences to the relatives who had appeared in town suddenly and were doubtless causing all kinds of gossip. Local opinion had always been that the relatives were wealthy, and that they had turned their backs on Madame in her need. But the neighbor Ariel had talked to said a couple, perhaps an adult grandson and his wife, had been to see her before she died, had even been helping her around the house, so perhaps they weren't as distant and unfeeling as rumor had it.

She was still unsettled about the nighttime prowler who had searched her car and wondered if that person was here today, maybe even watching her. It dawned on her suddenly that the brigadier ought to know if he didn't that they were in town.

She hurried to a quiet corner under an awning and dialed the gendarmerie headquarters in Avallon. No, the brigadier was not in. Would she like to leave a message?

'Please tell him that relatives of the woman killed in Reigny are in Noyers right now for her funeral. Their surname is Gaudet.'

The gruff voice sounded skeptical that the boss might want this information, much less that it was urgent.

'Please, he's been trying to find them to help in the investigation, but no one knew who they were.'

Grudgingly, the voice agreed to send the message to the brigadier.

'Your name please?'

'Madame Shepard. He knows me.'

'Well then, I will send the message to his car. He's on the way back from Paris.'

Inwardly, Ariel groaned. Allard might not get back in time. 'This is urgent. They intend to leave as soon as the funeral is over. Perhaps the brigadier can send another officer then? It really is important.'

As she ended the call, a voice close to her said, 'You are calling the police, Madame?'

She whirled, startled. It was the would-be real estate investor. His mouth was smiling, but his eyes were dark and glittering.

She waved her phone. 'Oh, it's nothing really. I think they should be here, don't you, given that she was murdered? They say killers often show up at the scene of the crime, or in this case, the funeral. I've heard that, at any rate.' Ariel heard herself babbling. He made her nervous, and why had he been listening?

He looked as if this was a particularly interesting theory. 'And will you be examining everyone for signs of guilt? Perhaps you know more than the rest of the villagers? You might even know who killed her?' He cocked his head then looked around. 'Do you suspect anyone right now?' He had already been standing too close, and now he stepped so close that his arm brushed hers.

A sudden thought made goosebumps rise on her forearms. The house he seemed too interested in wasn't worth a lot unless there were valuable items or money hidden there and he knew it. It couldn't be the box of old memorabilia or the gun. Was there still something there that no one had found, under the floor or buried in the garden?

She moved out from under the awning, cleared her throat and slipped the cell phone into her bag. 'Of course not. If you'll excuse me, I have to check the church. The choir, you know?' she said and hurried away, not daring to look over her shoulder to see if he was still watching her.

There were more cars than usual on the street that led to the church, a mix of sedans and SUVs, the latter all with tinted windows. Big cars, tinted windows – was it an American conceit

imported to France or an international obsession? She recognized
a decal in the back window of a dusty Peugeot – a concert logo
from Michael's last tour. Still another Peugeot, polished to a high
gleam, close to the church probably belonged to the man who
was making her nervous. She thought she remembered it from
the time he came to the château. One especially large model
hogged two spaces close to the café. Sadly, it had a broken taillight, which took away a little of its Mercedes prestige.

She stopped walking. A foreign SUV? The French neighbor
who had remarked on the car outside Madame's, the relatives'
car, with a Frenchman's sense of insult that it was German. She
closed her eyes. The vehicle speeding away in the pitch-dark –
yes – only one taillight. Could this be Madame's grandson and
his wife, out of sight until today? If it was their car, then they
had been last night's prowlers, searching it for something they
hadn't found at her house. The grandchildren and the unsavory
Mr Tremblay were like flies buzzing around poor Madame
Toussaint's property. One of them must have killed her. It was
the only answer that made sense.

Tremblay had been in her kitchen and had seen Raoul come
into the room from outside. He would know about that door. He
was working with them, she was sure. Maybe they couldn't bring
themselves to kill the old lady so they hired him.

Glancing around to make sure no one was looking, she circled
the car, trying to see through the darkened windows.

Nothing, not that she knew what she would find that would
prove her theory. Maybe if she saw them, it would trigger something. Were they in the church? She jumped when she heard her
name called.

'Ariel, wait for me.' It was Pippa, who had chosen what almost
seemed like cosplay for the event – a long black tunic over wide-
legged pants that flapped as she jogged over. What set her apart
from anyone they were likely to see was a hat, the kind of hat
one only saw at British state events. It sat at an alarming angle
over her spiky hair and looked like a thin black plate on which
was perched a stiff, curled feather, possibly from a large turkey.

'What on earth?' Ariel said, nodding toward the structure.

Pippa grimaced. 'Had to get it for a funeral back in London
a few years ago. Cost the moon, so I couldn't very well throw

it away, could I? Just waiting for a chance to use it again. Rather dashing, I think.'

Ariel bit her tongue and instructed herself not to laugh. It would be enough to keep a straight face when she imagined the villagers reacting to a tall, lanky creature who apparently thought Madame Toussaint was British royalty.

'The service doesn't start for at least an hour,' she said.

'I know, but I thought I'd hang around and see if anyone looks suspicious. Katherine said she'd do that with me.'

'Their car is here, I noticed, so I'm guessing she's either looking for remnants of artwork in the church or heading to Tony's.' She lowered her voice. 'Don't turn around but sneak a look behind me and tell me if you see a man in a leather jacket behind us. I said *don't turn around.*'

It was futile. Pippa had snapped her head back over her shoulder, her hat quivering with the effort to stay on her head.

'No, not unless it's the spotty teenager dressed like James Dean and his girlfriend, and his jacket is fake leather, by the way.' Pippa turned back and smiled. 'Don't tell me you're getting paranoid. Although after last night, I can understand why you might.'

'Last night?' She hadn't told Pippa about the person who had searched her car.

'You have to admit it was a bit creepy whispering and running around in the dark. It's a wonder no one called the gendarmes, and I can't think how I would have explained it if Philippe had shown up. I think we scared off a guy who was out for a walk. He practically ran in the other direction when I walked back to my house.'

'What guy? I didn't see anyone.'

'Oh, just someone walking one of those fluffy little dogs for a last pee of the day. Probably staying in the Belgians' rental cottage – cheap at this time of year because there's no heat. I almost didn't see him because he was wearing a black jacket.'

Ariel stopped walking. How many little dogs on leashes were there likely to be in a rural hamlet? 'Why didn't you tell me sooner?' Lowering her voice, she said, 'It could have been the thief – or even the murderer.'

Pippa's face registered her own shock. 'Do you think so? Was

I a few steps away from a killer?' She turned her head back and forth, surveying the street.

Ariel's head was spinning, and she felt a sudden pressure on her temples. Someone might have overheard them that night. If that someone was the husband of the woman the neighbor saw at Madame's with the little dog, and if that woman was the same one as the well-dressed tourist who came in to look at the elegant silverware in Katherine's shop the day before it was robbed, she and Pippa might be in major trouble.

'I'm going to head back to the café and will meet you there for the brief reception.' She needed to check out the relatives. 'Then we'll all go to the church together. Don't talk to an intense guy with a real leather jacket, whatever you do.'

The threads were coming together even if she couldn't figure out the why of it all. Monsieur Tremblay and the relatives were either working together or in a race to claim the house for whatever it contained. What was it? Massive loot stored under the floorboards? If searching her car was a clue, it must be something small but significant, something that would betray them. Madame's little treasures, or almost all of them, had been stolen from Katherine's shop shortly after the woman with the dog examined them and before the police could impound them. If the thieves had them now, why did they need to search her car?

Katherine said the pieces were lovely, very old and worth something, but nowhere near enough, she was sure, to commit such violence. Maybe the strange fork-like piece with a vermeil handle could implicate the thieves in a robbery somewhere else and that's what they were frantic to retrieve.

And Raoul? He had taken the box from Madame's house, hidden it and was now in jail, so he had something at stake in this business too even if there were no obviously valuable items in the box. What puzzled her the most was how some old war memorabilia factored into this, important enough for Raoul to steal. The dog was an entirely different mystery – or she hoped it was.

She needed to see the grandson and his wife and maybe watch to see if they spoke to Tremblay.

Tony's was crowded, and Ariel would have chosen to sit on a little metal chair in the town square across the street to observe without being too obvious if Regine hadn't seen her from inside and beckoned her over.

'Tony saved you a seat at the bar,' she said, her mouth close to Ariel's ear. 'The relatives are coming now, so your timing is good.' She worked her way to the open door and extended her arm to draw someone in.

The woman was probably in her forties, with enough makeup to blur the accuracy of a guestimate. She wore a short fur coat over a black skirt that hugged her thighs, high heels that probably didn't help her navigate the cobbled street and a lot of jewelry. The women of Noyers, who were parked at tables around the room, stared as if a peacock had flown into Tony's. Her eyes were like a bird's too, Ariel thought – round, black and alert.

The man who came in behind her made Ariel suck in her breath so fast she began to cough. He was common looking, ordinary except that his arms looked beefy beneath a sports jacket that strained to close over his belly. There was a tattoo peeking out over his open-collared shirt. None of that made her gasp. It was what he carried – a small dog nestled on his arm, its leash held loosely in his fist. A man walking a tiny dog where she and Pippa had tried to re-enact the scene of Madame's death but vanishing when Pippa came toward him. A man and wife who owned a distinctive vehicle that Ariel was ready to say was part of last night's search of her car. Madame Toussaint's loving relatives?

Regine was guiding the couple to the bar. Tony tapped a wine glass then, when that didn't work, shouted for everyone to be quiet. 'We are here today to pay tribute to our departed neighbor, and here are her grandson and his wife, Monsieur and Madame Gaudet, who have hosted this event.'

The room quieted and the woman in the fur jacket cleared her throat. 'We thank all of you for your kindnesses to our dear grandmother, rest her soul.'

The proprietor of the *épicerie* in Noyers, sitting next to Ariel, murmured, 'Not from around here.' Her partner, who habitually dressed in overalls and hiking boots and whom Ariel knew as the woman who carried in large crates of potatoes and cases of beer, nodded.

The woman waved a hand, bracelets clanking. 'Please stop by

here or at the church and share your memories of her with us. We'd love to know what you, um, know. Enjoy.' She, her husband and the dog sat abruptly at the table where Regine had placed a 'Reserved' sign, and Tony hurried over with a bottle of Crémant and two glasses.

Ariel thought Monsieur Gaudet looked bored, but as his eyes swept the room, she realized he was paying a great deal of attention. He focused on Madame's neighbor, who was oblivious as he talked animatedly with someone behind him, and his eyes narrowed. Then his lazy gaze continued until suddenly he and Ariel were staring at each other. Her face flushed, and Ariel turned to the bar, hoping to strike up a conversation with Tony, but the host was all the way across the room. She wondered if the stranger knew who she was? Had he heard her when she and Pippa acted out the murder scenarios?

She had to get out, but the café was more crowded than when she arrived, and the man was sitting at a table right next to the door. For a fleeting instant, she thought about the upstairs apartment she had stayed in when she first arrived in Noyers. It had a back stairs. No, the sneaky man was probably still there.

Just then, the *épicerie's* owner stood up. 'I've had my glass of red. You ready to walk down to the church?' she asked her friend.

'Yes,' Ariel said. 'I mean, I'll come with you if that's all right.'

'Sure,' the women said in unison, looking mildly surprised, and Ariel wedged herself between them as they made space and made it to the steps outside the café.

Ariel took a deep breath, but a moment later, a strong arm grabbed hers, and a small yip sounded behind her.

'I'll walk with you,' a husky voice said.

She didn't have to turn her head to know it was Monsieur Gaudet, still carrying the dog.

'I'm in a bit of a hurry,' she said now, 'and I'm with these people.'

'Don't bother,' the grocer said, waving her arm. 'See you in church. We're singing, so we have to get along quickly.'

The man said in a voice that pretended to be soothing yet was anything but, 'There, you see. Plenty of time for us to chat. You saw my dear grandmother die, I heard.'

'No, of course not.' Ariel twisted away, so he had to let go of her arm or risk showing anyone passing that he was using force. 'She's your grandmother? She was already dead when we saw her lying on the step.'

'My poor nana – sad, so sad. What else did you see? Understand, I'm just trying to piece together the facts of her passing. They think she was murdered, but why? Did you see a weapon?'

Ariel's throat was getting tight, and she fought to keep her breath even and her tone neutral. 'Really, the sheriff came within minutes and shooed everyone away, and the police came soon after, so, no, we saw nothing.'

'You say "we". Was the short woman who owns the junk store with you?'

Ariel paused. 'Lots of people showed up all of a sudden. It's hard to remember because the sight was so shocking. Other people saw her first.'

'Poor Grandmother, lying there so exposed,' he said in a tone so obviously false that she felt suddenly queasy. 'Was she wearing her usual old coat? We tried to give her a new one, but she wouldn't take it. Did you know that? Did she confide in you?'

Ariel forced a short laugh. 'Madame didn't confide, as you put it, to anyone. We all respected her, but she kept her distance, she and her dog.'

'Ah, yes, the dog. I met it once. It didn't like me.' Gaudet laughed. 'Here, wait a moment while I put my wife's ugly little thing in the car. Can't have him barking or peeing in the church.'

Ariel didn't want to wait but couldn't think of a way to escape the interrogation, which is what it was. She watched while he carefully lowered the windows on the driver's side a couple of inches before getting out and locking the car with his remote. She took a few tentative steps toward the church, and he was beside her again. Maybe it was her turn to ask a question.

'Do you live in Burgundy?'

'Not so close, more like Paris – near Paris anyway. And you?'

She felt like saying that he knew perfectly well where she lived but thought better of it.

'Here, in Noyers.'

'You're not French.'

'No.'

They walked along silently for a moment until the open door of the church came in sight. He stopped and took hold of her arm again. 'So, madam, the dog. Have you seen him? He seems to be missing.'

'I saw him often, always with her. I thought you might have adopted him.'

Gaudet chuckled. 'He would probably eat my wife's furry rat in one bite. No one has seen him. I wonder if whoever took him in was present at the time of the attack – maybe even the attacker, eh?'

Ariel wondered too, wondered if the man crowding her right now was that person. In a minute, she could detach herself and find Katherine, but she'd try one more question first. 'You visited her recently, didn't you? Were you helping her clear out some old things? I understand her place was kind of messy.'

Gaudet looked hard at her, raising his eyebrows. 'Now who might have told you that?'

'That her house was messy? Honestly, I can't remember. You know gossip—'

He cut her off. 'Who told you I was at her house?'

She opened her mouth to give him a vague non-answer but was cut off again, this time by Pippa.

'There you are. Brilliant. I just met Madame Gaudet and— Oh hello, are you Monsieur Gaudet? Your wife is looking for you.' She laughed. 'Although it's difficult hiding from anyone in Noyers, it's so small. Anyway, everyone's headed to the church.'

She put her arm through Ariel's and kept talking. 'I say, you must be broken up. I mean, Madame was a crusty sort of person, and here she was having to live on beans and toast, so to speak. Did you realize she was poor?'

Gaudet's face colored slightly. 'She did all right.'

'Well, maybe, but did you know she had to sell her pretty things to buy food?'

Ariel had been thinking Pippa was simply filling in empty air time, but now she understood her friend was aiming toward something.

'Things?' Gaudet said, his interest sparked. He turned away from Ariel. 'No, I didn't. What things?'

'I only saw a few pieces of old silver and vermeil, so charming. Shame that almost all the pieces were stolen from our friend's little shop, or maybe the *flics* took them away? I can't remember. Who would do such a thing?'

Monsieur Gaudet had stopped, rooted to the street. 'The police have some? But, you say almost. There are other trinkets?'

He fell for Pippa's bait. That did it for Ariel. Gaudet was still hunting for whatever was part of their stolen haul.

'Pippa, come on, we're late,' she said, yanking her over the step and into the dark and chilly church. 'Don't say anything in case we're being followed,' she said into Pippa's ear.

Pippa turned to her with a look of triumph and would have answered except that she stumbled over a protruding chair leg at the end of an aisle. 'Oops. Look, there's Katherine and Michael, and Katherine's holding places for us.' Pippa made her way along a row of chairs, pushing a couple out of alignment with the others, the chair legs scraping loudly on the stone floor.

At the front of the church, a handful of women and two men were clustered, their heads bent toward each other. Ariel noticed Regine, the owner of the grocery store and the couple who ran the hairdresser's, all wearing parkas to fend off the dank chill of the church. They were clutching sheet music and nodding earnestly in the direction of their probable leader, the woman who ran the post office. A man she didn't recognize, with long sideburns and a sharp nose, was bent over his guitar, strumming quietly and peering at a singer's sheet music.

Ariel was tempted to get out her phone and try the gendarmerie again. She had to let the brigadier know what she'd deduced before these awful people left Noyers.

'We saved you seats, darlings,' Katherine said and stood up for the ritual kisses, which in Pippa's case led to further confusion since Pippa always managed to plant the *bis* on someone's ear. In this instance, she almost lost her hat, and Katherine backed away from a collision with the hat's brim. 'This is quite an occasion. The church will be full, and I'm sorry I didn't know dear Madame better.'

'You didn't even know her name,' Ariel said.

Michael swallowed a laugh, and Katherine stood as tall as a short woman could. Ariel took in her outfit and wondered how

Katherine managed to look merely charmingly eccentric in what on anyone else – well, on Ariel at any rate – would look merely odd: a full-length black skirt, a little ragged at the hem; a black turtleneck top; a long taffeta coat of some undetermined mix of dark gray and purple; and a little fur headband from which sprouted a bit of black lace.

'She came to my shop. One pays one's courtesies in any case,' she said, her chin raised.

Ariel saw the hurt in her eyes. 'I'm sorry – of course you knew her,' she said and squeezed Katherine's hand, 'and you've shown you care by helping determine what might have happened. I'm just on edge.'

She leaned closer. 'I know who did it,' she said, barely breathing the information into Katherine's ear.

The sudden loud strumming of the guitar stopped Katherine from replying, although her face registered shock. The singers moved into a ragged line in front of the altar. The mayor, who had been sitting in the front row, stood up and walked to the pulpit. The audience was still sliding in through the doors and finding seats as far back as possible. Ariel looked around and saw Monsieur Gaudet beckoning to his wife, who squeezed past an elderly couple to sit right behind Katherine. When Ariel looked farther back, she was startled. Tremblay was parked a couple of rows behind them and was eyeing Katherine, Pippa and herself. When he saw her looking, he frowned.

'Friends,' Noyers' mayor said, 'we are here to pay our respects to a citizen of Noyers, a woman who lived in our town for many decades, whom most of us saw every day but did not really know.' He cleared his throat. 'I understand many of you are from Reigny, where she passed away, and you are most welcome.'

'Passed away,' Katherine said in a whisper that probably carried farther than she intended in the echo chamber of an old church. 'Well, that's one way of avoiding what really happened.'

Ariel shook her head at her friend, willing her to be silent. Katherine might not know that a trio of suspicious people were sitting behind her.

The choir began to sing. '*Je vis un ange qui volait . . .*' and the guitarist strummed the simple chords, mingling with the sopranos, the single tenor and the one bass voice, a stocky man wearing work boots who made up in volume what he lacked in musical nuance.

When the choir finished, the mayor stood up again, pulling his scarf closer around his neck, and turned to the audience. 'I know Madame Toussaint's relatives are here, and we are pleased they came.' He looked around the dim space. 'Would you care to speak, perhaps share a memory of her?'

A chair leg scraped against the hard floor, and Ariel turned to see Madame Gaudet standing up. 'No, thank you. We' – she gestured to her husband who was sitting stone-faced – 'would like to hear from those who have memories of her.'

Or show themselves as friends who might have the missing clue to their crime, Ariel thought.

Katherine had turned in her seat to see Madame Gaudet and suddenly gasped. She leaned toward Ariel and said in a whisper, 'It's her. That's the woman who came into the shop and wanted to see all the silver pieces I had, the day before the shop was broken into.'

The woman in question gave Ariel's friend a sharp look.

While the owner of the hair salon stood to speak about Madame and her loyal dog, Ariel's mind raced. She was sure now that the relatives were involved in the old woman's death, and it was absurd to think it was over a few pieces of pretty silver. They'd been using the unremarkable house in a tiny village to hide whatever it was they were here to take. Madame must have figured out they were stolen goods, maybe even confronted them after pulling out a few pieces she had to sell for food money. Maybe Tremblay, the so-called real estate investor, was the hired killer, hanging around because he, too, realized the house held something important and planned a double-cross. Or, and her stomach dropped, because someone else needed to die, someone they thought knew too much?

She didn't dare turn completely in her seat but slid her eyes as far to one side as she could and shifted. In fact, the man in the leather jacket was looking intently at Madame Gaudet, who was squinting at Katherine. Those pretty pieces of silver? That's why they wanted to grab them from her friend's shop, to keep anyone from linking the goods to Noyers, but they had been too late. Was there something else in the house? Something else they'd stolen that Madame might have hidden? Was that what the attempted burglary was about?

Every question she asked herself led to more. Had Raoul been forced to help them find it, he with access, gardening tools for digging, local enough not to be noticed? Was he getting paid? After all, he had wound up with the dog, so he had to have some part in this. The dog, she was convinced, had not simply run away when its mistress was knocked down. Maybe Raoul had been tasked with taking it from the poor woman. There must be something in that wooden box that pointed to the crime. Surely not that old pistol? No, she said to herself, there was nothing there except records of something, so it had to be in them. Those documents were blackmail of some kind. Raoul, a blackmailer?

She had to find Allard. She looked around openly. Surely the brigadier or at least someone from the gendarmerie was here by now? She needed to get to a policeman and make sure they detained the Gaudets and Tremblay.

A couple of people had risen to pay short, vague tributes to Madame Toussaint, but now the church was silent again. She stood up and, whispering apologies, sidled along the row away from Katherine and Pippa, who stared at her, and to the side aisle.

The choir had begun another song and the sixty or so people in the church were focused on them, when suddenly a voice began to sing so loudly that it drowned out the choir.

'*Allons enfants de la Patrie / le jour de gloire est arrivé / contre nous de la tyrannie . . .*'

'La Marseillaise', the French national anthem. Every head turned toward the back of the church, where in the dim light, Raoul was standing, his arm raised and his fist clenched, singing with such passion that Ariel was stunned. Out of jail? Here in Noyers? And why this drama? He moved his fist so it pointed directly at Monsieur Gaudet. Then, as far back in the shadows as possible, she saw the brigadier. Several men in street clothes hovered near him, all of them watchful.

'Shame!' Raoul shouted. 'I will give you a memory you can't escape. Disgrace is your family's curse. Your grandfather betrayed his friends into death here in the Yonne when the Nazis occupied us; your father shamed his whole family too, and now you have killed her. She said you would find a way to silence her if she didn't agree to your plan to use her house to hide the evidence of your latest crime, and now you have. Shame! She was a hero of France.' Raoul began to sing again. '*Aux armes, citoyens*!'

There was a scraping of chairs and Ariel looked around to see every person in the church begin to stand up, mouths open, faces moving from confusion to anger. The choir was silent for a moment, until the guitar player picked up on Raoul's lyric and then the choir and everyone in the church turned toward the trapped couple and sang in a mighty roar.

'*Aux armes, citoyens / formez vos bataillons / marchons, marchons, qu'un sang impur / abreuve nos sillons*!'

Ariel had goosebumps and a flash of understanding. The lyrics of the anthem were sung all over Paris and surely elsewhere on VE Day. The men and women, the teenage girl captured in the famous photo with her Sten gun, the letters and documents in the box. The old woman who quoted Sartre and kept Camus's first book must have been in the Resistance even as a teenager like so many, and the items in the box were her treasures. Raoul was surely too young, but he knew.

'*Marchons*', indeed. The fighters for France were dying of old age, those that had not been shot, captured, tortured or sent to the death camps, but their bravery was still honored in the Yonne. Tears pricked her eyes.

Was Raoul the catalyst to flush them out? Allard must have received her message. She moved quickly toward the back of the church.

A commotion broke out in the middle of the rows. Madame Gaudet had pulled Katherine from her chair and was shaking her, shouting something. Michael jumped up and shoved the woman away, and Monsieur Gaudet slammed his fist into Michael's side. The relatives started pushing their way past people roughly, Tremblay with them, even knocking over chairs as they made for the exit. The men clustered at the back of the church ran forward and the brigadier ran too, speaking into a piece of equipment on his shoulder as he moved. Monsieur Gaudet pushed someone so hard she fell to the floor with a cry. Ariel registered that it was the owner of the *épicerie* and that her partner then took up the chase, a look of grim determination on her face.

The choir and guitarist had quit trying to make music and stood at the front of the church, mouths open. Noyers' mayor held his hand up as if to speak but looked confused. Ariel took off after the brigadier, glancing at her friends as she reached the big doors. Michael was upright but grimacing and holding his side. Katherine was patting him, and Pippa had the look of someone who was memorizing every detail of what was happening.

The police were after the Gaudets but might not realize that Tremblay was part of the scheme. 'Catch him,' Ariel said in a croaking shout as she tried to reach the gendarmes. She pointed to Tremblay, who was running fast, right behind Monsieur Gaudet. 'He's a murderer.'

No one paid any attention to her. She had to stop to catch her breath and was transfixed by what was happening. Tremblay had caught up with Gaudet and was tackling him, dragging him on to the cobblestones. Fighting to see who would get to the treasure first?

She looked past them to see the other men who had been with the brigadier in the church closing in on Madame Gaudet, whose ankles were wobbling as she hurried along the cobblestones in her high heels. She made it to their car and in a second had started the engine and was headed toward her pursuers, who had to jump to the side of the street.

Ariel realized she was directly in the path of the car. The driver motioned wildly with one hand for Ariel to move, but Ariel stood paralyzed. If she moved, the woman would escape. She wouldn't deliberately run Ariel down? The car slowed a bit and the horn blared, but it was still headed straight for her.

TWENTY

All of a sudden, the brakes screeched and the big SUV shuddered to a halt. Madame Gaudet wasn't looking at Ariel though. She was looking down at her feet. As the police swarmed the car and opened the door, Ariel heard her crying, 'My darling, my sweet thing.' The gendarmes had a hard time pulling her out of the car.

While she was standing with her face pressed against the side of the car, being handcuffed, an officer reached in and lifted out the little dog. It was alive, Ariel noted through her own shock, but clearly distressed.

The woman wept and tried to push closer to the animal, but the police held her up against the car. 'My baby, my sweet thing,' she said. *'Il va bien?'*

'Yes, he's OK,' the officer holding him said impatiently. 'See? Just got his leash caught on the gear shaft. He's scared, but he's alert.'

He held the dog out to her, and she kissed its face. Then the gendarme pulled the animal away and began scanning the street, probably hoping, Ariel realized, that someone would take the squirming little thing and let him get back to the work he was trained to do.

It was Regine who waved a hand from the sidewalk opposite and took the little creature, still attached to its leash. She said something to the gendarme, who nodded before heading back toward the church at a trot while his fellow plainclothesmen stood with the weeping woman.

A half dozen police cars had materialized from the side streets, blue lights flashing, and a swarm of uniformed officers in full gear were trying to secure the street – difficult with most of the people who'd been inside the church milling around, clustering and regrouping every few minutes into pods of likely disinformation. Brigadier Allard was standing near the church being briefed by several officers. He looked up and saw Ariel, who had been walking slowly in his direction, waved off his lieutenants and strode up to meet her.

'Are you all right? My God, you could have been killed.' He took her elbow and steered her to a metal chair in the minuscule park across from the café.

'I know what happened,' she said, taking a deep breath to try and slow her pulse. 'It's the house. Something's there. They all want it.' She looked at him, wondering if she was making any sense.

He nodded. 'We think so too. The museum loot.'

'Museum?'

'The Gaudets are part of the gang that stole a quantity of valuable objects from two Paris museums recently. The national police of the Paris Police Prefecture were in charge of the investigation since these are French historical artifacts. It was they who found images on surveillance videos from the streets near the museum sites and alerted every gendarmerie in France. Took a while, but eventually they were identified. You gave us the final piece of the puzzle.'

'I did?' Ariel's head was pounding, her legs were shaky and she was so dehydrated she might faint. 'Could I have some water?'

The brigadier turned and instantly a young, uniformed man appeared at his side. 'Yes, sir?' It was the corporal who had been so eager at the gendarmerie. He gazed at her with such concern that Ariel smiled to reassure him, and at the brigadier's direction he trotted across the street to the café.

'You told us the Gaudets were here in Noyers but would be leaving soon, and when we had that information, we could finally tie them to the theft of the museum's antique silver. The Paris police had already identified them by name but couldn't find them. My sergeant called me with your message, and we put out a bulletin on the police radio for immediate help and, well, here we are. How did you know Gaudet was the killer?'

'Gaudet? No, I don't mean him. It's that man who calls himself Tremblay. Did your men see him running away? Have you caught him too?'

The corporal returned with several bottles of Badoit and was now hovering twenty feet away, poised like a gazelle to act on the brigadier's next command. Allard called him over, murmured something in his ear while Ariel drank deeply and then he took off at a trot.

'You connected the dots so well, my dear Ariel, but there was one piece you could not have known. See there?' He pointed down the street. The corporal was almost marching as he approached with the real estate investor, who was smoothing his hair and walking slowly.

When they reached Allard and Ariel, Allard stood up. 'Detective Barbeau, let me introduce Madame Shepard, who is very intelligent and a fine amateur sleuth. But you, sir, are an even finer actor.'

Ariel held on to her water with both hands. She was afraid to speak. Actor? Detective?

'*Enchanté*, Madame, and please accept my apologies for having deceived you.'

'I don't understand. You're not with them, the Gaudets?'

Barbeau pulled up a chair, and the brigadier sat down too. The eager corporal stood stiffly at attention at the other end of the little cobbled area, far enough away so he could not be accused of eavesdropping but close enough to take any further orders. Two teenage girls in torn jeans and fake fur jackets walking past eyed him admiringly, but he looked straight ahead.

'Your brigadier thought there was something distinctive about the stolen pieces, and the pictures they took were forwarded to the section of the Paris Prefecture I'm detailed to. Brigadier Allard is quite perceptive, and it was determined that those objects were part of a cache stolen from the display rooms of one of Paris's exceptional museums of decorative objects. We have now retrieved them from the Gaudets. You will have to visit some day when they are back on display.'

'I hope you're planning to search her house again. I have a feeling there's more stolen items there. Upstairs was quite a mess. There was even dog excrement in one room. Hey, that would be the best spot to hide things. No one would want to go in there.'

Barbeau said, 'You've been there?'

Ariel said nothing.

'I will fill you in later, Detective,' Allard said.

'So the little pieces Madame was selling you're saying her grandson and his wife stole?'

Allard shifted in his seat. 'They were only distantly related to her, and Monsieur Gaudet is the disgraced grandson of a Vichy sympathizer, despised by Madame Toussaint and everyone in her hometown.'

'How do you know all this? I thought she was a mystery to you?'

Allard nodded. 'She was until your gardener explained it all.'

'Raoul? I can't believe he had anything to do with her death.' She glared at the brigadier.

'He didn't, but he had another piece of the puzzle, and he finally shared it with us. He had promised the victim not to but realized the whole business was so tangled and that the scoundrels must have killed his old friend. I will tell you, but right now, I need to get back to the gendarmerie. I promise I'll come see you as soon as I can.'

'And I need to supervise the removal of the Gaudets to Paris, so I must leave also,' Detective Barbeau said. 'My Prefecture colleagues will be working at the victim's house for a while. They may need to visit your friend's shop also. As you say, Madame, with so much to hide, the old woman's house so far from Paris would have been ideal.'

Ariel had a sudden thought she didn't want to share. There had been that one odd piece of silver that had escaped the thieves' notice. Did Katherine have it, and would the police think she had stolen the stolen goods?

The detective looked at her and smiled as he stood. 'Perhaps I shall come back to visit this lovely little town when I have a few days off. I just learned it's one of France's hundred most beautiful villages, a great honor. I promise to come as myself and perhaps will stay at Monsieur Tony's little apartment again.'

'And I'm supposed to be content with that?' Ariel asked, jumping up from her chair. 'My friends and I have been worried sick and trying to help all along. You, Detective, frightened me once I realized you had no intention of buying real estate, and now we're left out of the solution?'

Allard laughed. 'I very much doubt you and your friends are left out of anything that happens around here for very long. Why don't you gather everyone for dinner at your charming café, say tomorrow, and I will be there, I promise.'

The Paris detective raised his eyebrows and looked at the brigadier.

'Yes, I know I can't reveal everything, and nothing that would impact the criminal investigation by our colleagues at the esteemed Paris Prefecture, especially since there's a murder charge pending in Paris.'

'Another murder?' Ariel said.

'The museum guard. As stupid and unnecessary as the old woman's murder,' Barbeau replied, his voice dripping disdain. 'Neither was armed, neither was about to kill the thieves. They just panicked and took what they figured was the easiest way out of trouble. Most crooks aren't half as smart as they think they are.'

'You did mention that,' Ariel said to Allard, 'but I didn't connect what was happening in Paris with our little village.'

Allard nodded. 'Frankly, neither did I until I saw the antique silver with its royal engraving.'

'Royal? So that's what it was. We looked at the pieces in the shop and just thought they were lovely and old, much too precious to belong to an impoverished old woman. We did think there was some kind of crest, and Katherine had planned to research it when she had a little time. I'm glad the museum will have them back. There's so much I don't understand about the connection between her history and the thieves.'

Allard said, 'Between Raoul and myself, I promise we will explain why a fearless Resistance fighter met an undeserved death at the hands of the Gaudets.' He turned toward his corporal. 'Corporal, please stay with Madame Shepard until she is reunited with her friends, who are in the church giving their witness statements, and make sure she gets home without incident.'

'Yes, sir,' the young man barked and promptly attached himself to her side.

Ariel hung on to two water bottles as she and the corporal walked back to the church. There were villagers still loitering outside, but a uniformed officer Ariel recognized as Philippe's partner was standing at the door. When she saw Ariel's companion, she broke into a smile. 'Sahli, look at you. Big man now, eh? No more making the station coffee.'

Ariel glanced at the corporal, who had turned bright red.

'Officer Lannes, Brigadier Allard has authorized this woman entry.'

'Not exactly,' Ariel said. 'I can meet my friends here when they've given their witness statements. Is there a place to sit? My legs are weak.' She made a face. 'I was running after the wrong man, as it turned out. They've all been captured, and my adrenalin has vanished.'

'Happens to me all the time,' Officer Lannes said. 'Corporal, get Madame Shepard a chair from inside, yes?'

He was gone and back in less than a minute, and Ariel sank into a hard wooden chair, one of the ones kept in the church for events. No wonder, she thought, that fewer people went to church these days. The chair was uncomfortable and small, but it was better than standing. Or falling down, she reminded herself. What she really wanted was her bed, a brandy and sleep. She closed her eyes.

'There you are. I've been so worried.' It was Katherine, Michael and Pippa right behind her, exiting the church. 'Where did you go? Did those bastards hit you too? My poor Michael suffered—'

'Kay, cut the drama.' Michael's voice held a mixture of annoyance and amusement. 'I told you, it was a temporary blow, mostly to my ego. Hi, Ariel. Did you fare better? Pippa says she saw you start running right along with the cops.'

Before Ariel could say anything, Pippa waved her arms. 'You obviously figured it all out brilliantly. Did you catch them?'

Ariel noticed her British friend had lost the black plate hat during the confusion but had her cell phone out. Before she could stop her, Pippa had taken photos of her and of the corporal and Officer Lannes. 'Research,' Pippa said.

'You know what?' Ariel said slowly. 'I'm so tired I don't think I'm up to talking much, only to say, no, I didn't catch a criminal.'

Corporal Sahli stepped close to her and spoke softly. 'But you did, Madame. You stood in front of the car she was aiming right at you, and you stopped her all on your own. She might have run you down. We all saw it. She is a hero,' he said, turning to the small audience.

'Wait. In front of a speeding car?' Pippa said in tones of awe.

'You could have been killed,' Katherine said, her voice rising, reminding Ariel of her mother from long ago.

Later, Ariel thought, she would describe the scene and the little dog, but not now. 'Now that I know you're all OK, I'd like to go home and sleep off what's rapidly turning into a major headache. Before I forget, the brigadier wants all of us to meet at Tony's for dinner tomorrow. That's when we'll learn what this has been about.'

Katherine opened her mouth, doubtless to ask more questions, but Michael put his arm around her shoulders and shook his head at her.

Pippa bit her lip and looked thoughtful. 'I want to know everything. I have so much material – general ideas of course.'

Officer Lannes cleared her throat. 'Philippe said to tell you he's off tomorrow and will call you.'

Pippa paused and looked cautiously at the policewoman. 'Good then, thanks.'

'He thinks we should go out together sometime. You and him, me and my girlfriend.' Lannes grinned and might have said something more, but her radio emitted loud static, and she turned away to deal with it.

Pippa opened and closed her mouth a few times before taking a deep breath and turning back to Ariel with a smile. 'Well, that's that then, isn't it? Anyway, I'm chuffed to know you're the hero of the day.'

Sahli insisted he would drive Ariel home in her car. 'It's a kilometer or more walk back,' she said, and he shrugged.

Officer Lannes had come back and she laughed. 'We do more than that at a run each morning, don't we?'

The small group began to walk up to the line of parked cars. Katherine and Pippa kissed Ariel, and Michael patted her shoulder before they maneuvered out of their tight space. Others were leaving, and the street was busy. Ariel used her remote to unlock the car, and Corporal Sahli walked around to take the driver's seat. She was settling into the passenger seat when a loud voice called her. She groaned. 'What now?'

Looking up, she saw Raoul half trotting toward her from the church, followed at a slow pace by what must have been his wife, a thin woman whose gait suggested she had hip or knee problems.

He was panting by the time he reached her. Holding on to the open door, he said, 'You are all right then. I was worried. Do you have Camus?'

'The book in the box? Yes. I'm sorry I took it from the church in Reigny, but—'

'Not the book, the dog – Madame's Camus?'

'The dog's name is Camus?' Suddenly, she started to laugh and found she couldn't stop. 'Oh my God, of course she would name him Camus. I remember that she quoted Sartre to me at the memorial gathering we held for Christiane last year. I always thought I would break through her reserve and we could discuss philosophy over coffee one day.' Tears were rolling down her cheeks, and Ariel realized she was finally ready to grieve properly for the mysterious woman who had spent her days walking, walking, walking, always with the dog she loved. 'Poor dear Madame Toussaint. Yes, yes, I have Camus and he's fine. He's at my house, waiting for his next meal. Do you want to take him?'

'No, no,' Raoul said and looked over his shoulder. 'My wife hates dogs. But I didn't know what other choice I had when I found him. I was afraid they'd shoot him.'

She had questions, so many questions, but Ariel realized she was too exhausted to ask them.

'Raoul, come to dinner at Tony's tomorrow. You too,' she said as his wife finally made it to the car. 'The brigadier is meeting with all of us, and he'll share everything he can. I hope you will too. There's so much I'd like to know about this woman who was such a mystery but who apparently had a history everyone should know.'

She put her hand over his where it lay on the open window. 'In the meantime, Camus is fine. I'll even bring him tomorrow, all right?'

Raoul's wife looked horrified.

'Not to give him back, I promise. In fact, I think Camus has a new home. Tomorrow then. Get some sleep.'

TWENTY-ONE

March 28

T here had been no brandy, which she decided would worsen her headache, but warm milk, a satisfied dog and a duvet to sink into had done their work, and Ariel woke up late. Camus had left the bedroom, and when she wandered down to the kitchen in her robe, noting the bright-blue sky, he was waiting, standing next to the sink, gazing earnestly at her.

'Yes, Camus, I do know it's breakfast time. Any chance I could let you out without a leash for your first pee of the day if I leave the back door open?'

Unlike his namesake, the dog had no doubts about the state of the world and five minutes later, he was back in, lapping up his meal while Ariel slowly pressed water through the freshly ground coffee beans and sniffed the aroma.

The phone rang before she took her first sip. Pippa. Feeling a bit guilty, she let it go to voicemail. She needed zero drama right now, no more demands for replays of yesterday's horrible activities at least for an hour. She needed the warmth and security of her home, the peace and quiet of her château.

Tearing off pieces of a roll she had left from her last trip to the boulangerie and smearing it with apricot preserves bought at last year's farmers market, Ariel fell into conversation with her late husband, speaking out loud to the kitchen, which was fast becoming her favorite room.

'So, Dan, would you have been proud of me or furious that I just stood there when that car came at me? We both know I'm no hero, but at least nothing happened. After everything I've been through to make a new home, it would have been so stupid to let myself get run over and have poor old Château de Champs-sur-Serein be abandoned again. How did I get mixed up in another murder? I have no idea, my love. I mind my own business – well, most of the time – but I'm not like Miss Marple nosing around, looking for trouble, I swear.'

There was a loud rapping at the big front door. Ariel pulled her robe closer and walked up the stairs. 'Who is it?'

'It's me, Katherine, and I've brought you something. Hello, darling,' she said as Ariel pulled the door open. 'I figured you need something to calm yourself.' She held out a plastic bag tied with a bow, through which a long sprig of rosemary was tied. 'Rosemary, lavender, chamomile and rose hips, aromatherapy from my own garden. I dry these all winter and no one could possibly deserve it more than you do.

'For the bath, my dear, for the bath,' she said when Ariel just looked at her. 'You do have a working tub – I saw that. I can dog sit while you rejuvenate, or you can use them tonight. I even brought Gracie to have a play date with what's-its-name.'

Ariel was close to speechless. A bath with a bag full of dried leaves? A doggie play date?

'Don't argue. I know what I'm doing. I'll bring Gracie in and we'll let the two of them sniff each other and make friends. Oh, and I brought croissants.'

With that, she was out the door and back again with the large black dog and a paper-wrapped packet and was halfway down the stairs to the kitchen before Ariel could marshal her thoughts.

Ariel trailed her slowly and was in time to see Camus standing guardedly near his bedding while Gracie, oblivious to anything but a possible new friend, trotted over in her roly-poly fashion. Her tail moved like a feather fan. The two women watched for a long minute while Camus tried to decide if this was friend or foe. Finally, his thin tail began to wave back and forth like a windshield wiper and Gracie's picked up speed.

As the sniffing and circling began, Katherine turned and said, 'See, dogs really aren't complicated.' She smiled and made a shooing motion. 'Bath time. I'll make myself coffee and start thinking about the frescos. Now that Madame has been exonerated, we can turn our attention to happier projects.'

Thirty minutes later, Ariel had to agree. An aromatherapy bath was bliss, or at least Katherine's own collected herbs and flowers were. It hit her that this would be a distinctive touch for her dream of a luxurious experience for guests, a locally made gift.

She dressed and ran down to the kitchen to share her idea. No one was there – no tail-wagging dogs, no artist friend. And the back door was open.

'Over here.' Katherine gestured from a place far down the back path.

Ariel didn't see the dogs as she hurried down to meet her friend.

'Don't worry,' Katherine said, pointing to the remains of a tall hedge off to one side. 'They're playing hide and seek.'

Sure enough, Camus came flying out of the shrubbery, mouth open, ears up, chased by the dog the size of a small black bear. The two circled Ariel a few times, then Camus threw himself down, tongue hanging out, sides rising and falling, and, Ariel thought, looking blissfully happy.

'You do realize there was once a maze here?' Katherine said. 'I wonder if Raoul, once he's back at work, can find the bones of the thing and replant the shrubbery. We can find some statuary to put on pedestals, have Jean bring over new gravel . . .' She stopped. 'I'm way ahead of myself, aren't I?'

Ariel grinned. 'A bit, but I agree the back gardens will eventually need landscape design I can't afford. Plus, I worry that Raoul is getting a bit old for the heavy outdoor work. After what he said yesterday, I realize I don't know how old he really is. Could he really be old enough to have been in the Resistance?'

'No. I talked to his wife when we got home.' Katherine answered the question on Ariel's face. 'Well, their house is a short walk and I did have to take the dogs out. Raoul was still at the gendarmerie, not as a suspect but to fill in some holes in his report of the Gaudets' invasion of her home to store their stolen goods.'

They walked back to the château, the two tired dogs loping along with them.

'Madame Descoteaux knew about the old woman's brave war activity all along,' Katherine said, 'but no one thought to ask her. She was worried about the long walks Madame Toussaint was taking to and from Noyers, knew she was selling silver for food money, but couldn't persuade the fiercely private woman to ask for government help. So they did the next best thing – driving her when they could.'

'Raoul says very little,' Ariel said. 'I knew she was married and that she keeps a vegetable garden, but that's it. All this time, we had a possible source for help with the stash of material I found.'

'She wouldn't have told us anyway. She didn't agree with her husband's determination to keep the story secret but said it was his story to tell. A few weeks before the poor woman was killed, she told him if anything happened to the old woman, he should tell the police about the thieves but keep her Resistance work quiet.'

'But why, I wonder? She should have been proud.'

'Raoul's wife only said his own family is part of the story, and that he was finally driven to call out the crooks masquerading as her relatives. Oh, I keep meaning to tell you. The letter in French handwriting that you found? I finally had time to translate it. Needed a magnifying glass because the writing was so small. It was from someone's mother, maybe her own, but only signed "Maman." It was an account of what this writer knew about a Nazi ambush that killed her son and several of his friends. She was telling this person, who she called Yvonne, never to forget, but wrote "How could you, Petit Chien?" Apparently it was some kind of family secret not to be shared.'

'This might be something for Pippa to research if her French reading skills improve. Sounds like a Resistance story that might be in the local historic record in some form. Maybe the letter should go to whatever local historical society takes these things, or the museum Katherine wants us to visit.'

Ariel closed the door and put down an extra bowl of water for Gracie. 'The brigadier told me the couple were related to Madame, but not as closely as they claimed.'

Katherine made a noise of frustration. 'Raoul's wife said that Madame Toussaint had no children, much less grandchildren. I feel stupid. She and Raoul live a few minutes away from me, and I never met her until all of this. Pippa has already asked to interview her for the historical novel she's determined to write. Imagine Pippa with her imperfect French and Madame Descoteaux with no English.'

'I expect you'll be invited to serve as the translator.'

Katherine sighed and accepted a fresh *café crème*. 'Right now,

I miss painting. I haven't done any decent work for two weeks. I'm curious though, so, yes, I expect I will do it. Michael has a trip to the States coming up that I have no desire to take with him, and I'll be able to focus on my work for a bigger part of the day. I love him madly, but he has a habit of hollering for me when he's sitting on the patio making his wonderful music, expecting I will drop everything and come running, whether it's to bring him a cup of coffee or find a dog's leash.'

Ariel laughed. 'If you're hoping to make having a husband seem like a bad thing, forget it.'

Katherine pushed absently at the hair that had escaped her ponytail. 'I'm sorry I never met him, but your Dan gave you the château, so I know he was generous, romantic and had a great sense of adventure. The partner you deserved.'

Ariel swallowed and looked down at her coffee cup. 'All of that.' She paused. 'Listen, I had an idea after taking that delicious bath with your herbs and flowers. What if I hire you to make some as gifts for my clients? And if they're the hit I think they will be, you could run a side business of making aroma-therapy packets if I open a small gift shop somewhere inside this place?'

'I have my own little shop, remember? I paint. I hunt the *vide greniers*. The last thing I could take on would be an obligation to forage for wildflowers, dear friend.'

Ariel had to agree. She was reaching for help from friends who had already done a great deal for her. Scratch that.

Katherine held up her forefinger. 'However, I have an idea. The flowers and herbs are more abundant in summer. The bunch I gave you were dried from last year. Jeannette is out of school in the summer and needs work. Her young brothers need some-thing – anything – to keep them occupied and out of trouble when there's no school.'

She looked at Ariel, who said, 'If you can train them so they don't deliver bouquets of poison ivy or hemlock, it might work.'

'You can count on Jeannette, and I'd double-check their harvests. She keeps those boys in order – has to, really, since their father is off doing whatever he does all day.'

They agreed it was worth a try and that Katherine would bring the teenager over to meet Ariel some weekend day.

'I don't suppose you'd consider moving your shop in here?' Ariel asked.

Katherine threw herself back in her chair. 'Goodness, where did that come from? One step at a time, Ariel dear. That sounds too much like a real business, and my little folly is, well, my own folly.'

'Sorry, didn't mean to push. Just another bit of brainstorming. Will you and Michael be at Tony's tonight? Allard promised to fill us in as much as he can, given that the investigation and arrest means there's a criminal case he can't jeopardize.'

'Of course, but I'm almost more interested in what Raoul is willing to share.'

'He and his wife will be there too. I'll bring the box. I feel guilty keeping it another minute, although I would like to under-stand why it was so important to him and, I assume, to Madame Toussaint.'

'And the dog?' Katherine glanced over at Camus, who was curled up on his bed, with Gracie on the floor next to him.

Ariel frowned. 'I didn't plan on a dog in my life, but Raoul can't take him. He's so noble looking and so French. Am I crazy to think I can care for him properly? What if I want to go to Paris for a couple of days?'

'Look at them. There's your answer. He stays with his friend Gracie of course. When you're at home, having him here with you will be safer.'

Ariel shivered, remembering the late-night skulking and the search of her car. She described it to Katherine and admitted having Camus with her had offered a crumb of comfort. 'Maybe if he comes to know this is his real home, he'll be more of a watch dog.'

Katherine looked at her watch. 'I'd better get back. We'll be there tonight. Shall I remind Pippa?'

'Of course, although I expect she'll have to be restrained from turning this whole business into a novel.'

While Ariel was saying goodbye to her friend, Andre's little truck bounced in over the ruts on the drive and the plumber jumped out, meeting her on the steps, a rolled sheaf of paper in his hand. '*Bonjour*, Madame Ariel,' he said. 'I have your solution – two of the most beautiful bathrooms in all of Burgundy.' Seeing her expression, he added, 'And not expensive.'

'I don't have a lot of time, Andre. You know there was a crisis yesterday and I have to visit the gendarmerie to give a statement.'

Andre's face showed that he had no idea what she was talking about. He lived in Tonnare, not quite an hour away.

'Never mind. Let's go upstairs and you can show me what you and the architect have in mind. I'm glad to hear they won't be *trop cher.*'

Andre spread the papers on the worktable that had resided in the big center hall of the bedroom level. He was right about the plan, which set the new bathroom in such a way that there was easy access from the two bedrooms on the right side of the house. It was a large room made possible by taking the space from an alcove in one bedroom. The drawing showed double sinks, a long counter that echoed the color of the exterior stone of the château, a walk-in shower with double shower heads and a slightly chis-eled floor 'so no one will fall'. The lavatory was a separate room with its own hallway door as well as one from the large bathroom. 'We will have enough heated towel racks and wall hangers for occupants of both rooms to leave their belongings apart from the others, you know? Nothing crowded.'

'Why won't it be too expensive?' Ariel asked.

'Local stone, plumbing aligned without much demolishing of walls, only two new doors.'

Ariel wondered how many doors they would have suggested had money been no object. She also wondered what counted as 'not too expensive', but she said she liked the design, so if Andre or the architect was prepared to get contractor bids, she was ready to make a decision.

The other bathroom was similar, if somewhat simpler since there was already a lavatory and a bathroom in the space. 'So no more holes in the walls?'

Andre's face registered his professional sorrow. 'Alas, more holes, but,' he added as Ariel's mouth opened to protest, 'only a few and not disruptive.'

After some further delicate negotiating back and forth, Andre left with his drawings rolled under his arm and a springy step. Ariel understood that she might quibble over the fittings and the flooring but that she had to have those bathrooms, and the plumber knew it. She had a mental image of euro notes wafting up and away over the château's slate roof like autumn leaves in a high wind and decided a high priority was research into the going tariff for staying at a château in Burgundy.

'Income, income,' she said as she gathered a jacket against the gray skies and headed to the kitchen to offer Camus a walk. It would be a relief to get back to restoration problems after two weeks of high emotion, illicit acts and murder. She flushed at the reminder of how completely she had misjudged Tremblay, who was actually not Tremblay. Fortunately, he had said he was headed back to Paris with the murdering crooks, so there was no chance she'd see him at Tony's tonight.

She had forgotten about the kitchen goods catalog she had ordered before all hell broke loose and that now sat on a counter near Camus's bed. It showcased stainless-steel and copper pots, massive paella pans, standing mixers, machines to slice, dice and otherwise slash fresh food into enticing shapes, fancy espresso makers with their own milk steamers. Enough to have paralyzed her but now possibly an enticement for Regine to take on the role of teaching chef at Château de Champs-sur-Serein. She'd bring it with her tonight and maybe there would be a quiet moment to plant the idea in her friend's mind.

The sun was shining and the breeze was mild. Heading down the overgrown path to the end of the back gardens, Ariel's eyes were attracted to several small bits of purple in one area. Camus sniffed at something on the path as Ariel stepped off it to look closer. 'Hyacinths!'

Looking around, she saw other small announcements of spring poking up between weeds and scrub – what might be a daffodil over there and several curled-leafed plants that she thought she recognized as tulips. Perhaps this area had been planted specially as a bulb garden. Last year, she had rarely ventured out this way. Had the previous owner, the ne'er-do-well offspring of the pater-familias, or a girlfriend done this? No, it wasn't likely because no one had lived at the château for decades. Perhaps a friendly interloper. If so, Ariel hoped they would come back for a visit so Ariel could say thanks for leaving such a positive message.

Later, she nibbled at an omelet with herbes de Provence and a handful of small, oblong strawberries from Switzerland with a flavor that sang of fresh mountain air and realized she was rest-less, impatient to hear Brigadier Allard's account of Madame's death and Raoul's explanation of the box of historic photos and papers.

'Six o'clock won't come any faster if I fill the time with chocolate wafers and too much coffee,' she said to Camus and got up from the kitchen table to look for the notebook with her previous to-do lists. Bathroom designs done and cost almost negotiated, wallpapers from Katherine collected. Dinner at Tony's with the Goffs, although she thought they might make a special evening of it at the restaurant the brigadier had taken her to in Montbard. Maybe she'd invite him to make a fourth if she ever learned his first name. She stopped when she came to the last item: 'Decide if Madame's death was homicide, and if so, make sure the crime doesn't go unsolved'. Well, she and her friends had done that even if parts of the 'why' still weren't clear.

In just a couple of weeks, the house would be full again with construction noise, Jean-Paul's French pop music, the front door opening and closing, the cell phone pinging with messages about fixtures, deliveries, needs for meeting and approving projects, trucks parked in the forecourt. These next few days might be the last quiet moments she had for a while, so she started a new to-do list.

1. Ask Katherine for the name of a veterinarian.
2. Take Camus to the vet.
3. Buy Pippa's first book before she realizes I haven't read it.
4. Call financial advisor in NY to see if I'm going to be broke by the end of the year.
5. Find websites that advertise châteaux stays.
6. Do something to start the renovation of my tower.
7. Do a real plan with Raoul – if he's still speaking to me – for the back gardens.
8. ~~Talk to Regine~~ Convince Regine to become my guest chef.

Suddenly, she remembered the look on Lucas's face when he had dropped by to tell her he had added a duck confit with lentils and leeks to his growing repertoire of dishes. He had nowhere near Regine's mastery of a score of dishes, but he might be thrilled to help her as sous chef at château weekends, or perhaps even at the café if she would ever let anyone else into her kitchen.

9. Talk to Regine about Lucas.

Looking at what she'd written, Ariel added two more items.

10. Spend two days in Paris communing with great art and shopping.
11. Ask the mayor of Noyers if Raoul and I can create a commemorative garden for Madame Toussaint in a quiet spot where she and Camus used to walk.

TWENTY-TWO

The handwritten sign taped to the door of Tony's café read, 'Closed for private event.' The door wasn't locked, and when Ariel and Camus entered, Pippa, Katherine and Michael were already at the bar, holding glasses of red wine and chatting with the host.

'Come in, come in,' Tony said. 'Red, white or Crémant? From what I have heard, you have earned the right to drink everything I have.'

'Then I will have earned the world's worst headache, no thanks,' she said. 'I just got over the one yesterday's drama gave me, but a glass of bubbly sounds delicious.' She put the box she was carrying on the floor next to her. Katherine and Pippa eyed it but said nothing.

Pippa said in tones of abject sorrow, 'I missed it. When you get over your trauma, I need you to tell me what it felt like as the car came at you and you were almost killed.'

'Easy, Pippa,' Michael said, holding up a hand. 'If Ariel didn't have PTSD before, you're giving it to her now.'

Ariel chuckled. 'No trauma, no nightmares yet. It's still sinking in probably. My life didn't flash in front of me. Until then I thought she was probably an unwilling accomplice, but she proved me wrong. I have to admit, I'm pretty angry to think she had no plans to stop before slamming into me.'

'I thought she changed her mind,' Katherine said. 'I heard the car stopped right in front of you, and she was crying.'

'That's true, but she only stopped because her little dog had gotten its leash tangled in the gearshift and might have been strangled. When the officers pulled her out, she was weeping because her poor little dog might have been hurt. Me? Not a thought.'

Tony made a growling sound. 'What's worse, that yappy mutt is at my house. My soft-hearted Regine agreed to take it for a day or two until the police tell her how to surrender it. And it nips. If it's not careful, Regine will serve it here one day as rabbit.'

'Heavens,' Katherine said. 'I'll take—'

'No way. Kay, don't even think it,' Michael said and took a large swig of his red wine. 'Two unruly animals are more than enough in our small house.'

She shrugged. 'I only meant I'd take it to the humane society rather than have to look at my plate every time we come here for a meal. There's one in the Yonne department.'

The door opened and Brigadier Allard came in dressed in a tweed jacket over a turtleneck sweater, followed by Corporal Sahli in a sharply pressed uniform.

'Hello, everyone,' Allard said. 'Have your pulses returned to normal?' He stepped close to Ariel. 'And you, have you recovered from your near collision with that woman's car?' He put his hand on her arm briefly but withdrew it.

'Wine, Brigadier?' Tony said. His voice was a step shy of friendly, but he wasn't openly hostile, which Ariel noted with relief. 'And you, young man?'

Corporal Sahli drew himself up as tall as possible. 'No, sir, I am on duty, and officers in the gendarmerie are not permitted to drink while on duty.'

Ariel thought he sounded as though he was reading word for word from a training manual.

'Corporal Sahli is my driver today, so if you have sparkling water?' Allard grinned. 'I have every confidence that if I were not here, he would say the same thing.'

'Yes, sir,' Sahli said and nodded several times.

'I asked him to join us because he was on the scene yesterday and saw everything from his post near my car.'

Sahli's eyes shifted to look at Ariel, and she thought she saw a measure of awe in them. Sahli looked at his boss that way too, she remembered. He was like a well-behaved puppy.

Aha, thought Ariel. *This is the moment.* 'Brigadier, may I introduce you to Monsieur Goff? I don't think you've met.'

'Michael, please,' Katherine's husband said, sticking the unlit cigarillo he had been playing with into his shirt pocket and holding out his hand. 'We met briefly last year under trying circumstances.'

'Matthieu. You are a singer? I heard you are very good.'

'Must have heard it from my wife. Kay's slightly prejudiced.'

Matthieu then. Matt for short? They were speaking English, Ariel noted with relief.

'Where is Regine?' she asked, looking over at Tony. 'I smell something wonderful coming from the kitchen, but I'm not hearing pots banging or dishes clattering.'

'She assures me everything is under control. She ran out to pick up something from the boulangerie up the street. I expect,' he said, his voice deeper, 'that she also stopped at the butcher shop. It's closed, but knowing her, she asked the butcher to save a few juicy bones for that little mutt, plus a few for Madame's dog.'

'Camus,' Ariel said and looked down at the dog, who was sitting at attention, his luminous eyes checking everyone out. 'Camus is his name, the one Madame gave him. I'm sure he'd love a break from kibble and canned food.'

'Will he be going to the humane society too?' Tony asked, leaning over the bar to look more closely at the animal. 'He's a good dog, yes? I've never seen him this close up. Madame kept him firmly under her table when she stopped here for her morning espresso.'

Ariel turned to Allard. 'I want to adopt him. He's such a wonderful creature, and we seem to have hit it off. Would there be a problem with that?'

Allard shook his head. 'He was a stray when you found him, and you can just claim him as such. By the way,' he added, raising his eyebrows, 'where did you find him? The last I heard, he was missing and presumed far from here.'

Ariel was saved from answering by the door opening again. Raoul and his wife came in – he hesitantly, she even more so. His eyes swiveled from the brigadier to the uniformed gendarme in confusion and he stopped. Madame Descoteaux peered around him.

Behind them, the door opened yet again, and Regine came in, shooing them forward with clucking sounds. 'Welcome, welcome. Let me get to my kitchen so the *lapin à la cocotte* doesn't get dry.'

Everyone stared at her. 'What? It's too late to tell me you don't like rabbit stew,' she said with a hearty laugh, 'and even if you did, I dare you to try mine and not say it is delicious.'

In the silence, Pippa cleared her throat. 'Um, where did you get your rabbit meat?'

Regine cocked her head and said, 'Where I always get it – at the butcher shop right here. Why?'

Tony's laugh filled the room. 'Never mind, my angel – we love your stew and cannot wait for it to be on the table.'

'Well, it will not be if I do not get going. Had to get the late-bake baguettes to mop up the sauce, eh? And I made a chocolate mousse but could not resist the last almond cake she had on the shelf. She is a talented baker beyond her breads. I told her to add more pastries to her offerings when the summer visitors arrive.'

With that, she disappeared behind the curtain, and the sounds of a busy chef began in earnest.

'Come on in, man,' Tony said to Raoul. 'Wine? I have not met your wife.'

Ariel realized suddenly that Camus was not at her side. He had trotted over to Raoul and stood close, his tail wagging furiously. Raoul squatted down and held his muzzle gently, speaking softly to the dog. Behind him, Madame Descoteaux looked on, her lips shut in a tight line.

'Monsieur Descoteaux, please. Our investigation has ended, and you are under no suspicion,' Allard said, 'but we are all most anxious to know about your friend's history. First, wine.'

'Come sit with me, Madame Descoteaux,' Katherine said in French, picking up her glass and heading to a table. 'I want to hear every word. I also want to apologize. Here we are close neighbors and, while I know Raoul, you and I have never met.'

Pippa trailed the two women, and Tony ambled over with a glass of white wine for Raoul's wife. Returning to his post behind the high zinc counter, he said, 'So, Raoul, I gather Madame Toussaint was something in the war? And the Gaudets?'

Raoul patted Camus's side gently and led him back to Ariel. 'He is a good dog.'

'I know. I think Camus has found his new home with me. But you saved him, and I'm so grateful.'

From her spot at the table, Raoul's wife was paying intense attention, and when Raoul brought the animal back, Ariel noticed her face had relaxed. *Definitely not interested in taking on a dog,* Ariel thought. *Lucky me.*

Raoul drank some of his red wine and cleared his throat. 'She was a true hero and just a girl. This branch of the Gaudet clan have proven themselves to be a disgrace to the extended family since the dark days of 1943.'

Allard took Ariel's arm again and steered her to another table. She liked the feel of his arm on hers, she noted, but what of it? 'So then tell us about this woman.'

Raoul took another sip of wine then placed it on the zinc bar. 'I grew up here in the Yonne. My father died six months before I was born in 1944, but my mother and uncles told us about his sacrifice, the story of his work with the Maquis. Starting in 1942, the Resistance movement took shape here. My mother said almost everyone was involved somehow, sneaking food and supplies to the Resistance fighters, finding ways to fool the Nazis when they came to raid the farms for their food. The Nazis and the Vichy collaborators started rounding up and shooting villagers to show us they could if we caused trouble for them. My father joined a brigade in the Morvan forest when he was just nineteen, and his cousin did as well. So many people in the village were related. Madame was a young cousin to my father's cousin also, and so was related to me, although only distantly. For a while, they tried to derail Nazi trains moving troops southward and supplies stolen from the farmers northward to feed their piggish appetites.'

He stopped and gulped his wine.

'My mother said there was one girl, this relative of a cousin, just fourteen, who was the bravest of everyone in the village. She wore a dress that was too large for her size and her mother had sewn secret pockets in the skirt and top. She looked fat. She rode her bicycle everywhere, spoke cheerfully to the German patrols and as a result delivered messages, replacement parts for guns, even small amounts of ammunition.'

He laughed suddenly. 'My mother said the Germans must have been fools because sometimes you could hear her dress clanking. But when she realized it, the girl just smiled more and sang nursery songs at the top of her voice.'

Ariel said, 'That girl was Madame Toussaint?'

'Yes, and she never got caught, not even when the brigade was betrayed.'

'I've heard about French sympathizers who turned their own

people in, not only the ones who outed Jewish neighbors. Your father's brigade was caught?'

Raoul nodded. 'In late 1943, there were two brigades hiding in the Yonne forest near my mother's village. His group caught a dozen Nazi soldiers on a bridge while they were escorting trucks of supplies. Shot a few of them and blew up the bridge. The occupiers vowed to kill half the village to make a point that resistance was impossible. My father's brigade planned to ambush the soldiers hunting for innocent citizens. Madame Toussaint – well, Mademoiselle Gaudet as she was then – was entrusted to deliver the message about what the Nazis swore they were about to do. This time, the Nazis weren't as friendly, but she talked her way out of trouble even though they searched her bike and bike bag before they let her go. And then . . .' He paused, gulped down the rest of his wine and waited while Tony poured more. The café was silent, everyone waiting for Raoul to continue.

'As my mother told it, and as I came to understand it was witnessed by the survivors, she was pedaling along the dirt lane in the forest when she saw some soldiers in a clearing. They were looking at a map, and she saw the Gaudet cousin she and my father shared pointing straight to the place where the Resistance brigade was camped.'

A hissing sound jolted everyone. It was Corporal Sahli, and his eyes were burning. 'Traitor,' he said softly.

Raoul looked at him and nodded. 'My father's cousin, a Gaudet, the disgraced side of a big family that fought in the Resistance. He betrayed the fighters and the village.'

Regine had come out of the kitchen, her hands holding a towel, and she muttered something.

Katherine said in a whisper, 'Did the Nazis kill them all, the fighters and the villagers?'

'Not all. Mademoiselle Gaudet – her first name was Yvonne – crept past the soldiers, biked to the camp quickly and warned them. She was still there when the soldiers surrounded the group. One of the survivors said she grabbed the Sten gun of someone who had been killed and shot the Nazi leader. The survivor grabbed her and took her with him. Almost half of the brigade managed to escape because of her warning, and the Nazis were too crippled by the two attacks and their captain's death to carry out their vengeance. But my father was killed. It was late 1943.'

Michael cleared his throat. 'She was just a child.' The rest of them were silent.

Regine nodded. 'And the war continued. Did she go into hiding, that poor girl?'

Raoul shook his head. 'She was still in the Resistance in 1945 like so many of them. They kept doing what they could. Many were captured, tortured, killed. She changed her looks and moved north where she would not be recognized easily.'

'How come she isn't in the history books?' Pippa asked.

Raoul said, 'But she is, only with her code name, Le Petit Chien.'

'I remember that nickname in the paper records in the box,' Katherine said, snapping her fingers. 'And that's who the letter describing what must have been the same ambush was addressed to, you remember, the letter you took . . .' She stopped. The Brigadier turned to Ariel and raised one eyebrow.

Katherine coughed and turned in her chair to look at Ariel. 'That's it – the name of my shop. That's how I can honor her.'

Raoul clasped his raised hands together in front of him, a gesture of approval and appreciation. '*Idéal*. She told me years ago, when I introduced myself, that she would never forget the shock of taking someone's life, that it was nothing to brag about. She changed her code name when she left the Yonne. She remembered my parents and told me she chose that code name because one day in the forest my father had teased her for her spunk by calling her that.'

'She married at some point,' Ariel said, 'because she became Madame Toussaint.'

'No, she took the name of one of her favorite teachers who was killed for hiding a cow.' He turned to look at Ariel. 'If you found the dog, you have the box. A few photos from the years before the war, one with my father and his cousin when they were kids. Also one of Gaudet that she took with my cell phone several weeks ago when I asked. I printed it out and brought a copy to her to keep with her things as insurance the next time I worked in the garden.' He shrugged. 'It was not much help, but I showed my copy to the gendarmes when they brought me in for questioning. I said they were harassing her but said I did not know their names. She said not to ever say their names, said it was a stain on all Gaudets.'

He paused, and Ariel thought he would have spat if he wasn't in Tony's café, drinking his wine. 'When she couldn't get rid of the *voleurs*,' he looked over at Ariel, 'I mean the crooks, she gave me the box for safekeeping.'

Ariel went to the bar and pulled out the box. 'We had no idea if it had anything to do with what happened to her, just odd pieces of paper and photos.'

'And the gun,' Pippa said. 'Don't forget the gun.'

Allard and Sahli both stared at the young English woman. 'You found a gun, and you didn't think it was important?' the brigadier said.

Raoul opened the box, set the papers aside and unwrapped the odd-looking pistol. 'This. A relic – the Liberator. They did not work well, and Madame told me she never fired it.'

'I will take that please,' Allard said and held out his hand.

Raoul shrugged. 'Cheap, single shot, you know, and the fighters abandoned them immediately for better pistols and the Sten guns.'

Everyone came over to look at the gun, which was as primitive looking as Ariel remembered.

'It is not loaded,' Raoul said.

The brigadier cleared his throat. 'I think I can tell part of the current story. The judge will forward the charges here about Madame's death. Both of the Gaudets were involved, she as the driver that morning. She has decided she does not like the idea of prison so much and is spilling all she knows about the gang and the crimes. The gang knew Paris and its environs were too hot, especially because one of them had lost his head and shot the museum guard. They needed somewhere remote to store the stolen goods and Gaudet had the idea to use Madame's house. They roughed her up and threatened her with beatings. It gave them a base to distribute to black market dealers across the continent in small amounts, carefully. Gaudet and his wife had traveled down from the Paris suburb where they lived to take away another dozen or so items to sell in Antwerp. They hadn't realized the old lady was herself filching an item here and there to pay for food. There are more people involved, and they are being arrested in Nantes, Marseille and Nice as we speak.'

Katherine cleared her throat. 'Just so you don't have to round me up,' she said and opened her vintage hobo bag. 'The Gaudets didn't steal this from my shop because they didn't see it. I'd left it on a table and forgot to give it to your men with the rest. I still have no idea what it is.' She held out the archaic serving piece and Allard accepted it with a slight bow of his head.

Ariel realized that because it was so distinctive, and the engraving identified it immediately as coming from the stolen collection, of course the Gaudets needed to find it. Hence the desperate search, even in her car. They had probably been following her too, to see where else she might hide it.

Allard continued, 'Madame Gaudet heard the old woman rummaging around, and when she looked, she saw her open a box and take out a piece of silverware. She told her husband, so they followed her to find out where the pieces were ending up. When she made it to the outskirts of Noyers that morning, they forced her into his car and he shook her until she admitted she was selling things to pay for her food. The coroner found bruising on her arms.'

'I saw bruises earlier. She told me she fell. He admitted this?' Regine said, her face red.

'Some of it, and other parts we got from his wife, who insists she had no part in the violence – a claim, by the way, that we do not accept as truthful. She tried to bite one of the arresting officers last night. He planned to break into your shop' – he nodded in Katherine's direction – 'and recover the goods. But the victim started to shout for help and he hit her. He swears he didn't mean to kill her, just to silence her. As you know, she was in her late nineties, and it didn't take much. He grabbed the bag she was carrying, and they drove off, leaving her to die.'

Regine broke into a stream of curses. 'That son of a whore; those bastards. I hope he dies for this.'

She whipped her towel in the air as if the killer was standing in front of her.

She stopped suddenly. 'Oh, my *lapin* – I think it may be burning,' she cried and fled into the kitchen.

Tony moved slowly around the room, filling glasses. Allard handed the ancient pistol, still wrapped in cloth, to his corporal.

Ariel sat down and Camus came to sit close to her. 'And the dog?' she asked.

Raoul sighed. 'Poor boy must have been in the car, and when that bastard pulled Madame out and marched her to the shop door, I'm betting he got out and stayed close.'

'The dog probably panicked when our neighbor came close waving her hoe because she thought the old woman was sleeping,' Katherine said.

Raoul nodded. 'I found him with the leash and by then we knew Madame was dead. I didn't know what to do, but I was afraid the cops would think that made me a suspect, so I just hid him.'

Allard said, 'Raoul had connections with her that we didn't understand right away. As soon as he explained, he was released, and then he helped us capture the Gaudets after Ariel told us where they were.'

'Another thing to punish them for,' a voice said.

They looked to see Regine coming out of the kitchen with dishes and napkins.

'The rabbit was ruined. It cannot be eaten.'

Ariel noticed relieved looks on several people's faces.

'So, I am making omelets with mushrooms and tarragon. We have bread, a nice Époisses cheese and salads, and the desserts. Tony, my love' she said over her shoulder as she slammed plates on the tables, 'we shall need a great deal of wine to wash the bad tastes from our mouths and then to toast the memory of the brave woman who helped save France.'

'So many pieces to this puzzle,' Ariel said thirty minutes later, looking around the room. 'We all had pieces but couldn't see the complete picture. The only thing we knew for sure was that we cared about this wizened old woman who walked and walked, always with her faithful dog and her secrets. May she rest in peace.'

Raoul stood up, and the others raised their glasses. 'To Madame Toussaint – *liberté, égalité et fraternité*.'

Ariel leaned down to where Camus was licking the last of his omelet from the plate Regine had given him. 'And to you, my boy, and our new life together,' she said in a whisper and patted his head.

Matthieu Allard looked over at her, raised his glass and smiled. 'To the future.'